Monica Belle is an Oxbridge graduate and the author of several successful *Black Lace* novels, including *Black Lipstick Kisses*, *Bound in Blue*, *Noble Vices*, *Office Perks*, *Pagan Heat*, *The Boss*, *The Choice*, *To Seek a Master*, *Valentina's Rules*, *Wild by Nature* and *Wild in the Country*.

Also By Monica Belle:

Black Lipstick Kisses
Bound in Blue
Noble Vices
Office Perks
Pagan Heat
The Boss
The Choice
To Seek a Master
Valentina's Rules
Wild by Nature
Wild in the Country

French
Lessons

MONICA BELLE

BLACK
LACE

1 3 5 7 9 10 8 6 4 2

First published in 2014 by Black Lace, an imprint of Ebury Publishing
A Random House Group Company

Copyright © 2014 by Monica Belle

Monica Belle has asserted her right to be identified as the author of this Work
in accordance with the Copyright, Designs and Patents Act 1988

The Random House Group Limited Reg. No. 954009

Addresses for companies within the Random House Group can
be found at: www.randomhouse.co.uk

A CIP catalogue record for this book is available from the British Library

Penguin Random House is committed to a sustainable future for
our business, our readers and our planet. This book is made from
Forest Stewardship Council® certified paper.

Printed and bound in Great Britain by Clays Ltd, Elcograf S.p.A.

ISBN 9780352347787

To buy books by your favourite authors and register for offers visit
www.randomhouse.co.uk

1

'Elise, my office, five minutes.'

'Yes, Mr Curran.'

I watched him go as he continued on towards his office, taking him in: the carefully untidy hair, the perfectly fitted but slightly rumpled designer suit, the handcrafted Swiss watch. No other man I'd ever known carried himself with such an air of easy, casual arrogance, or took his good fortune in life so much for granted: Aaron Curran, a man born with a golden spoon in his mouth and who clearly felt he was entitled to it, and to me.

It wasn't going to happen. Nobody makes me their toy, no matter how rich and good looking he is, and I knew that was how it would be, because it had happened before. I don't know what it is in particular about me, other than the obvious, but men often seem to think I'd make a good mistress, or just a handy plaything. Not that I'd have minded in Aaron's case – in some ways, at least – and he wasn't even married. But he had been through most of the girls in the office, and I do have my pride. He liked to show off, too, and he liked control.

He didn't even really need to see me now, I was fairly sure of that. What he really wanted was to make me do the walk of shame, the full length of the office, with everybody staring at me and wondering what I'd done to be called into the inner sanctum. Worse still, our premises are modern but built within a traditional old building, and his office is beyond a big, solid oak door with no way of looking in or knowing what's going on inside. Once I was through that door, the office gossips would be having a field day outside, happily speculating about whether I was being given a ticking off, propositioned or offered a promotion in return for five minutes on my knees under his desk.

I was going to have to go, anyway, but the five minutes' grace he'd allowed me meant I just had time to deal with the post I'd snatched up from the floor as I left the flat. There were three letters: a bill from a catalogue, an invitation to contribute to a charity and a large envelope of expensive, cream-coloured paper with a name printed across the top in gold letters: Clarke, Conway & Clarke, Solicitors of Lincoln's Inn Fields. It looked pretty ominous, and there was a lump in my throat as I imagined myself being sued or summoned to court, and at the same time I tried to think what I could possibly have done to deserve such a fate.

The headed paper within matched the envelope, and the letter printed on it began with old-fashioned formality, addressing me as 'Miss Sherborne' and moving straight into long-winded legal jargon, the upshot of which was not that I was being taken to court, nor anything else unpleasant, but that I was the sole beneficiary of Madame Adèle de Regnier. I couldn't even recall who Madame Adèle de Regnier was, at first, but then it came back to me: she was my mother's much older sister, who had been through a series of tempestuous marriages, providing the family with endless scandal.

It was hard to remember the details, and my parents had kept most of it from me anyway, but I could remember the house, La Fleur. I closed my eyes and tried to think back fifteen years and more, to wonderful sunny summers deep in the French countryside. La Fleur had seemed to me like a fairy-tale castle, complete with high walls and towers, odd little nooks, and rooms so secret and dusty it was as if nobody had been inside for years. There were grounds, too – a magical garden where I'd been able to lose myself for hours, in among beds bright with flowers, mysterious little paths between high hedges of dark-green yew, a little walled garden full of the scents of herbs, with colourful butterflies everywhere. Beyond the grounds had been the vineyard: row upon row of plants hung with fat golden grapes that made a wine like the nectar of the gods. When I was little, I'd sneaked down from my room in the evenings and begged for sips in return for going to bed and leaving everybody in peace, unless Aunt Adèle snapped at me, in which case I'd flee.

She'd been magnificent – tall, elegant, refined, yet also sensual and comfortable in her own womanhood in a way I'd never experienced before or since. I'd looked up to her as a child, and later, years after I'd last visited La Fleur, she had always been the role model to whom I aspired. Yet I'd had no idea she'd married again, or who Monsieur de Regnier had been. Whatever the situation, unless there had been some terrible mistake, or Aunt Adèle had somehow managed to lose everything before she died, it seemed I had been named in her will as the inheritor of her entire estate, and I was now the owner of La Fleur. All I had to do was call in on Clarke, Conway & Clarke and sign the official documents.

I read the letter three times, the implications slowly sinking in. The two years since I'd left college had been the dullest of my life, a slow start to what might turn out to be a remunerative career but wasn't going to be an exciting one. I'd expected so much of life, through a wonderful childhood and great college days, but here I was, helping Aaron Curran do clever things with money while I earned just enough to keep myself in a one-bedroom flat on the wrong side of Hoxton. Only now I was mistress of La Fleur, if the letter could really be believed, owner of a château in the Dordogne and a vineyard that had to bring in tens of thousands a year, maybe hundreds of thousands. There'd be no more commuting, no more nine-to-five, no more bossy bosses and office politics and petty jealousies and pointless meetings and stupid little rules and . . .

'Elise. I said five minutes.'

'Sorry, Mr Curran.'

My answer was automatic, and so was the blush that coloured my cheeks as I hurried down the long aisle between my co-workers' desks to where he stood waiting in the doorway of his office. It was only as I drew close that I considered the possibility of resigning on the spot, but it was all too sudden and I went in meekly enough, stopping in front of his desk as he closed the door behind me. I'd always hated his desk, a huge thing made of highly polished oak and topped with sage-green leather, partly because having to stand in front of it made me feel as if I was back at school, and partly because of the way his knees showed underneath the open mid-section, always set slightly apart as if in invitation for me to crawl under and take him in my mouth. From the knowing, calculating smile on his face, I was fairly sure he was thinking the same thing, and that he knew I was fighting a terrible compulsion to do exactly that.

I don't know what it is with me but whenever I'm in a slightly demanding situation, I get a terrible urge to do the most embarrassing, inappropriate thing possible, like tweak somebody's nose in a crowded tube train, strip naked at a family wedding, or in this case give my boss the oral sex I was sure he wanted and felt entitled to. Fortunately, I have good self-control, and merely raised my chin a little as he took his seat.

'Elise,' he began, 'you've put in quite an impressive performance over the last few months, so I've decided to give you an opportunity to step up a pace. As you know, I'm going to New York next week. I need a PA to come with me, somebody who understands how I work and who will be ready to support me, and the company. That person might be you, if you think you're up to the challenge?'

So this was it, the move I'd been expecting for weeks, and had carefully set up. If I refused, it would look as if I lacked ambition, but despite the veneer of professional respectability of the offer, it was obvious what he expected: me, as his plaything, performing every dirty little trick in his dirty little mind, with the preferment he'd offered constantly dangled in front of my nose like a carrot for a donkey. I knew this because he'd taken Vicky Bell to a conference in Amsterdam, spent the evenings practising the Kama Sutra on her, and on their return promoted her from junior docketing clerk to senior docketing clerk. Now it was my turn, and it wasn't just that he *hoped* I'd say yes and let him seduce me; he *knew* I'd say yes and let him seduce me.

But not me; not Elise Sherborne. My defiance rose with the angle of my chin as he carried on, telling me what a wonderful opportunity he was offering me, before deliberately taking it right to the edge of what he could expect to get away with, just as he had with Vicky.

'But you mustn't think this is going to be a holiday. I'd need you to be on call twenty-four-seven, to deal with anything that comes up, and I do mean anything . . .'

'Like your cock?'

He stopped talking, looking at me in blank astonishment that changed to a broad grin as he decided I was being deliberately brazen. I took my cue, gave him a slow, suggestive wink and stepped over to where a new ten-litre flask stood by the water cooler next to his desk. He raised a finger as I undid the top of the plastic container, but didn't speak, maybe thinking I was going to pour it over my chest and unsure if the view would be worth a soggy carpet. I smiled as I carefully lifted the heavy vessel, set my feet apart, curved my back into a provocative S shape, and tipped the water bottle over to pour it into his lap.

'Maybe that will cool you off a bit?'

It didn't seem to. As the first splash of water hit his crotch, he tried to push his chair away and jump up at the same time, but only succeeded in going over backwards to end up with his legs kicking in the air like an upturned beetle. He was cursing pretty freely, too, and calling me all sorts of things, of which 'crazy bitch' was the mildest, so it seemed a good time to make myself scarce. Placing the now-almost-empty container on his desk, I made for the door, pulling it

wide to reveal the familiar rows of desks with their
familiar occupants, every single one of them now
craning their head to try and see what was going on in
Aaron's office, and most of them babbling questions at
me as I walked out.

I didn't say a word but simply sauntered down the
aisle with a deliberate sway of my hips for Aaron's
benefit and left, a dramatic exit only partially spoiled
by having to come back to pick up my things from my
desk, including the letter announcing my title to La
Fleur.

The rest of the day passed in a blur. I had my fingers
firmly crossed all the way to Lincoln's Inn Fields, half
convinced that it would turn out to be some dreadful
mistake and that all I'd achieved was to resign in
spectacular fashion. Even while I was actually in
the solicitors' offices, it was hard to accept my good
fortune, as Mr Conway handled everything as though
it were all completely ordinary and routine, calmly
going through the paperwork before handing me a
set of large iron keys. He also informed me that, in
addition to the property, I'd been left just under one
hundred thousand euros, after inheritance taxes had
been settled.

Only as I left Clarke, Conway & Clarke did it
really start to sink in, and suddenly my heels no longer
seemed in contact with the pavement and my face
broke into a grin so dopey, I soon began to get funny

looks. I wanted to celebrate, but everybody I knew was at work or impossibly far away from central London, while the crowds around Holborn tube and the smell of hot asphalt along Kingsway made me yearn to be far away too: in France, with a glass of chilled golden wine in my hand and not a care in the world.

A true romantic would have gone straight to St Pancras and simply left everything behind, but I have a stubborn, sensible streak, and even as I fought the temptation to sing out loud, in the back of my head I was making a list of what needed to be done and who I'd have to see before I left. It wasn't a very long list, though, as there was no current boyfriend and only a handful of people I knew in London, while my old friends were scattered from Bristol to Beijing.

In the end, I went back to my flat and set to work sorting things out, with the promise to myself of a bottle of wine if I made all the phone calls and sent off all the emails I needed to before six o'clock. I made it, just, but had no sooner popped the cork than a text arrived on my phone, from Vicky, telling me she was coming over. It was typical of her – of course knowing nothing about La Fleur – to be genuinely concerned about me because of what had happened at work, and also to be eager for gossip. I wanted to talk anyway and told her she could come, eliciting a ring on my doorbell so quickly she had to have been in my street already. She didn't waste time asking the vital question either.

'Well, that happened? What did you do?'

She was full of excitement, and something close to awe, so I gave her a quiet smile and poured us each a glass of wine before answering her.

'Don't you know? I emptied a water-cooler bottle into Aaron's lap.'

'But why?'

'Oh, just to cool him down a little. He wanted me to be his bit of stuff on a business trip to New York.'

She looked shocked and envious, but a little hurt too, so I went on quickly.

'It was on your behalf too, Vicky, and for the others as well. He can't just use women like that, and I'm sure you'd have done the same before Amsterdam if you'd known what he's really like.'

She gave a doubtful nod and sat down, toying with the stem of her glass as she spoke once more.

'I wouldn't. I wouldn't have had the guts, and I need my job. Anyway, he really likes you.'

'Yes, of course he does, because he hasn't had me yet. That's the way he thinks, Vicky, a conquest at a time. He probably has notches on his bedstead.'

'No, but he does call out your name when he comes.'

'You're joking!'

She obviously wasn't, as she'd gone cherry red and looked as if she was about to burst into tears. I'd been about to tell her all about La Fleur, but didn't want to seem to be boasting, and I was also fascinated to hear what she had to say. There was plenty.

'He does. That was the worst thing about what happened in Amsterdam. I thought I had a chance, just maybe, and I did like him so much. He's good in bed too, fun . . . a bit kinky, but in a good way . . .'

'Kinky? How kinky?'

'Oh, you know, the usual, but the way he does it meant I could let go completely, and I did. Then, after all sorts, and I do mean all sorts, when he finally came, he called out your name!'

'Sorry.'

'It not your fault, Elise, but can you imagine how I felt?'

'Yes, but what a prat! I can't think why he'd prefer me to you anyway – you're gorgeous – but couldn't he have held it in?'

'He explained, and he did apologise too, but it seems he's wanted you from the moment you walked into his office.'

'Why didn't he ask me out, then? Okay, I'd have refused, because I don't believe in mixing business with pleasure, but why all the sleazy stuff?'

'He's not actually that confident with women. Apparently, it's because he was at an all-boys' public school and finds it hard to relate to women, especially beautiful women.'

'So he says. More likely he was just trying to play the vulnerable little boy so he could get into your knickers.'

'Well, he only told me that after we'd been to bed.'

'Okay, so how about this: he has his fun with you, deliberately calls out my name when he's coming to put you off, then gives you the vulnerable little boy routine knowing full well you'd pass it on to me to help his chances of getting into *my* knickers.'

'Do you really think he could be that calculating?'

'Yes! This is Aaron Curran we're talking about, a man who makes his money by out-thinking his rivals in the City. He starts where Niccolò Machiavelli left off.'

'I'm sure that's not true. He says he's in love with you.'

I answered with what was supposed to be a snort of contempt but which came out more like the sort of noise you'd expect from a distressed hamster.

She carried on. 'I think he was telling the truth. He was very emotional, and he asked me not to tell you, so what you've just said doesn't really make sense, don't you think?'

It was hard to know what to think, let alone what to say. I'd always had Aaron down as the classically arrogant public schoolboy, rich enough and good-looking enough to get away with treating women as pretty things to be used and discarded at leisure. He also had a reputation for playing life as if it were a game of chess, with each move calculated to bring him maximum advantage in the long run, and while that might well include me as one in a long line of girls to amuse himself with, if he was planning on marrying at all, it would no doubt be to some high-flying female executive, or maybe the daughter of some major figure in the City. The fact that he'd told Vicky not to pass on what he'd said to me meant nothing, as he'd no doubt known perfectly well that she would, if not immediately. Yet for all my scepticism, I couldn't help but feel a lingering sense of doubt.

Not that it mattered, because whatever his feelings for me might be, I'd burnt my bridges with a vengeance by humiliating him, and effectively in public, too. No man with any real pride was going to accept that, and certainly not Aaron Curran. I was off to France anyway, and had sent in official notice of my immediate resignation that afternoon in a curt, formal letter that showed no hint of remorse or even interest. Just possibly he deserved the benefit of the doubt, so after a few moments spent pretending to busy myself with cooking preparations, I turned back to Vicky.

'It's too late, anyway. I've been left some property in France, a small wine-growing estate in the Dordogne, so I'll have some income too. That's why I poured the water over him: I knew I could afford to do it. But if you do speak to him, please explain that I might have made a mistake. If his feelings for me are genuine, and only if they're genuine, then I'm sorry; but I wouldn't want to be with him anyway, so it's probably all for the best.'

There was a lump in my throat as I finished, even as I told myself that I was simply responding to his carefully judged manipulation. Vicky nodded in response and then took a swallow of wine, perhaps no more keen to delve deeper into the situation than I was. I couldn't help but feel sorry for her, so offered to cook for her, rustling up some fresh pasta and a pesto sauce with anchovies. We shared a second bottle of wine as we ate, leaving me feeling warm inside and a little dizzy by the time she left, but also strangely dissatisfied.

It was a Wednesday, and Vicky had work in the morning, so I'd drunk far more than she had, but it didn't matter. I could have another bottle if I wanted to, or go out on the town and come back at dawn, or wind up in some good-looking young man's bed in an effort to satisfy the sexual tension inside me, but I knew it wouldn't work. What she'd said had unsettled me, and I found myself wondering what might have happened if circumstances had been different, if I hadn't been safe in the knowledge that I could leave.

I knew full well that I'd have reacted in much the same way, not actually tipping the contents of the water cooler over him, perhaps, but either declining his offer, or, more likely, telling him I'd come with him to New York, but only on the clear understanding that our relationship remained strictly professional. Nevertheless, now that I'd stood my ground, it didn't hurt to think about what might have happened if I'd accepted his offer, or had felt unable to refuse and found myself having to do as I was told.

Once he knew I was his, there'd have been no holding him back. He'd have been keen to make my status clear from the very start, both to me and to other people. We'd meet up, probably in an executive lounge at Heathrow, and his hand would go straight to the curve of my hip before planting a gentle but proprietorial pat on my bottom. I'd feel embarrassed and ashamed, but there would be nothing I could do. Maybe we'd be alone, and maybe I'd have threatened to pour the contents of the water cooler over him before giving in to the inevitable. There would be a cooler in the lounge, too, and he'd demand that I pour some of the water over my chest. I'd do it, splashing my face and neck, soaking my blouse and bra to leave my breasts showing through as if I was in some smutty, drunken wet T-shirt contest.

The thought made me shiver. All my life I've been a little goody two-shoes, well brought up and well educated, polite and reserved, also secure in the knowledge that I would never have to sell myself, which makes it great fun sometimes to imagine doing exactly that. I could do better, though, much better, and I was smiling at my own dirty imagination as I made for the bathroom. Proud I may be, and no man gets away with treating me that way in real life, but I'm also strong enough to enjoy my fantasies without feeling bad. This one had a lot of potential, too, as I wouldn't even have the embarrassment of having to face him again and remember what I'd been thinking about the night before. Better still, there was no hurry at all, and the wine had made me feel easy and uninhibited.

I was feeling deliciously naughty as I kicked off my shoes and climbed into the shower, still fully dressed. The previous evening I wouldn't have dared do anything so silly, let alone on a weekday night, but none of that mattered any more. I was going to soak my clothes and play with myself in the shower while I imagined how Aaron Curran would have handled me, had he had the chance – making me dance for him in my soaking blouse, a slow striptease with my lower clothes coming off first to leave me in nothing but a sopping wet, see-through top before he put me on my back, or making me kneel in a chair with my bottom stuck up in the air, or just taking me up against the wall.

My hands were shaking so badly, it was hard to work the shower control, but I eventually managed to get it on and the water to the right temperature, just a little too cold to be comfortable. Next came one of those moments I enjoy the most: the final chance to stop being silly and back out, knowing full well I'm going to go ahead with whatever I'm planning. I held it for several seconds, with the shower head pointed away from me, although my feet were already wet, the cool water bubbling up through my stockings and between my toes, then twisted the shower head around to play it full in my face.

I was left gasping and spluttering, but that was

exactly how I'd planned it, with my eyes already closed as I imagined Aaron making me stand still in the middle of the washroom at the executive lounge as he slowly and deliberately poured the entire contents of the water cooler over my head. He'd soak my hair, turning my glossy brown curls to sodden rats' tails. He'd order me to open my mouth and make sure plenty went in, laughing as it bubbled out over my lips and ran down my neck and into my cleavage. He'd wet my breasts, his grey-blue eyes alight with amusement and arousal as he watched the water soak into the cotton to leave the lacy pattern of my bra on plain show, with the dark outlines of my nipples beneath.

Even as I let my imagination run, I'd done it, playing the shower hose over my head and into my face, soaking my jacket and blouse, the water pouring down to wet my skirt and legs. It felt good, very good, but I needed more, a long, slow rise before I finally gave myself what I was coming to need so badly. I leant back against the wall, playing the shower hose over my breasts and belly, enjoying the pressure on my skin as much as my dirty thoughts as I began to speculate on what Aaron Curran liked that was kinky. Vicky said it had helped her let go, which suggested that he'd restrained her in some way, perhaps handcuffing her to the bed or tying her hands behind her back while they had sex. It was an appealing thought and a nice added detail to my fantasy, imagining my wrists bound securely behind my back as the water was poured over my head and chest. I'd be defenceless, allowing him to have a good leisurely grope of my wet breasts before ripping my blouse wide and jerking my bra up to get me bare.

There was a twinge of regret for sixty-five pounds' worth of designer blouse as I ripped the sides open, but one has to make sacrifices. I wasn't going to need buttons at La Fleur anyway, and could wear it tied beneath my breasts, even with no bra if I felt so inclined. For now, though, it was ruined, open wide with my wet bra cups my only protection, and that not for long as I pulled them up sharply, the way I imagined Aaron getting me bare. He'd be gloating by then, both for my half-naked, vulnerable state and because it would be quite obvious that I was turned on, as helpless in mind as I was in body.

If I were tied up, he'd have to strip me, pulling off my skirt and panties, rolling down my stockings and making me step out of the puddle of sodden cloth around my feet to leave me naked from the waist down. I've always liked that. Topless is acceptable in the right circumstances, even rather chic, but bottomless is just plain rude. Not that I'd have anything at all covered with him – nothing important, anyway – and he would take full advantage of me. I'd probably be spread out on a table with my ankles held high and wide as he used me, or be made to kneel in the sodden ruins of my smart office suit and taken from behind with his hand twisted in the ropes that secured my wrists.

I'd slumped down and was now sitting in the corner of the shower with my skirt rucked up around my thighs and my legs wide to let me play the hose across the front of my panties as well as on my bare breasts. A little more attention to the right spot and I'd have come, but I was determined to hold off a little longer, deliberately teasing myself so that when the moment came, it would be stronger still. The thought of being tied up and had from behind was too good to miss, but I needed to be as close to the situation I was imagining as possible. It took a moment to wriggle out of my skirt and panties and stockings, all the while with my eyes closed, imagining Aaron's strong, male hands doing the work instead of my own.

Now nude from the waist down, I twisted over into a kneeling position on top of my wet clothes, face down and bottom up as if about to be penetrated. I couldn't tie myself and there was no Aaron to take me, but the powerful jets from the shower hose felt so good between my open cheeks and against my sex that my mouth was wide in ecstasy in an instant. Holding back was no longer an option, and I was playing the hose between my legs and using the rounded metal head to rub myself as I let my thoughts run wild. I'd be on the floor, bottomless, soaking wet, held by my tightly bound wrists as he pushed into me, hard and fast. He'd be talking to me, too, telling me how rude I looked and how he'd always wanted me this way, stripped and helpless at his feet, every intimate detail of my body on plain show as he pushed his cock in and out of me.

His name was on my lips as I started to come, and I couldn't stop myself, screaming it out over and over again as wave after wave of pleasure swept through me – pleasure mingled with more than a little shame for my disgraceful behaviour, but that only made the ecstasy more exquisite. Besides, to judge from what Vicky had said, he was no better than me, so it was really only fair that I'd given in to my feelings, if not to him.

2

A week later, as I stepped from the air-conditioned cool of the taxi into the warmth of a French summer's day, it was as if I'd been transported back in time and was once again a little girl. From the crumbling stone arch over the gates to the black iron weathervane in the shape of a woodpecker at the top of the tower, La Fleur was everything I remembered: as beautiful, as romantic, every bit the fairy-tale castle I'd so often visited in my dreams. The taxi driver had got out to unload my things and was standing behind me in anticipation of his fare while occasionally making those odd little clicking noises Frenchmen substitute for wolf-whistles, but I didn't care.

It was all so wonderful that tears started in my eyes as I drank in the courtyard and crumbling yellow stone walls with their patina of red-leaved Russian vine, the faded, peeling grey-blue paint and rusting iron of the doors and the shutters that closed off every window. It seemed a good deal smaller, though, especially the tower, while the old red tiles on the roof were not only thick with grey and yellow lichens, but also broken in places. The gate into the old stables and gardens hung askew, while what little I could see of the hedges and flowerbeds had largely been given over to weeds. The only sign of life was on the right-hand side of the courtyard, where a short flight of stone steps led down into the winery, and where somebody appeared to have been trying to make a seat out of old barrel staves.

The taxi driver was beginning to get impatient, so I paid him off before returning to the contemplation of my property, my sense of awe now tinged with dismay. Beautiful and romantic it might have been, enough even to tempt Monet or Fragonard with its state of picturesque dilapidation, but I wasn't planning on painting it: I had to live there, and it was in desperate need of some very expensive repairs. Suddenly, one hundred thousand euros didn't seem very much at all. However, I consoled myself that the vineyards stretching down towards the river would bring me in a decent income.

With the taxi gone, I was left in peace with just the faint singing of a cicada somewhere in among the bushes. I made for the side door, wheeling my baggage behind me, and had soon managed to find the right key for the huge, forged-iron lock. After surveying the exterior, and recalling my discovery before I left home that Aunt Adèle had spent the last year or so of her life in a care home, I was expecting cobwebs and dustsheets inside, so it was a pleasant surprise to find the interior gloomy but clean, more like what you'd expect of a holiday home on first arrival than a mothballed château. The electricity was on, too, allowing me to illuminate a long, low-ceilinged kitchen, all more or less as I remembered from nearly two decades before.

I lost my bearings a little at first, because the driver had brought me in by the courtyard, which was at the functional end of the house, while, on previous visits with my father, he'd always parked at the front, where a fine façade imperiously faced the sweeping carriage driveway and lawns extending to the valley beyond. Now that I was in the kitchen, everything began to make sense once more as I remembered the hall and the finely appointed but seldom used rooms that led off it to my right, and the old part of the house with the tower to my left. There were two staircases: a rickety, winding set of wooden stairs that led from the corner of the kitchen up to what had once been the servants' quarters, and which I'd been expected to use as a child, and the main stairway rising up from the hall in a double sweep of marble, with an iron balustrade carved with leaves and exotic birds.

Despite being a grown woman and the owner of the château, I still felt a touch of guilt as I made my way through to the hall, as if Aunt Adèle was likely to step out from the music room or the library at any instant to admonish me for any one of a multitude of minor sins, or simply for being there. I don't believe in ghosts, so I knew it was all in my mind, but I could feel her presence, which grew stronger as I ascended the grand main staircase, to reach a peak as I pushed open the doors to the master bedroom.

I'd only ever glimpsed inside before, but if anything had changed, it wasn't immediately obvious. The huge four-poster bed still dominated the room, and yet it was only one of several pieces of massive, dark-wood furniture, even the smallest of which made the sort of stuff I was used to seem frail and cheap by comparison. The furnishings were either the same as I remembered or had been redone in the same style, in blue and gold, while the relics of Imperial France that Aunt Adèle had seen fit to use as ornaments were exactly as before: the ancient, brass-mounted globe with the meridian marked through Paris, the display cabinet of brilliantly coloured, if somewhat moth-eaten, stuffed tropical birds, and even the grotesque, half-human mask some ancestor had brought back from central Africa. For a moment I reflected on the mysterious scandal that had been the final straw in ruining the relationship between Aunt Adèle and my mother. I'd never discovered what it was about, and now it seemed that I never would.

My sense of being somewhere I shouldn't had grown painfully strong as I entered the room, but I forced myself to walk to the window, pull the curtains wide and throw open the shutters. Light flooded in and, after a moment of blinking in the sun, I found myself looking out at another familiar sight: the lawns with the six gravel paths arranged in a sunburst around the central fountain, now somewhat unkempt and with the water turned off, but not entirely derelict. There was a man walking towards me along the central path, a man who very much drew the eye.

He was big and muscular, with a shock of midnight-black hair above a face you'd never call handsome but which showed immense strength, and which suited his body. All he had on was a pair of boots and tatty jeans, leaving his powerful, sweat-streaked torso bare and dirty from the soil he'd been working. His muscles moved as he pushed a wheelbarrow loaded with what appeared to be vine clippings, and he seemed to be singing to himself – the words inaudible but adding to his aura of carefree power and virility.

My first thought was that it was hard to imagine anybody more different to Aaron Curran; my second that I had staff, which made sense but still came as a surprise. He was quite interesting, too, and I continued to watch as he made his way across the lawns and disappeared through an arch beside the tower, unsure whether he was appealing or repulsive, but very sure that he was intensely masculine. I was obviously going to need to talk to him, anyway, which would be my first chance to exercise my rather rusty French properly. Now seemed as good a time as any, especially as my sense of intruding in my aunt's room had come back stronger than ever. I'd reached out to close the shutters when a voice spoke from directly behind me, loud, sharp, commanding and in French.

'Who are you? What are you doing here?'

I twisted around, seriously expecting to find the tall, imperious figure of Aunt Adèle looking down a ghostly nose with the air of disapproval I remembered so well. She wasn't, but the stocky, grey-haired woman in the doorway looked no less disapproving and no less formidable, which had me stammering out an immediate explanation.

'I . . . I'm Elise Sherborne, the new owner. Who are you?'

'I am Madame Belair.'

'Ah . . . have you been looking after the house? Thank you, that's so kind of you. Um . . . here's my passport, you know, just in case you thought I was a burglar, or something.'

I was trying to be funny, but her expression didn't soften at all as she took my passport and subjected it to a careful inspection. That gave me long enough to get over my surprise and remind myself that it was my house, something she seemed to have accepted, if grudgingly, as she went on.

'I keep house. You'll be wanting dinner, I suppose?'

'Yes, please, but don't put yourself to too much trouble. A salad will do nicely.'

'My husband has some rabbits.'

With that slightly unnerving remark, she left, apparently having at least accepted my right to be there and to be fed. I made to follow her, keen to ask about her husband and find out just how many people I was responsible for, and what their duties were, but she'd disappeared towards the back stairs, and when I got down to the kitchen, she wasn't there. She wasn't in the yard, either, but a faint, rhythmic chinking noise coming from the winery suggested that somebody was at work. I made my way towards the noise, quickly finding myself in the long vaulted chamber with its racks of golden bottles I remembered so vividly from childhood, unchanged but seemingly half the size, so that I had to duck at the bottom of the steps to avoid banging my head. The noise was louder now and came from beyond another low arch, where a complicated machine was filling and labelling bottles under the supervision of an elderly, weather-beaten man in faded *bleu de travail*. He looked up as I entered, clicked his tongue just as the taxi driver had done, and reached out to turn the machine off before giving me an enquiring look. I began to explain who I was, but he interrupted immediately.

'I remember you – the little girl who was always hiding. I am Luc Belair.'

The name meant nothing to me, but as he spoke, his age-worn face had seemed to change, the years slipping away as I remembered the younger of the two men who'd worked the estate, and his son, a dark youth who'd been forever teasing me, and who had to be the man I'd seen earlier. I still didn't remember the woman, evidently his wife, but then Aunt Adèle had always taken a very old-fashioned attitude to her staff, keeping a firm distinction between family and what were effectively servants. The idea was alien to me, and I was determined to treat them as equals, so returned a bright smile before I spoke.

'I remember you too, and your son . . . Jean?' Suddenly the name came back to me. 'I've met your wife as well. Didn't you get the email to say I was coming today?'

He merely shrugged then reached out to take an open bottle from the top of a nearby barrel that seemed to have been set out for tasting. I waited as he poured a glass, sniffed, sipped and poured a second, which he passed to me, grinning. It was a familiar ritual I'd seen my parents go through many times as a child, and I'd always had my own small glass with a little water added, so I returned his salute. Unlike his wife, he seemed friendly and eager to please, so I put to him the question that had been uppermost in my mind for some time.

'This is all wonderful, and I'm delighted to be here, but can I ask roughly what we bring in a year, after all the outgoings?'

He shrugged. 'The estate? We lose money. Every year, we lose money, except the best. Three years in ten, maybe, we will make money. It is not an easy thing – making Monbazillac is not easy – and it is hard to get a fair price. People today, they drink beer, or water in bottles.'

He spat as he finished, a gesture of utter contempt for the modern world. I carried on, trying to fight back my sudden dismay.

'So, overall, across a ten-year period, say?'

'We lose money, but if the years are good, maybe if the Chinese come to understand the true quality of our wines, then maybe . . .'

He trailed off with yet another shrug, which did nothing for my rising sense of dismay. Now I knew why my Aunt Adèle had married a string of rich men – not for the sake of passion and luxury, as I'd assumed, but because otherwise she'd have ended up broke. My hundred thousand euros was presumably the tag end of the late Monsieur de Regnier's fortune. That at least gave me a breathing space, although only for so long. But while Luc Belair seemed fatalistic, or possibly was hoping that I'd take Aunt Adèle's cue and find myself a string of wealthy and indulgent husbands, he evidently wasn't quite as bucolic as he looked.

'Chinese? What Chinese?'

'Rich Chinese, the ones who pay a thousand euros a bottle for the First Growths in Bordeaux and buy every château that comes on the market. You're not going to sell.'

The way he said it sounded more like a statement of fact than a question, which gave me a twinge of irritation, but he was right. Despite the difficulties I was facing, I had no intention of selling La Fleur, but it was clear that I would have to modernise. I'd assumed that there would be some sort of separate entity to run the vineyards – a management company, perhaps – and that I could simply run an eye over the books now and then, while the profits would be my income. Now I could see that I'd been wrong, very wrong, in assuming that the systems I was familiar with from the City would also apply in rural France. With me as the owner, and the Belair family doing the work, if La Fleur had a system at all, it was feudalism.

The idea was actually quite appealing, to the romantic side of my nature, but to the sensible side it was obvious that there would have to be major changes. Unfortunately, I knew nothing whatsoever about making wine, which meant I'd have to bring in a consultant, another expense, and there was sure to be resistance from the Belairs. Luc was friendly and voluble, but the way he clicked his tongue at me, and his general attitude, showed a marked lack of respect, while his wife seemed taciturn to say the least, and I couldn't imagine the hulking, hyper-masculine Jean accepting my authority. I had a struggle on my hands.

Luc had gone back to working the bottling machine, evidently deciding that with his brief ritual of welcome complete, it was more important to get on with what he was doing than talk to the new owner. I considered turning the machine off again and giving him a version of the sort of carefully balanced pep talk and telling off Aaron Curran had used to keep his staff in line, but immediately abandoned the idea. It was too

soon, and too aggressive an approach. I needed to be
subtle, applying charm and common sense to achieve
what was needed, and even then not until I had a better
idea of how things worked. For the moment, I would
allow them to continue as before, and to believe I was
content with things the way they were.

I went outside again, through the huge double
doors of the new part of the winery into the work
yard, an area that had been largely off-limits when I
was a child. That alone made it quite satisfying just
to be there as the owner, but there was nothing to see
beyond two pallet loads of new bottles and the ancient
high-wheeled tractor, a curious contraption designed
to straddle a row of vines as it went along. Beyond, the
gates stood open to the road, a dusty strip of tarmac
running between tall, overhanging trees that made
patterns of sunlight on the ground.

That was more how I remembered La Fleur, and
I walked a little way along to where the trees gave
way to an open hilltop covered with vines. The front
gate to the château was only a little further along, with
twin pillars ten-feet tall and carved with fleur-de-lys
to either side of massive wrought-iron gates bearing
the same motif. A wrought-iron arch curved over the
top, with the name of the estate in tall letters above
the legend: 'Propriétaire Mlle Adèle Montaubin'.
Montaubin had been my mother's maiden name,
and the ironwork evidently dated from before Adèle
had taken her first husband – or perhaps, knowing

her, she'd simply declined to adopt her married names, to reinforce her keeping her ownership of La Fleur sole and unchallenged, and her independence uncompromised.

The overall effect was to make the gates look almost fortified, like the entrance to some ancient castle, which had always struck me as a bit odd when there wasn't even a fence to either side, but just the ditch that marked off vineyard from road. It had always been journey's end for me, a vast relief after the long, long drive south from Calais, a memory that brought me a touch of sadness for my parents, and while the gates had always stood open in welcome, they were now not only shut but seemed to be rusted into place.

I walked around the gates and started down the drive, keen to push away the sudden melancholy that was making my already mixed feelings yet more complicated. The sight of the front of the château helped, bringing home just how grand a property I'd inherited, and also prompting the thought that, had it been in London, it would have been worth tens of millions of pounds and made me the envy of the likes of Aaron Curran. I wished he could have seen it anyway, if only to puncture his air of ineffable superiority just a little, but I wasn't even sure if it would. He had enough wealth to buy a similar estate, if it suited his fancy, but at least I was no longer obliged the play the eager, obliging office worker, and my mouth curved up into a smile once more as I remembered the look on his face as I poured water into his lap. That brought me to what I'd done afterwards, and more mixed feelings arose – a delicious sense of naughtiness strongly tinged with embarrassment.

The drive was an odd shape, an elongated S that seemed to have been designed to allow carriages to draw up to the front door and then move on to the stables without getting in the way of the carriage behind – or at least that was how Aunt Adèle had explained it to me. I followed the drive around, meaning to continue on to the maze of hedges and the little walled garden that had been my favourite place as a child, only to have my attention caught by a flash of scarlet among the line of trees beyond the lawns. That was another familiar haunt of mine, the line of big poplars growing along a low bank providing the perfect cover when I'd wanted to help myself to a bunch or two of ripe grapes.

I changed course, partly from simple curiosity, partly because I wanted to be sure that whoever was there had a right to be, as none of the Belairs had been wearing scarlet and didn't seem very likely to, either. Whoever it was had gone down the bank, presumably in among the vines, and I had nearly reached the trees when I heard laughter, youthful, joyful and distinctly feminine. I slowed a little, and instead of striding boldly between the poplars and down the bank, I paused to peep out from behind a tree trunk.

The vines stretched away down the slope below me, the summer-green foliage shifting slightly in the faint breeze, the grapes already golden and speckled with brown, but there was nobody to be seen. That could only mean she'd gone left, in among the hedges. I turned the same way and immediately caught the sound of her laughter a second time, but now answered by a deep, masculine growl followed by a squeak of happy surprise, again very feminine. Whatever was going on was clearly both intimate and private, but it was also on my property and I hesitated only a moment before moving on.

Too many years had passed for me to remember all the little ins and outs of the hedges, but the voices seemed to be coming from near the bottom corner, where I recalled there was a little circular space sheltered by a huge oak, with a swing hanging from one massive overhanging branch. I could see ropes, so the swing was presumably still there, and as I drew closer, the ropes began to move, accompanied by more laughter, quieter now and more than a little excited. Again I hesitated, and again I went forward, doing my best to focus on my sense of indignation at what might very well be a trespass, while trying to ignore the feeling that I was being a Peeping Thomasina.

The yew hedges didn't seem to tower up the way I remembered them, but they were still a lot taller than me. They were also quite badly overgrown, and scruffy in places, so that before long I'd come to a bit where a hole allowed me to duck down to get a moderately clear view of the swing. As I'd expected, a girl was using it, younger than me if not by all that much, with a riot of jet-black curls framing a pretty, rounded face, her figure petite but with quite full curves, although it wouldn't have been fair to call her overweight. I could be very sure of that, because she'd let down the front of the brilliant scarlet summer dress she had on to show off her bare breasts, and, as she swung back and forth, the short, loose skirt would rise with the air, revealing the fact that she had no knickers on, to me and to the man who was watching her: Jean Belair.

All of that would have been shocking enough, but what really left me with my eyes wide and my mouth hanging open was not the show she was giving him, but his reaction. He was seated opposite her, on an ornate iron bench that might well have been placed there for the purpose, his trousers round his ankles, his massive, knot-muscled legs splayed apart, and his hand wrapped around the biggest cock I had ever seen. Not that I claim to be an expert on the relative sizes of male genitalia, but he was huge by any standards, and not only that but gnarled and veined and dark, more like something you'd expect on some grotesque piece of erotic statuary than anything flesh and blood.

There was no doubting that he was alive, though, very much so, and while the sight of him had me wincing and tightening my thighs, the girl on the swing seemed delighted. She certainly knew what she wanted, and wasn't the slightest bit reticent about getting it, either, suddenly jumping down from the swing to twist around, laughing as she flipped up the back of her dress to show off her bare bottom, then lowering herself onto him with a little wiggle. He responded by taking one plump breast in either hand and settling back onto the bench with a grunt, allowing her to ride him as he used his thick, gnarled fingers to stroke her nipples and squeeze at the softness of her chest.

I was a little surprised, having pictured him as the sort of man who'd take control during sex, if only by simple, rude power. A moment later he had, moving his hands from her chest to her waist and lifting her off his cock as if she weighed nothing at all. Her response was the same delighted squeak I'd heard before, and she gave no resistance as he laid her down over the swing and eased himself into her once more. My hand had gone to my throat as he begun to push into her, hard enough to make her gasp, with his hands now locked into the flesh of her hips.

She looked impossibly small, like a doll in his massive hands, while the sheer force of his thrusts was making her entire body shake and had set her panting and crying out in a helpless, abandoned ecstasy I couldn't help but envy, and pity. I also couldn't help but imagine myself in the same situation, pushed down and held in a grip I could never hope to break as I was taken in that most revealing, most undignified position, kneeling and bottom-up to my man.

It looked as if he was going to finish like that, to

judge by the sound of his bestial grunting and the expression of pleasure on his face, but he proved to be less selfish than I'd expected. He slowed down, his expression switching to a happy grin as he changed his grip, taking hold of the swing to rock her back and forth on his cock, slow and easy, to change her gasps and squeals to gentle sighs and little whimpering noises. She'd been clinging on to the swing to stop herself going face down in the patch of bare soil underneath it, but now moved her hands to her breasts, stroking and squeezing gently.

I made to slip away, telling myself I'd seen enough and that I was intruding, but he'd taken hold of his cock and was rocking the swing with one hand while rubbing himself on her, an act at once so rude and so desirable, I simply couldn't pull away. He was going to make her come, deliberately, and for all the triumphant, even cruel grin on his face as she began to gasp once more and to clutch at her breasts, it was a wonderfully kind thing to do. I for one would have been more than happy to indulge his sense of power and control over my body in return for that supreme moment of bliss, and as she screamed in climax, I was urgently wishing that I were in her place.

He was patient, too, waiting until she was spent before he pulled back, but clearly wasn't the sort of man to go easy on her just because she looked exhausted. She had gone limp over the swing, her head hanging low and her face slack with pleasure, only for her mouth to come wide in a fresh cry as he pushed himself back inside her with a single hard thrust. His hands closed on her hips again and he began to pump, once more jerking her back and forth like a rag doll. Only she no longer had the will to cling on to the swing; she went over, face down on the dirty ground, as he rammed himself into her ever harder, his face set and his mouth tight, only to spring wide in a cry of triumph and ecstasy as he came, deep inside her.

I just ran. It was too much, to see her handled that way and his sheer, animal power, so primeval, so male, that it had me as scared as I was turned on. I had to come, and I had to come while my emotions were still raw and fresh, allowing me to feed on my immediate reaction to his overwhelming virility. All I needed was a few minutes' peace somewhere I wouldn't get caught, and I knew exactly the place. At the far side of the hedges there was a blind alley with a high-backed, circular bench at the end, a bench no doubt intended as a lovers' seat. That was more or less what I wanted to use it for, if I could only remember the way.

It took three false starts, and I nearly ran into Jean and his girlfriend on their way back up to the house, but I got there, giggling at my own silly, dirty behaviour as I dropped into the warm gloom of the little alcove made by the seat and the tall yew hedges. A moment to gather my courage then I pushed my jeans and knickers down to my ankles. It felt lovely to be bare, so free, so rude, and after another moment I pulled up my top and bra to leave myself completely exposed. My hand slipped down between my legs and I closed my eyes, already in a state of bliss as I began to tease myself. There was a touch of jealousy and regret that it hadn't been me on the swing, but I pushed that aside, along with all thoughts of Aaron Curran, who'd been the only man on my mind for some time. Now it had to be Jean Belair, big, muscular, powerful Jean Belair with his enormous hands and his great tree trunk of a cock.

I thought of myself in his girlfriend's place, teasing him until he gave me what I wanted. He'd have appreciated my body, I was sure of that, his primitive masculinity too strong for anything but a straightforward reaction to my naked breasts and open thighs. I wouldn't have got on his lap, though, the way she had done; that was far too deliberate for me. Instead, I'd have carried on teasing him until he lost control, rising from the bench with his monstrous erection in his hand, grabbing me by my hair to push it deep into my mouth, twisting me around and throwing me down over the swing to take me roughly from behind.

My mouth came open in a cry of ecstasy, completely involuntary, but I held off from the final moment, teasing myself as I ran through my dirty fantasy again, from the moment of baring my breasts to him until I came with his beautiful cock pushed inside me to the very hilt. A third time and I'd begun to rub faster again, unable to hold back, with one hand clutching at my breasts and the other busy between my thighs, my mouth wide as I began to babble, begging out loud to be bent over and taken from behind over and over again, until at last my orgasm exploded in my head like a choreographed firework display, peak after glorious peak, until I finally let my body go limp – and opened my eyes to find myself looking full into the face of Madame Belair.

3

There may be more embarrassing things in this world than being caught masturbating by your new housekeeper, but not many. It certainly made it difficult to exert my authority over a woman who was not only more than twice my age, and had been doing things the same way for year after year anyway, but who also seemed to think she had some sort of undying mandate from my late aunt. Whatever I suggested in the way of changes or improvements at La Fleur would be met with the same response, that the old way was the way 'the lady' had ordained things should be done, and that therefore I should be content. There was also the implication that, while Aunt Adèle had been a lady, I wasn't, and not just because ladies didn't play with themselves in the shrubbery. To her, I was clearly an interloper, and while she was prepared to put up with the situation, she didn't have to like it.

Then there was Jean. When I met him later the same day, he treated me with a mixture of condescension and grudging respect, much what I'd have expected from my memory of him as a young man and given that I was now his boss. The next morning he was very different, and kept giving me the most disturbing looks – pensive, knowing, slightly amused. I was sure his mother had told him what had happened, no doubt in the most unflattering terms, and that he rather liked the idea while also thinking of me as easy, a little English tart. It also seemed likely that he'd worked out the full story, knew I'd been peeping and how I'd responded, a thought that was enough to bring the blood to my cheeks every time I saw him.

That was rather a lot, as he and his father spent the morning giving me a guided tour of the winery and the vineyards, explaining how things were done, which grape varieties were planted in which plots, and why. I could tell they were wary of change and expecting some sort of challenge, or perhaps a demand for modernisation, but the more they told me, the more I realised how little I really knew about the business. Only as we walked back towards the house did Luc come up with something I felt I could get my teeth into, phrased in his usual assertive manner.

'You will want to attend the fair in Bordeaux.'

'To market our wines? Yes, of course . . .'

'We belong to an association of independent growers. There are fairs in Bordeaux, Paris, Lyon, Marseille, Lille. Liselotte will show you what to do.'

'Okay, but who is Liselotte?'

I'd already guessed the answer from the grin on Jean's face, but he had to rub it in.

'She's met Liselotte, but Liselotte hasn't met her, not yet.'

Luc looked puzzled for an instant, then shrugged and carried on.

'Liselotte makes for a pretty face behind the stall; always good for business. She'll soon teach you the right way.'

I finally gave in to my rising exasperation at his attitude.

'I'll certainly study your marketing strategy before making any changes, but it's clearly inefficient. I'll need to inspect the accounts as well.'

'You must speak to Liselotte, and to my wife. Now, lunch.'

As he finished he moved to one side, ducking down to inspect a bunch of grapes. It was a move clearly intended to end the conversation, and I was going to say something more when I caught sight of Jean's grin. He looked more amused than ever, no doubt looking forward to my attempt to challenge his father's authority, so I held my peace. As we continued back towards the house, I found myself starting to plot in my head, something I always do when challenged.

Having staff was one thing, and I knew it wasn't realistic to expect a selection of obliging and respectful peasants, but the Belairs really were a bit much. My first thought was to sack them and bring in new staff, preferably trained wine professionals from elsewhere in the region. Unfortunately, that would make me

deeply unpopular, and they undoubtedly knew everybody within miles and were probably related to a good
many of them. I wanted my new home to be a friendly,
easy-going place, free from the stresses and rivalries
I'd hated so much in London. Besides, they knew how
the place worked, and there was no doubt that Luc
Belair was a skilled winemaker and perhaps the only
person capable of teasing out the qualities that set La
Fleur apart.

The obvious alternative was to attempt to exert my
authority, as I'd done when placed in charge of teams
back in the City. Even before I'd left university, I'd
known that it was as important to work on my skills as
a team leader as it was to be able to do my actual job. I'd
been good enough to gain Aaron Curran's confidence,
but everybody I'd worked with had been part of the
same rat race and keen to look good. I couldn't see the
Belairs reacting well, especially as I was younger and
less experienced than any of them. All I'd get was grief.

A much better technique was to appear to accept
their ways while gradually building up a power base,
and I could see how it ought to be done. First, I'd work
on Liselotte, who was more or less my own age. She in
turn would influence Jean, being his girlfriend, while
he was plainly the apple of his mother's eye and so
would influence her in turn. Luc would then fall into
line for the sake of marital peace. It all made sense.

Another advantage was that if I made an effort to be
friends with Liselotte, I had the perfect excuse not to

allow my natural attraction to Jean to get the better of me. I believe in respecting other people's relationships, and have always found it far easier to turn down a man who's with a friend than merely because I know it's a bad idea. Jean was a prime example: altogether too virile, too primitive in his masculinity, for me to reject unless I had a compelling reason to do so. The knowledge that if I gave in to my desire, I'd probably end up well and truly under the thumb of his awful mother might not be quite enough to stop me, but loyalty to a friend would be.

I was smiling by the time we got back to the house, and made a point of complimenting Madame Belair on the salad of cold meats and artichoke hearts she'd laid out for us. Luc had disappeared into the winery and came back with a jug of red wine, which he poured out into beakers with a casual hand. I could remember how it had been with Aunt Adèle, who would take lunch in the dining room with family and usually a guest or two, while the staff ate in the kitchen. Evidently, I wasn't to be accorded the same privilege, but it was the last thing I'd have wanted, anyway.

Liselotte soon joined us, greeting Jean with an easy kiss before turning to me to introduce herself with a respectful curtsey and a knowing look that sent the blood to my cheeks again, hotter than ever. She was dressed much as she had been the day before, in a light summer dress, only blue instead of scarlet. The cotton clung to her curves, making it quite plain that she had no bra on, and probably no knickers, either, but she obviously didn't care. Nor did the others, apparently, even Madame Belair, although she seemed to go through life with an air of general disapproval anyway.

It was at least easy to talk, as Luc never stopped and Jean contributed his fair share of witty remarks, while Liselotte was completely without pretence, her talk and her manner as free and easy as the wind. They soon had me laughing, and for the first time since my arrival at La Fleur, I began to relax properly, while as we ate Luc continued to pour from the wine jug with a liberal hand. I was hungry after the long morning's walk around the estate, and ate my fill of the salad, but I'd forgotten how long the French take over lunch. When it was finished, Madame Belair produced a plate of cheese and then a *tarte Tatin*. By then I was full, but it seemed rude to turn down her efforts, or the bottle of old Monbazillac that Luc retrieved from the cellar.

The ancient brass and mahogany clock on the mantelpiece had struck three before Luc Belair muttered something about needing to get on with his work and left, closely followed by his wife. I knew there was any number of things I ought be doing, but it was very easy to convince myself that my priority was making friends with Liselotte, and I really didn't want to move. The wine had left me pleasantly tipsy, too, and drowsy, watching tiny dust motes dance in the beams of sunlight streaming through the windows as I sipped from my glass and listened to Jean teasing Liselotte. He was getting quite personal, certainly more than any man I'd been with would have dared in front of another woman, but she didn't seem to mind. I did, unable to hold back my blushes, which they could hardly help but notice. Jean laughed and gestured towards me.

'The English, so reserved.'

Liselotte answered immediately.

'Not too reserved. Shy, maybe.'

Jean laughed again as my cheeks grew hotter still. I should have had some snappy answer, but I couldn't think of anything to say, and my French is good but not really up to witty rustic repartee. So I just sat there, grinning like an idiot and trying vainly to hide my blushes behind my glass. I knew exactly what she meant – that I couldn't be all that reserved if I'd been playing with myself in the garden. Her voice was bold and easy as she spoke again.

'Did you see us, on the swing?'

I found myself nodding automatically, my face burning hot, and hotter still as she responded with a delighted laugh, making her heavy breasts move beneath the light cotton of her dress. Jean's grin had become broader than ever, and it was impossible not to picture them as they had been the day before, with Liselotte showing off on the swing, or thrown over it as he took her from behind. My nipples had grown stiff, making two painfully obvious little bumps in my dress, which they could hardly fail to notice, so I made what was supposed to be a casual gesture and tried to find a joking remark to go with it, but no words came, only a weak croak. Jean began to speak again, perhaps to defuse the tension, but Liselotte got in first, her eyes glittering with wine and mischief.

'Did you like what you saw? He is fine, isn't he?'

Jean laughed. 'Liselotte, that's not kind!'

She turned to him, taunting. 'Oh, but you are, like a great big bull. I don't suppose Mademoiselle Sherborne has ever had a man like you, not in London, have you, mam'selle? So big, so strong.'

Jean lifted one thick, calloused finger and wagged it at her, playfully enough but with more than a hint of physical power.

'Don't tease her, Liselotte, or maybe I'll put you across my lap and spank you, right in front of her, and don't tease me, because you know what will happen then.'

My reaction changed in an instant, to shock and indignation that any modern man could suggest such a thing, even a man like Jean, but Liselotte's voice was full of laughter as she answered him.

'You'd like that, wouldn't you, Jean, to show me off for Mademoiselle Sherborne . . . to show what a big, strong man you are?'

Jean's eyebrows rose in surprise and he started to get up. Liselotte gave a squeak of mingled alarm and delight, jumped up and fled. Jean turned to me with a brief grin and followed her through the kitchen door, leaving me alone at the table.

For a long moment I just sat there, fiddling with my wine glass as I struggled to calm down. My emotions were in a tangle; embarrassment, outrage, curiosity and completely involuntary arousal all vied for first place in my head, but were completely unable to compete with a strange sensation of weakness, a sensation I was desperately trying to tell myself had nothing whatsoever to do with Jean's threat to Liselotte and how she'd reacted.

It couldn't have, not for me, not for Elise Sherborne. I knew there were women who liked their bottoms smacked as a prelude to sex, but I'd always thought of them as mixed up, weird, even. Liselotte didn't fit the image at all, with her enviable curves and her open, unashamed sexuality. I certainly didn't, and yet, as I sat there, it was impossible to bite down my excitement, or the urgent need to follow them and watch her get it, and more, because he was sure to take her all the way once he had dealt with her bottom.

They'd pretty much invited me to watch, but left me in the agonising position of having to follow them down among the hedges instead of being able to say yes or no. I'd look like a Peeping Thomasina again, but this time they'd know I was there. They'd know how excited it made me, too, perhaps even invite me to play with myself while I watched, or worse. Maybe Jean would use my behaviour as an excuse to spank

me too, down across his knee with my dress turned
up and my knickers pulled down in front of Liselotte.
It was a thought at once so unbearably inappropriate
and so exciting that a sob broke from my lips, and I
found myself glancing around in sudden guilt in case
Madame Belair was within hearing range.

She wasn't, but noises from upstairs suggested that
she was doing something in the bedrooms, which
meant she was safely out of the way, removing one
more excuse for not following Jean and Liselotte. Still
I hesitated, trying to tell myself that they'd actually
left the house because they wanted some privacy,
but I knew it was a lie. They'd included me in their
flirtatious game, at least to the point at which it was
clear they wouldn't mind if I came down to watch,
although Jean for one seemed to think of me as a poor
repressed little English girl who wouldn't dare, not
when he knew what they were planning to get up to.

That was what decided it for me. He'd always treated
me as if I was a little girl, and I had been once, but not
any more. Liselotte was as bad, deliberately taunting
me so that I'd go down and watch. Only I wouldn't let
them see what they'd done to me; I'd be cool, calm and
collected, thoroughly British, standing casually to one
side with my nose in the air as I watched Liselotte get
her bottom laid bare and smacked. Maybe I'd even add
a few teasing comments, embarrassing her until her
blushes were as hot as mine had been, so that her face
ended up the same colour as her bottom.

I swallowed down the rest of my wine then decided that it would make a good prop and refilled my glass, emptying the bottle. Outside, the afternoon was hot and sultry, the air still and quiet but for the faint buzz of bumble bees among the flowers growing against the old wall – that and distant, happy laughter. They weren't exactly being quiet, and I found myself glancing nervously to the windows at the back of the house. Getting caught by Madame Belair was definitely not part of my plan, and I nearly went back indoors, only to realise that I could use the risk of being overheard as an excuse for following them, making me seem cooler still.

They'd gone through the arch that led from the old courtyard to the stables and gardens, the same way I'd walked back in disgrace the day before, which made it more than a little difficult to maintain my poise. It was going to be harder still if Jean caught up with Liselotte in the little blind alley where I'd been playing with myself, or by the swing, but her laughter seemed to be coming from much further away. Sure enough, when I came out at the bottom of the maze of hedges, I found myself looking down over the lowest part of the vineyards, where Liselotte was dodging among the vines as Jean tried to catch her. She was fast and agile, and hitching up her dress to show off long, bare legs allowed her to climb over the wires every bit as nimbly as he could.

It looked like stalemate, while his increasingly

desperate efforts to catch hold of her were quite
funny. I stood to watch for a while, sipping my wine in
a pose that I hope suggested casual amusement, but if
they had noticed I was there at all, they gave no sign,
and when Jean stumbled and went headlong into the
mud between two rows, I couldn't resist calling out a
comment.

'Don't worry, Liselotte, he's too drunk to catch you,
and too old!'

She laughed and waved, but as he got up he threw
me a glare that that made my stomach go tight with
apprehension. For one awful moment, I thought he
was going to turn his attention to me, and I nearly
ran, only for him to twist around, vault the wires and
grab at Liselotte. She was taken by surprise and had to
jump back, squealing in alarm and avoiding his fingers
by inches, but she was next to a vine and couldn't get
over the wires in time. He caught her dress, pulling
her in, then ducked quickly down to catch her around
the back of her knees. The next instant, she'd been
hauled up over his shoulder with no more effort than
had she been a doll, with her legs kicking and her hair
flying as she struggled to escape, calling him a pig and
thumping her fists on his back and buttocks, but still
laughing.

Jean paid no attention whatsoever, but set off down
the row with Liselotte slung across his shoulder,
carrying her with no more thought for her dignity
than he'd give a sack of potatoes. I hesitated, not sure

if I dared come closer, but my curiosity quickly got the better of me and I followed, telling myself that they were only playing, and that I'd be able to call a halt if things started to get out of hand. That was the theory, anyway, but from the way my heart was hammering, and the weak, yielding feeling in my belly, I wasn't at all sure if I'd be able to say anything to stop him, or if I even wanted to.

The vineyard ended where a belt of trees shrouded the river, but wild vines had sprung up here and there, creating a screen of green and gold heavy with grapes. At one point, the trunk of a fallen willow stuck out a little way, creating a perfect seat for a rest, maybe a solitary picnic, or in this case a spanking. Jean obviously thought so too, carrying the frantically wriggling Liselotte across to it and making himself comfortable at the exact centre. She immediately tried to escape, but he was far too strong for her, casually moving her from her perch on his shoulder to a yet more undignified position, across his legs with her bottom lifted to make a round, tempting ball under her skirts.

I stopped, a safe distance away, my throat dry and my heart hammering fit to burst from my chest, staring open-mouthed as he took a firm grip around her waist and began to pull up her dress. It was unthinkable – an impossibly rude, inappropriate thing to do to any woman – and yet he'd didn't so much as hesitate, and while she was wriggling like an eel and calling him as fine an assortment of names as I'd ever heard, she couldn't stop herself from giggling, too. Not that it made any difference. Up came her dress, and I discovered that she did have panties on after all – big, rather tight ones in plain white cotton that clung to the contours of her bottom.

They got pulled down in one casual movement, baring her so suddenly and so completely, I found my mouth coming open in a gasp of shock and sympathy that echoed her own cry of indignation. Jean didn't care, but set to work, landing a single firm swat across her bottom to make her flesh jump and shiver as she cried out in pained reaction. I started forward again, not really sure if she was enjoying herself any more and determined to intervene if he'd gone too far, but I'd barely taken a half-dozen steps, and he'd only landed another couple of smacks on her bottom, before he stopped spanking and instead slipped a hand between her thighs to cup her sex from behind.

Her back arched tight and she cried out once more, only now in ecstasy as he began to rub her, with her bottom pushed high against his fingers, the full pale moon of her cheeks now marked by a set of rapidly reddening handprints. I stopped, watching in astonishment as he deliberately masturbated her, my face flushed hot with embarrassment but also arousal, my fingers twisted into the front of my dress. He turned towards me, just long enough to give me a grin and a wink, before he began to spank Liselotte once more.

She immediately started kicking her feet and wriggling in his grip, and it dawned on me that she enjoyed making a fight of it, either that or she simply couldn't help reacting to the pain and shame of her spanking in the most natural way possible. There was no doubt about Jean, though. He was grinning and laughing to himself as he spanked her, and showing off too, deliberately smacking her cheeks one by one with an upwards motion to make them bounce and jiggle, and ensuring that every single rude detail of her rear view was on full display, to him and to me.

He wasn't exactly being discreet about it, either, but rather was clearly visible from the entire sweep of the vineyard and the windows of the top floor of the house, but he didn't seem to care, spanking away merrily until poor Liselotte's bottom was a glowing red ball and her yelps and squeals had given way to gasps and sighs. I wanted to point out the risks he was taking, and perhaps suggest going in among the trees, but that would have an admission of my own desire and I held back, only for Jean to stop, sling Liselotte over his shoulder once more and stand up from the tree trunk.

There was no struggling this time. She lay limply across his shoulder, her hot red bottom pointed at the sky and her feet cocked apart in her panties, which had fallen right down as she'd been spanked. As they disappeared in among the foliage, I hesitated only a moment and then followed. It was cool and dim beneath the willows, with the wild vines shielding the sunlight, but there was an open area right beside the river. Jean laid Liselotte down in the long sunlit grass, her thighs wide and accepting, her knickers still on one ankle. He hadn't even bothered to undress, but simply unfastened his working blues at the front to pull out his already hard cock before mounting her without preamble. One long smooth push and he was inside her, his hips thrusting hard as her arms came up and around his shoulders.

I stayed back in the shadows, concealed from the house and partially concealed from them, not that they seemed to notice, now too wrapped up in their shared ecstasy to worry about me, or what I was doing. They had invited me to watch, though, more or less, and teased me about how I'd behaved the day before, which made it so much easier as I bunched up my dress and pressed my knuckles to the sodden cotton of my panties. I was going to do it, I couldn't stop myself, for all my shame at being so impossibly rude; and as I began to rub, I found my thoughts going back to the spanking.

My sense of overwhelming weakness had never really gone away, but as I thought of how he'd dealt with her, it came on stronger than ever. It had been so effortless, so casual, a grossly inappropriate act carried out as if it were the most natural thing in the world, and for all Liselotte's struggles and cries, she'd obviously enjoyed it too. At the very least, she'd known it would turn her on; and if Liselotte, then why not me? He'd have taken me so easily, hauled up across his broad, muscular shoulders and carried down to where he could sit in comfort. I'd be put across his knee, my dress pulled up and my knickers taken down, utterly without ceremony, as if it were perfectly reasonable to bare my bottom to the world for a good, firm spanking.

I was clutching at myself, my fingers pressed deep into the wet cotton of my panties as I rubbed at the still wetter flesh beneath, already on the edge of orgasm, when Jean suddenly pulled free. He twisted Liselotte over and onto her knees in a single smooth motion, presenting himself with her rosy red cheeks pushed well up for rear entry. I thought he'd take her, but instead he grabbed hold of his erection and pushed it into the soft, wet groove between the lips of her sex, not in her, but rubbing on her clitoris. It was the same filthy, wonderful trick he'd played before, using the head of his cock to make her come, but maybe no more for her pleasure than to enjoy the helpless surrender of her body.

She certainly couldn't help herself, gasping out her ecstasy and clutching at the grass beneath her while the grinning Jean began to smack her bottom once more. The sudden change had broken my concentration and I was stroking myself more gently as he pleasured her, keen to watch her come and perhaps have them watch while I did it to myself. It wasn't going to take long, either, with Liselotte's gasps and moans growing rapidly more urgent and little shivers already passing through her body as he pushed her higher still.

When it hit her, she screamed, every muscle in her body seemingly locked tight, with Jean rubbing hard and fast while still spanking her to a firm, even rhythm. I could guess what was going on in her head, and I needed the same, if only the fantasy, but even as I began to rub more firmly, once more Jean pulled back, leaving Liselotte to collapse into the warm grass, her smacked bottom still cocked high and her knees wide open. He turned to me, his monstrous erection straining out from his dishevelled working blues and his mouth spread into a sloppy, meaningful grin.

'And you, Elise?'

'No . . . thank you, I . . .'

My words broke off in a sob and I was going down, onto my knees in the warm grass, but even then I didn't have the courage to stick my bottom in the air for what I really wanted, and as he reached me, brandishing his cock, he spoke again.

'Okay, in your mouth, if you like.'

I didn't have it in me to argue, my sense of weakness too strong to resist. My mouth came wide as to accept his cock and I'd taken him in, sucking eagerly as I gave way to my arousal. My dress and bra came up as one, baring my breasts to him in a gesture as much of surrender as of desire; my fingers went down the front of my panties and I was masturbating shamelessly as I sucked on his erection. I still wanted more – a good hard spanking and then the same rude treatment he'd given Liselotte – but I couldn't bring myself to ask.

He was getting too excited anyway, pushing deep with his hand tangled in my hair, while Liselotte had rolled onto her side, her head propped up on one hand in a languid, sleepy pose as she watched me suck her boyfriend from beneath half-closed eyelids. There was something about the quality of her attention that brought back my sense of shame, stronger than ever, and it was no surprise what happened next. There I was, on my knees to her boyfriend, with his cock in my mouth and my hand down my panties, masturbating over what I'd seen and what I was about to do. Then it had happened and she was laughing as she watched me eagerly swallowing everything Jean had to give me, down into my belly, even as my body went tight in one of the longest and hardest orgasms of my life.

4

When I set out to build my power base at La Fleur, I hadn't intended to kick off with a *ménage à trois*, let alone a kinky one, but there was no denying it was a good tactic. Liselotte and I now shared a guilty and delicious secret, always a good way to bond, although she was extraordinarily casual about what had happened, taking a moment to make sure I knew that Jean was her man, but otherwise treating it all as harmless fun. Jean was more casual still, and seemed to accept how I'd behaved towards him as no more than his due. Not that he was conceited about it, as most of the men I knew would have been. He was more like a prize bull, taking female attention absolutely for granted.

For me, it was very different. I've always thought of myself as sexually liberated, and it wasn't even the first time I'd had a threesome, but previously it had been with long-established friends. There had always been some sort of excuse as well, such as the night at college when my friend Lucy and I stripped to give a male colleague a birthday treat, and ended up providing him with a helping hand. He'd had a good feel, and I hadn't minded, but that was as far as it went. I'd played it very cool, barely letting my own arousal show at all, at least until later on, when I was alone in bed, and even then it had all been very conventional. This time, I'd really let myself go, with comparative strangers, and it had been distinctly kinky. Not only had I enjoyed watching another woman being spanked, but all it would have taken was a gentle push and I'd have been over his knee in her place and probably enjoying it just as much. That was the difficult bit, because it went against everything I'd believed in about how men and women should relate. Sex as equals was one thing, but to be spanked, on my bare bottom, while held down across a strong man's lap, was impossibly inappropriate, and impossibly exciting. Fortunately, or unfortunately, it hadn't actually happened, but that didn't stop me thinking about it – quite the opposite – and wondering if there might be a next time, and if so, how I could make sure I got it without admitting to my need.

Over the next few days, my feelings wavered between guilt and desire; I was appalled by my own reactions, but unable to fight my need. In my calmer moods, which prevailed most of the time, I'd tell myself I'd take advantage of the situation by capitalising on the bond of friendship I'd formed with Liselotte, while politely declining any further involvement; but after a few glasses of wine, or lying alone in bed of an evening, the strange, weak feelings would come back and I'd find myself unable to deny that, if the situation was right, it would happen again, and more.

I was kept busy, anyway, learning the business from the Belairs and from Liselotte, who was fast becoming a close friend – I even told her about Aaron and the water cooler incident. I found it surprisingly easy to fall in with the routine of the house, and within a week, London and my previous life seemed impossibly distant. I quickly abandoned the fashionable clothes and carefully judged look that had been so essential to working in the City, but which were both pointless and impractical at La Fleur. Liselotte's style made much more sense: loose, cool dresses with the minimum of underwear. I even took to putting my hair up in a bandana the way she did while she was working, and abandoning my shoes to pad around the house barefoot. Only Madame Belair took the slightest notice, and it was clear that she'd already decided I was more on a level with Liselotte than with my late aunt in any case.

Had Madame Belair had her way, I'd have done little or no work, both because she plainly doubted my competence and because she felt it unsuitable for the owner of the château. The others disagreed, a minor victory on my part but one I deliberately didn't try to exploit, simply agreeing to accompany Liselotte to the local market in Bergerac that weekend and to let her decide how things should be run. It sounded simple enough, with our stall one among many selling local produce; all I had to do was offer samples of our wines to customers and make myself pleasant, while ensuring that nobody took unfair advantage of our generosity.

We were up early that morning, with the sun striking gold from the old yellow stone of the house and a touch of chill in the air to hint at the approach of autumn. Liselotte had made more effort than usual, with a red bandana wrapped around her forehead to hold back her black curls, giving her an exotic, slightly Andalusian look clearly designed to draw attention. I followed suit, attempting to match the air of playful charm she'd achieved, although it wasn't my usual style and I ended up looking a bit of a ragamuffin. Jean at least seemed impressed and gave me several distinctly hot looks as he loaded the van with cases of wine.

I'd assumed he'd be coming with us, but apparently there were more important things to do, and Liselotte and I set off together, down from the hills and into Bergerac. It was a trip I remembered from childhood, although everything now seemed so much smaller. Even the great spire of the cathedral was far less imposing than the image I'd kept in my head, and the old town no longer seemed a huge and slightly sinister maze, but small and quaint. Yet even then I realised that my perceptions had changed far more than the town. The riverfront was certainly no different, with the huge grey carp nuzzling at the walls just beneath the water's surface, and the black wood gabarres coming and going from the quay with their cargoes of tourists. The cluster of restaurants and specialist shops was also much as I remembered from my last visit, when I'd received a sharp word from Aunt Adèle for giggling at the enormous nose on the statue of Cyrano de Bergerac. I could have happily spent all day just wandering around the town, revisiting old memories and perhaps watching the world go by from one of the cafés in the Grand Rue, but I'd left Liselotte alone to set up our stall and eventually made my way back to the old town, where I was given a look that would have done my aunt credit, and quickly joined her in trying to sell our wines.

We were soon busy, and while there were several other stalls selling wine, we had one great advantage. I'd always known that the Dordogne was popular with reasonably well-off ex-pats, as that was how my parents had met, but I'd never realised just how many British people there were in the area. They seemed to like the sound of my voice, and talking in English, as well as flirting. I did my best to respond in kind, while politely turning down the bolder spirits, most of whom were much too old, and in any case my life was quite complicated enough. Before long, I was doing most of the selling, while Liselotte struggled to keep up with the orders, and I'd told my story at least a dozen times, with every single listener commending me on my decision in coming to France.

One of my admirers was particularly persistent: John Lambert, a tall, white-haired ex-barrister with the look of a practised if old-fashioned Lothario. Had he been thirty years younger, I might even have been interested, and he did have the knack of making me laugh, but when he suggested a gabarre trip that evening, I couldn't help telling him that it would be too much like being taken out by my grandfather. His eyebrows rose in indignation, only partly put on, then he laughed, picked up his purchases and walked away from the stall.

I turned to another customer, assuming I'd successfully put John off, but kept a half-eye on him as he moved away. He was taller than most of the people there, and easy to keep track of as he crossed the square to a flower stall with a magnificent display of roses. I realised he was going to buy me a bouquet and immediately felt that burst of oddly mingled delight and irritation with which every woman must be familiar – emotions that multiplied tenfold an instant later and which now had nothing to do with John Lambert.

Next to him at the flower stall was another man, equally tall but a great deal younger and unusual for being dressed in a smart designer suit rather than casual dress; a man I recognised at once, even from behind – Aaron Curran. I was immediately praying I was wrong and cursing myself for the sudden hammering of my heart and the butterflies that seemed to be holding a party in my stomach, but as he turned side-on, holding up the enormous bunch of red roses he'd bought, the last of my doubts were pushed aside. It was definitely Aaron. Curiosity swept in as I wondered what he was doing in Bergerac, then I felt a completely involuntary but painfully strong stab of jealousy for whoever was about to get the roses.

He held a large box of extremely expensive chocolates as well – the local, hand-made sort. I'd always yearned after them as a child, staring longingly through the shop window, entranced by the pink-and-gold foil wrappers. Aunt Adèle had always kept a small box of them at La Fleur, carefully locked away, but if I'd been good enough to meet her exacting standards during the week, I would be permitted a single one after church on Sundays, never more. Now some lucky girl was about to get about a kilo of them, along with two dozen or so huge roses with petals like red velvet, and whatever else Aaron chose to buy, as he clearly wasn't finished. To cap it all, he'd moved to one of the rival wine stalls and was accepting a glass of clear golden liquid from the proprietor. I stifled a curse, completely unable to listen to the voice of logic in my head telling me that he was nothing to do with me and that I'd well and truly burnt my bridges anyway. Emotion ruled, wild and stormy, jealousy and regret and self-reproach, along with a healthy dose of embarrassment as I remembered how I'd behaved in the shower the day I'd resigned.

Voices finally penetrated my brain, first a man's, then Liselotte's.

'Please can I taste the Vieilles Vignes?'

'Elise, what's the matter?'

I snapped back to earth, mumbling an apology to the customer as I poured him his tasting sample, then turning to speak to Liselotte in a hiss.

'The man by the Domaine Saint Laurent stand, the tall man. That's my ex-boss!'

'The one you poured water all over?'

'Yes!'

She laughed.

'It's not funny, Liselotte. He . . . I . . .'

I broke off, flustered and not really quite sure why I was making such a fuss, but before I could explain my feelings, Liselotte leant close to my ear, whispering.

'What is it? Do you think he'll come over here and spank you?'

I went crimson, the blood rushing to my face to set my cheeks on fire, and my mouth opening and closing as if I were a hungry goldfish, while Liselotte dissolved into giggles. Several people wanted my attention and were giving me odd looks – puzzled, amused, or disapproving – so I tried to cover up my embarrassment by attending to them, but all the while my head was spinning with an image clearly conjured up in my mind's eye by Liselotte's cruel remark.

Aaron would come over to taste with us, recognise me, give me a single, hard look, then come behind the stall, sit down on the pile of wine cases and put me over his knee. I wouldn't even have the strength to put up a fight, but he'd still take a firm grip, with my arm twisted up into the small of my back. He'd hold me like that, helpless across his knee, wriggling with embarrassment but unable to resist, either physically or mentally, while my dress was turned up and my knickers were taken down, laying my bottom bare to the entire market. Then I'd be spanked, hard, squirming in his grip and kicking my legs in my panties as I apologised over and over again for what I'd done.

'Elise! It *is* you, isn't it?'

'Aaron, hi.'

He'd appeared from one side, taking me by surprise, and it had been all I could do to keep my voice level as I answered him, still with that awful picture in my head, so vivid I actually took a step back, although with Liselotte behind me and the wine cases to the other side, there would have been no escape. I knew full well he wouldn't do anything of the sort, and that it was highly unlikely even to have crossed his mind. He didn't even look cross – the complete opposite, in fact, the expression on his face nothing short of delighted as he carried on.

'I thought you might be here when I saw the wine stalls. Vicky Bell told me you'd hidden yourself away somewhere down here, so I thought I'd stop by and say hello.'

'Hello. But . . . but isn't it a long way to come, just to see me?'

'Oh no, I've been thinking of buying a property in

France for a while, Provence probably, but I like to consider all my options before making a decision.'

'Oh. So who's the lucky girl?'

'The flowers? They're for you, of course. I got your address from the tourist office, and I was going to drive up after lunch, but seeing as you're here . . .'

He held the bouquet out to me and I took it, unable to hold back my flush of gratitude and too confused and surprised to know what to make of the situation. Aaron had no such difficulties, holding out the chocolates as he spoke again.

'And these, too. I'm told they're the best.'

'They are. Thank you.'

'My pleasure. Do you break for lunch?'

It was as good as an invitation, but I just wasn't ready to accept, or sure if I really wanted to.

'No, I . . . This is my friend . . . my colleague, Liselotte. We've been very busy and she needs my help.'

He turned his best schoolboy grin on Liselotte and spoke in French easily as good as my own, if slightly tinged by his very English accent.

'Charmed, and what a shame you're so busy.'

'Not at all. We've been doing so well, I'm going to have to call the château to bring more stock anyway. Enjoy your lunch, Elise, and Jean or Luc can come and take your place until you get back.'

I turned to her with what was intended to be a significant glare, but probably looked more like panic as I tried to think of another viable excuse, but Aaron was too quick for me.

'I'll come back just before twelve, then. That will give me a chance to sample your wares first. For now, I'd better look around and pick a decent restaurant. Until later.'

He simply walked away, leaving me with my hands full of roses and a good half-dozen customers vying for my attention. I wanted to explain the situation to Liselotte in more detail, or to smack her bottom for her, seeing as she seemed to regard that sort of thing as fair play, but there were far too many people around. In any case, she was wearing a quiet, self-satisfied smile, and I was fairly sure she'd just have laughed at me. I swallowed my feelings and got on with work, only to find myself presented with the perfect target when she had to crawl into the back of the van to get out the last few wine cases. The doors were open, shielding us from most of the crowd, while her bottom made a tempting ball beneath her dress. One firm smack, a most satisfying squeak of surprise from Liselotte, and I drew away, only to realise that I'd been spotted after all.

John Lambert had been coming towards us along the narrow strip of pavement at the back of the stalls and had just emerged from behind another vehicle, a single red rose in his hand. For an instant, I thought I'd got away with it, only for his expression to shift to a distinctly smug grin as he drew close.

'A spot of discipline for the staff, eh? That's what I like to see. This is for you, and my offer remains open, including dinner on the water, if you don't mind being seen with a man who looks like your grandfather, that is?'

'Um . . . thank you, but I am actually busy.'

'Ah, so I have a rival, eh? The young man with the enormous bouquet, I imagine?'

'Yes, um . . . Ow!'

Liselotte had climbed out of the van and immediately given me the same treatment I'd given her, indifferent to the presence of a man, and one who was trying to chat me up at that – or, knowing her, deliberately showing off in order to embarrass me. I was tempted to retaliate, but the grin on John Lambert's face was now almost a leer and I didn't want to give him any ideas, so I contented myself with wagging my finger at her as she turned back to the stall and carried on with her work.

'Sorry about that. Um . . . look, it's very sweet of you to ask, and thank you for the lovely rose, but my life is far too complicated as it is, so I'm afraid the answer is no. Sorry.'

It was the kindest and most sensible thing to do, turning him down while doing my best to leave his ego unscratched. Clever put-downs and dramatic rejections are all very well, but as I was discovering with Aaron Curran, they don't always have the intended effect. I needed John Lambert to go quietly away, not to fix me in his mind as unfinished business, or, worse, as a cause for resentment. He gave a sad smile in response and I knew I'd hit the right note even before he replied.

'So be it. I admit defeat, but I trust there are no hard feelings and that we'll be able to get along as neighbours?'

'Are we neighbours?'

'If you're working at Château La Fleur we are. Fairly close, anyway. I live in Colombier.'

'That's not far, I suppose, but I don't work at Château La Fleur. I own Château La Fleur.'

I'd said it automatically and immediately wished I hadn't as the light of interest in his eyes changed from pure old-fashioned lust to something more calculating.

'I see. I knew Madame de Regnier had passed away, of course, but . . .'

'I'm her niece.'

'Ah, then that explains a great many things. I deal in property and had hoped to buy. I was surprised when the domaine didn't come on to the market.'

'Well, now you know.'

'I do indeed, and if you ever consider selling, please do at least give me the chance to make an offer, Mademoiselle de Regnier.'

'Sherborne, Elise Sherborne, but I'm not selling.'

He'd offered me his card as he spoke and as I took it, he gave me his sad little smile once more, and then went on.

'It seems it's not my day. At least allow me a glass

of your superb Monbazillac, if I am to face rejection at every turn.'

It seemed rude not to, and I poured him a full glass of the '05, which he accepted with a gracious nod before holding it up to the light to admire the golden gleams in the sunlight. I took the opportunity to break away, returning to the other customers, but he was in no hurry, stepping just a little to one side and lingering over his wine with obvious enjoyment. When he finally finished, he put the glass back down on our stall, thanked me and gave me his sad little smile one more time before moving away.

I quickly put him out of my mind, but I couldn't do the same for Aaron Curran. He'd shaken me quite badly, more so than I'd have expected, even allowing for our past history. I didn't believe he'd just happened to be in the area, either, not when he'd obviously made an effort to seek me out and had been buying chocolates and roses. That was hardly the behaviour I'd have expected of him, given my stormy exit from his company. Admittedly, I've known men who seemed to be encouraged by rejection, but I wouldn't have numbered him among them, and had been assuming that even if what Vicky had said was true, he would have moved on to somebody else. Now it seemed he hadn't, and was prepared to go to considerable effort and expense to be with me, or at the very least to take me to bed. I couldn't deny that I felt flattered, but I wasn't at all sure how I wanted to react, if at all.

There was no denying one thing: he gave me butter-flies in my stomach in a way I hadn't experienced since I was a teenager, along with feelings of excitement and confusion and doubt. That was all very different to the way I reacted to Jean Belair, who made me wet and weak, not so much in need of kisses and tender words as being put on my knees and taken roughly from behind. I wondered if I was in love with Aaron, only for my pride immediately to rebel at the thought, then die down as I told myself that he was no longer my boss, and any relationship between us no longer needed to be unequal.

By lunchtime, I'd managed to regain my composure. He came back to the stall a few minutes before twelve, as he'd promised, carrying two bulky shopping bags. I greeted him in a friendly but casual manner, and he was concentrating on tasting our wines when Jean arrived with the new stock. The instant Jean climbed from the car, I sensed a change in Aaron, a sudden wariness and a shift in the way he stood, which made me think of a tomcat sizing up a potential rival. Not that Jean seemed to care or even notice, accepting Aaron's handshake with his usual bluff masculinity before kissing both me and Liselotte. Aaron made a point of buying one of the most expensive bottles we had on tasting, our single vineyard *cuvée* from the hot '03 vintage, and when we left the stall, he couldn't help but comment.

'He's a bit forward for the help, isn't he?'

'He's French, and anyway, I don't really see them as my employees. I've known Jean since I was a kid, when I used to come here on holiday.'

'And he's Liselotte's husband?'

'No. They're lovers, but . . .'

I broke off with a shrug, keen to leave Aaron guessing, and then changed the subject.

'Where are you taking me?'

'On a picnic. I looked at the restaurants, but there are so many delicious things in the local shops – along with your wine, of course. Besides, everywhere is so crowded.'

'Well, yes, but the riverbank will be too, I expect.'

I'd guessed that was where he was taking me, as we'd turned down one of the little alleys that led to the waterfront, but he smiled at my objection, and when we reached the road, he hurried me across instead of turning towards the bridge. The quay was thronged with tourists, mostly either admiring the view or waiting for the next gabarre, but a number of smaller boats were moored to one side. He led me across to them, paid the attendant and helped me into one that was already afloat – a low-sided rowing boat with a rudder worked by strings. To judge from the bleached wood and cracked blue paint, it looked as if it had been doing service for the last half-century, and I got in more than a trifle gingerly. Aaron followed, casting off and taking the oars in a businesslike fashion before starting upstream with long, powerful strokes. I did my best to

steer, enjoying myself despite a touch of uncertainty
about his motives in getting me so alone; but while we
could talk privately, we certainly weren't unobserved,
with the town rising above us to the left, and both
banks speckled with fishermen and sunbathers.

We'd soon passed under the bridge, by which time
I'd realised that he could steer perfectly well using the
oars and didn't need my assistance. I made myself busy
with the picnic, discovering cold smoked duck breasts,
pâté aux cèpes and a cheese I didn't recognise, as well as
bread and the wine, along with plates and glasses, all
newly purchased. Given the way we'd parted, it was
difficult to know what to say and I was a little cautious
about our conversation, but he seemed content to
ask me questions about La Fleur, and my holidays in
France as a child, so the last of my misgivings quickly
faded. I'd opened the wine, too, pouring my own glass
and his before I realised that it would be impossible for
him to drink and control the boat at the same time. He
quickly found a solution, though, or else had worked
it out beforehand.

'Put the glass to my lips.'

I hesitated only an instant before complying, but as
I carefully tilted the glass to his mouth to let him drink,
I couldn't help but wonder if he'd set it all up for me to
perform the gently intimate and ever so slightly servile
task on purpose. Admittedly, I'd opened the wine and
poured the glasses on my own initiative, but I knew
him well enough to realise that he was quite capable

of factoring in the chance of that happening. It felt
nice, anyway, and even seemed to make up a little for
soaking him, so I continued to feed him sips of wines
as he rowed.

Before long we'd left the town behind and were
moving between thick belts of trees that hung right
down over the water. There were no more fishermen,
only water birds, with the only obvious human
constructions a pair of bridges far ahead and a single
gabarre moving back the way we'd come. The first
bridge carried a railway across the river, with the
wide stone pillars rising straight up from the water to
support a lattice of ironwork that cast a complex pattern
of shade on the grey-green water of the Dordogne. As
we passed underneath, Aaron turned the boat carefully
to one side, then shipped the oars, leaving us caught
against the side of the pillar by the weak current, and
pleasantly shaded from the heat of the sun.

Moving to one side of the boat, he patted the bench
next to him, a clear invitation that set the butterflies
in my stomach into motion once more. I hesitated,
wanting to join him but still held back by the thought
of him as my boss. But he wasn't any more. London
was behind me, and we were alone amid the beauty of
the French countryside, a boy and a girl in a situation
not so far from the fairy-tale imaginings of my later
teenage years. I went to him, cautiously sitting myself
down on the bench, which was too narrow to let me
avoid contact had I wanted to.

His arm came around my waist and I gave no resistance, nor when he reached out to tilt my chin a little upwards, allowing his lips to meet mine in a soft, lingering kiss. I felt his tongue touch my lips, gently, then again with greater urgency, and I'd given in, letting my mouth come wide beneath his. Both his arms were now around me and mine around him, in a tight, needy embrace that left me wanting to melt completely into his kiss, the last of my resistance quickly giving way to lust.

A moment more and his hand had moved to my breasts, stroking gently and tentatively at first, then more eagerly as he found me willing and realised I had nothing on under my dress. His grip grew tighter, the front of my dress had been pulled down and my breasts were bare to the warm, still air, and to his hands, with his fingers teasing my nipples until I'd begun to shiver in his grip and cling on tighter still. He responded in kind, tugging my dress off my shoulders to leave me naked from the waist up, as my hand moved to his crotch to squeeze the firm, expectant bulge of his erection beneath the material of his trousers. A moment's fumbling and I'd got him free, his cock hot and hard in my hand.

My panties had been levered down to the top of my thighs as I got him out, and my dress followed, pulled to my ankles, which left me deliciously bare save for the tiny scrap of cloth tangled around my legs. I was lost to him, perfectly willing to be laid down in the bottom of the boat, stripped and taken on the bare wooden duckboards, save that I could hear the faint chug of the engine of a gabarre, and it was getting closer. Aaron didn't seem to have realised, or didn't care, his kisses growing more passionate and his caresses more heated. As I let go of his cock and pulled away, he gave a moan of disappointment, then spoke, his voice urgent and pleading.

'It's all right. Nobody will see. Not in the bottom of the boat.'

'Yes, they will! There's a gabarre coming up. That means tourists . . . and cameras. Go in under the trees or something, please?'

Aaron nodded and stood up, grinning as he struggled to put his cock away. I was already trying to pull my dress back on, with the noise of the engine growing steadily louder, but one of the straps had snagged on a rowlock. Aaron reached out to try and untangle me as I twisted around, just as the gabarre shot out from between the pillars of the bridge. The wash caught us and I lost my balance, taking Aaron down with me as I sprawled forward over the bench, to land on top of him with my bare bottom stuck high in the air just feet away from several dozen onlookers, and as I twisted around in a desperate and pretty futile attempt to preserve my modesty, I found myself faced with a row of gaping people, including one I instantly recognised – John Lambert.

5

I wasn't doing very well when it came to preserving my maiden modesty, such as it was. First Madame Belair and now John Lambert had seen me in highly embarrassing and intimate situations, not to mention at least two dozen tourists from countries as far flung as the USA and Japan. The only consolation was that my new status as owner of La Fleur meant there would be no real-time consequences, such as losing my job or being reprimanded by some prissy official. Nevertheless, I was fairly sure some of the tourists had taken photos, and it was galling enough to imagine them chuckling over their computer monitors with mingled amusement and disapproval as they admired the picture of the girl who'd got caught with her knickers down.

Aaron took a more relaxed attitude, but then he was a man, and nobody had seen his face, because I'd been on top of him. His only real regret seemed to be that the gabarre had spoilt the moment, but at least he'd been enough of a gentleman not to expect me to carry on afterwards. In fact, he'd handled it all rather well, with far more cool than I'd have expected of a man interrupted during the throes of passion. The wash of the gabarre had dislodged our rowing boat and pushed it out into the current between the adjoining pillars, leaving us drifting down the Dordogne in midstream. It was only when we'd both made ourselves decent that we realised we'd lost an oar, but he had used the other one like a canoe paddle in order to retrieve it.

By then we'd been well downstream, and the gabarre had turned around beyond the bridge and was coming back, so Aaron had moved us in under the trees to spare my blushes, before rowing us back towards Bergerac and dropping me upstream of the bridge so that I'd have a decent chance of getting back to the market without running into any of the people who'd seen us. Some were sure to visit the market, though, and I very definitely did not want to run into John Lambert, so I called Liselotte on her mobile and managed to persuade her to have Jean pick me up on the far side of the bridge and drive me home.

I'd been exchanging texts with Aaron ever since, at first sympathetic and then with a humour that surprised me but also made the situation easier to handle. When something like that happens, there's nothing worse than everybody being shocked and consoling, as that only makes whatever has happened seem all the more dreadful. As it was, he helped me see the funny side of things, as did Liselotte once I'd plucked up the courage to tell her. She was also intrigued, and pleased by my bold behaviour, which was very much in accord with her own attitude. Jean just thought it was funny.

Aside from the incident with Aaron, everything had gone very well. I'd proved my worth at the stall, selling so much more than usual that even Madame Belair felt obliged to show a little grudging respect. My success also put me in a much stronger position when it came to suggesting changes and new ideas, the most important of which was to start selling overseas. Aunt Adèle had apparently refused even to consider export, excepting only a few private customers in Belgium, Germany and the Netherlands, all ex-pat French. According to Luc, she had felt that nobody but the French would be able to properly appreciate the wines, and I could well remember her haughty attitude to my father's tastes, which ran towards the sort of heavy, rich New World wines she most despised. Luc's own objections were the paperwork and the logistics, but those were both things I could easily cope with. I also had contacts, if not in the actual trade then among the sort of people who'd be content to pay a fair price: first and foremost, Aaron Curran.

That also gave me the excuse I needed to invite him to visit La Fleur, because, despite what had happened between us, and our almost constant texting, he hadn't come to see me or even suggested a date. He was supposedly busy looking at properties, but I wasn't entirely sure that he wasn't playing with me by pretending to be less interested than he really was, in order to make me run after him. It seemed unlikely, given his open enthusiasm in Bergerac, and while a lot of men do trophy-hunt and quickly lose interest once they've had their fun, I was hoping Aaron wasn't like that. Besides, he'd got close, but he hadn't actually had me.

I arranged for him to lunch at La Fleur the following Sunday, which meant that we'd have a long, drowsy afternoon together to sort out unfinished business. Whether that would involve him taking me to bed or not, I wasn't sure, but I was at least content to consider the possibility. Sunday also had the advantage that Liselotte and the Belairs would be at church in the morning. I had already explained to Madame Belair that I was not religious, lowering her opinion of me by another notch, but ten years at Catholic schools had left me with a deep-seated distaste for the whole charade, while it had been so long since I'd attended confession that I'd have kept the priest busy for a week. Not attending church meant I would be alone when I greeted Aaron, and able to show him around without interference.

On the day I was up bright and early, eager to pick flowers and generally arrange things in a brighter and more cheerful fashion, as Madame Belair either had naturally Gothic tastes or felt the house should still be in mourning. What arrangements she did consisted of roses and lilies, which I felt rather too formal, even staid, so I gathered several huge bunches of cornflowers, and mixed in poppies and a few big sunflowers to create a wild, slightly unkempt look that went much better with the image I wanted to project of playful, rustic beauty, rather than Aunt Adèle's crystal and ice. A blue summer dress I'd picked up in Bergerac, with heels to match, complemented the flowers and my mood.

I'd left the wine to Luc, instructing him to set out to impress, which meant one of our reds from the year I was born, plus an even older Monbazillac, while I was able to greet Aaron with a glass of a neighbour's sparkling rosé as he stepped from his Mercedes. He accepted it gratefully, kissed me and took a sip before looking up at the façade of La Fleur, clearly impressed.

'Good heavens, you have fallen on your feet. I had no idea.'

'Nor did I. My Aunt Adèle left the estate to me.'

'I didn't even know you had an Aunt Adèle.'

'There was no reason I'd ever have mentioned her, certainly not at work. I hadn't seen her for years, and my only memories of her are as a very haughty *grande dame* who carried herself like a duchess while managing to scandalise the entire family.'

'How very French.'

'She was. I don't think she ever forgave my mother for marrying an Englishman, but she did believe in family, and I suppose I'm her only surviving relative. According to her solicitors, Aunt Adèle always retained sole ownership of La Fleur, so none of her husbands' relatives could ever have a claim on the estate.'

'Lucky you, but this is magnificent.'

We'd entered the hall and he was admiring the staircase.

'I used to slide down the bannisters when I was little. It all seems quite normal to me.'

He gave a thoughtful nod and I continued the tour, sticking to the grander parts of the house as we sipped our wine and thoroughly enjoying his astonishment while pretending it was all quite ordinary to me. I knew I was showing off, but I couldn't resist it, not after all the time I'd spent at his beck and call, in awe of his wealthy background and casual assumption of superiority. He didn't seem to notice, anyway, admiring the rooms and making the occasional apparently erudite remark about this or that, although most of what he said meant nothing to me. I'd expected him to be a little more ardent, considering that we were completely alone in the house, but he remained cool and easy, until I'd begun to feel a little neglected and allowed my hand to brush his as we returned to the hall.

The staircase was right next to us, and all he needed to do was take me by the hand and lead me upstairs, under the pretext of continuing the tour if he wanted to be coy, or simply to take me to bed. He didn't, but asked to see the winery. A glance at the grandfather clock beside the drawing-room door told me that I now had less than an hour until the Belairs returned from church, so I decided that if he was going to play it cool, then so would I, and we would see what happened after lunch.

I took him down into the cellar, where the vaults we used to store the better wines for aging connected to the main area beneath the winery. He was more fascinated than ever, admiring the ancient, dust-shrouded bottles and commenting on the different vintages and comparable wines he'd drunk or owned back in London. Time ticked by, a quarter of an hour and then a second quarter, and all the while I was finding it increasingly difficult to cover up my rising frustration at his lack of attention to me. Finally, we came out from beneath the house into the long, low cellar that housed the barrels in which the previous year's wine was stored. The scents of oak and fresh wine were strong in the air and he gave an appreciative sniff before speaking again.

'What a wonderful scent, and what a wonderful place. Where is everybody, by the way? I thought you had staff living in?'

'They're at church.'

'Ah, I see.'

He had reached out as he spoke, to run one finger gently down my cheek. My heart instantly started hammering, and the butterflies in my stomach had gone wild even before the gaze of his grey-blue eyes locked with mine. I tried to speak, but only managed a soft moan, quickly silenced as he leant forward to press his mouth to mine. My lips came open, easily this time, and we were kissing. His hands found my waist and mine came up and around the breadth of his shoulders, each clinging to the other as we kissed before he lifted me with casual strength and sat me down on top of a barrel. My legs came wide as he moved in close, so close that I could feel the heat of his body between my thighs, then the firm, resilient bulge of his cock pressing through his trousers and the thin cotton panties that were the only thing shielding me.

If he'd taken me then and there, I'd have given in, because just being with him had left me wet and ready, but he was in no rush. Just as he had in the boat, he gently eased my dress down over my shoulders and then my breasts, his fingers brushing my nipples and caressing the curves of my flesh as he laid me bare, and once again with my exposure came a delightful sense of liberation and of vulnerability too. His kisses had grown hotter as he stripped me, but he was still very much in control, teasing my body even as he got me ready for sex. Only when he lifted me a little to tug my dress down over my hips did his mouth leave mine, planting a slow trail of kisses down my neck and across my shoulders before finding my breasts.

I closed my eyes in bliss as he began to explore my breasts with his mouth, kissing each in turn in what seemed almost an act of worship before taking one already stiff nipple between his teeth. By then my fingers were locked into his hair and I held on tight, my pleasure rising swiftly as he continued to kiss and caress, with his fingers now gently teasing the nape of my neck as his mouth worked on my breasts. I'd begun to moan, unable to hold back my reaction, but he seemed determined to render me utterly helpless before going any further, kissing and teasing me until I began to wriggle in his grip and beg for more.

Still he took his time, easing me gently back onto the barrels as his kisses traced a new path, down over my belly, briefly brushing the front of my panties before moving to the silky smooth skin of my inner thighs as he lifted my legs. I was now laid back on two barrels, open and helpless to my own need as much as to his strength as he quickly levered my panties down and off my legs, taking my dress and shoes with them. That left me in the nude, with not a single stitch on, while he was still fully dressed in the smart designer suit he seemed to find indispensable, without so much as a button out of place.

Not that I minded. It felt right to be naked in front of him as he worked his magic on my body, his lips and tongue concentrating on my thighs once more, ever closer to what had become the very centre of my being – my open, ready sex. I thought he was going to do it, to lick me properly, perhaps even take me to orgasm before taking his own pleasure, and as his lips found my lower belly once more, I spread my legs as wide as they would go in eager, dirty anticipation, only for him to start work on my thighs again.

At that I was begging, filthy, painfully intimate

words spilling from my lips as I clutched at his hair, desperately trying to pull his head in where it belonged. He gave a single quiet chuckle, curled his arms around my thighs to hold me wide, and his mouth was on my sex, kissing, lapping, nipping at my clitoris. I screamed, taken to the point at which pain meets ecstasy, and to the very edge of orgasm, but no more. He pulled back, to quickly free his cock from his suit trousers, already fully erect and rearing high above a pair of heavy balls. Then he was on top of me, easing himself in deep, and at last we were together, joined in the perfect lovers' embrace as I pulled myself up to take him in my arms and let his wrap around me. Our mouths met, opened, and we were kissing once more, in a blissful union that seemed to last an eternity as he eased himself slowly in and out.

I could have come, so easily, with just a little more, but even as my muscles begun to squeeze in the onset of ecstasy, he suddenly lifted me once more, twisting my body over to lay me back over the barrels, now face down and bottom up, a thoroughly undignified position in which he entered me once more. He'd taken me completely by surprise, and I was laughing in shock and delight too at the sudden change from abandoned intimacy to something far ruder and far from equal.

We'd been making love, but now I was being fucked, fucked naked over a barrel with the man inside me getting himself off over the sight of my bare rear view as he pushed into me, but the pleasure was simply too strong to let me find a voice for my instinctive resentment. As it was, all I could manage was a weak, breathless protest, calling him a bastard between gasps of ecstasy as his cock pushed deep, over and over again; yet, even as I cursed him, I was imagining how it would be if he were to smack my bottom as he fucked me.

I nearly said it, surrendering any last shred of dignity I might have held on to by begging to be spanked as I was fucked, but even as the words begun to break from my mouth, he'd pulled free once more, this time to take me firmly by the hair and haul me around to push his erection at my face. My mouth came open by instinct and he started to come just as his cock went in, making my eyes pop and my cheeks bulge as I struggled to swallow. I heard him groan and he pushed himself deeper still, his grip too strong and too fierce to break, the head of his cock well down my throat so that I was left gagging and struggling to breathe until he was fully satisfied.

He let go of my hair and I slumped to the floor, gasping for breath and dizzy with reaction, feeling used and sore but far too excited to stop myself as my thighs came wide. I had my back to the barrel, my head was thrown back and my eyes closed in ecstasy as I began to masturbate, blatantly showing off in front of the man who'd just taken me so cruelly, and wishing he could do it all again only longer and harder as I tipped myself over into a beautiful orgasm.

Aaron watched as I came, his eyes glittering with delight at my dirty behaviour, and his mouth curved up into a happy and ever so slightly cruel smile. I was calling him a bastard as I hit my second peak, but even to my own ears my voice sounded soft and pleading, while his smile had spread to become an evil grin by the time I was finished with myself. As I went slowly limp, he spoke up once more.

'That good, huh?'

I nodded, unable to deny what he'd done for me, but I couldn't help but feel a little resentful at the way he'd handled me, and I wanted him to know it.

'You were a bit rough, towards the end. I'm not just some sort of sex doll, Aaron.'

'Sorry. I suppose I did get a bit carried away, but you're too lovely to waste.'

I wasn't entirely sure what he meant, but time was getting on and I needed to sort myself out before the Belairs got back from church. Even as I tugged my dress on over my head, I caught the faint sound of tyres on gravel, filling my head with images of Madame catching me the way I'd been for Aaron, even though there was no reason for her to come down into the cellar. Aaron had clearly realised why I was in such a hurry and seemed more amused than anything, but he did at least have the decency to point out that we'd passed an old mirror in the other part of the cellar, so I could check my hair and make-up.

By the time I felt ready to face the world, Madame

Belair was busy in the kitchen, with Liselotte assisting her, while Luc and Jean were nowhere to be seen. A minute of conversation and it had been made very clear to me that I was in the way, so I took Aaron outside once more to show him the vineyard and grounds, apologising as we left the house.

'I'm sorry about Madame Belair. She's a terrible old dragon.'

'A virago and a half.'

'Yes, and I just can't win. She obviously thinks I'm far too common, but when I try to help out, like just now, she gets cross because I'm interfering with what she sees as her job.'

'If she wants you to play the *grande dame*, do it, or sack her and find somebody more pliable. When you're the boss, sometimes you have to make hard decisions.'

'I couldn't. I have to live here, and they know everybody. The last thing I need is a reputation as a hard-nosed bitch. Besides, the Belairs come as a package, and Luc's the only one who knows how to run the winery.'

'Nonsense. There must be dozens of skilled young winemakers coming out of college every year.'

'It doesn't work that way. You tasted our wines and you know how good they are. The estate is good, but without Luc we'd be making one more soulless commercial product.'

'There must be others as good, if not better, and not all the youngsters are going to be incompetent.'

I shrugged, not wanting to argue the point or get on to the topic of how he'd behaved as a boss, although it did occur to me that he was much the same when it came to sex, coaxing me carefully into a state of helpless submission before using me as if I were some sort of toy. The thought gave me a sudden and completely unexpected thrill, like a jolt of electricity to my belly and between my thighs. Aaron had turned to look out over the valley and didn't seem to notice, but I was left feeling hot and flustered as we walked on.

He was the exact opposite, calm and easy, apparently taking what had happened between us as part of the expected course of events, inevitable even, an attitude I couldn't help but find a little irritating. Yet I didn't want to come across as insecure or needy, so I did my best to match his air of cool detachment, pointing out landmarks and discussing the possibilities of the London market as we walked up between the long rows of vines, but all the while I was thinking of how good it had felt to be held tight in his arms and how utterly helpless I'd been to resist his advances, whether loving or lustful.

At length, we were interrupted by a single deep note I recognised immediately as coming from the gong that stood just inside the dining-room doorway, but which I hadn't heard since my childhood visits. That meant lunch was ready and we turned back, reaching the house to find Madame Belair standing in the hall. She somehow managed to look deferential and put-upon at the same time as she ushered us towards the dining room. I'd known we'd be eating in there, but I hadn't expected the splendid array of china, crystal, silver and linen set out in front of me. Nor had I expected only two places, as if we were to discuss the possibilities of running tastings in London and exporting to the UK, it made sense for everybody involved to be present. Evidently Madame Belair thought otherwise.

She didn't seem to agree with my efforts at decoration, either. My deliberately haphazard clumps of wild flowers had been replaced by careful arrangements of fat pink roses, each in an identical crystal vase and placed with an almost obsessive symmetry. Lunch was no less formal, and very different to the usual casual affair in the kitchen, with soup, fish, a ragout, cheese and finally dessert served and cleared alongside each of five wines. It was far too much for me, and all a bit uncomfortable, but Aaron took it all in his stride as if he was born to it.

By the end, I was very full, quite drunk and more than a little sleepy, a combination that made the idea of retiring upstairs to bed with Aaron distinctly tempting, especially as Madame Belair would no doubt have been outraged. He seemed indifferent, infuriatingly so, sipping a glass of Luc's home-distilled *eau de vie de mirabelle* and speculating on the worth of the oil paintings that decorated the walls. I prefer men to take the lead, but there are limits and I finally spoke up.

'Would you like to come upstairs, to bed?'

He turned to me with a brief grin.

'I'd rather go for a walk, if it's all the same to you?'

I hesitated, eager for my afternoon of sleepy, easy sex, but no less eager to please. His suggestion made sense too, as we'd be outdoors, safely away from the disapproving eye of Madame Belair, as while it was tempting to provoke her, I could see it was also unwise. Not only that, but I could imagine myself walking hand in hand through the vineyards with Aaron before he laid me down in the warm grass beneath the trees and made love to me, slowly and gently. It would be a wonderful memory.

'Okay, if you prefer.'

He took my hand as we left the house, as naturally as if we'd been lovers for months instead of hours. My heart was singing as we walked through the vines once more, further this time, and down into the valley towards the line of trees fringing the river. Somehow it seemed wrong to lead him to where Jean had spanked Liselotte before our little threesome. That had been good, but it had been raw sex, very different to what I wanted from Aaron; although even as he took me in his arms and kissed me gently on the forehead, as we stood at the edge of the vines, I couldn't help but remember how he'd handled me in the cellar.

It's a curious thing about French vineyards, but there are seldom clear boundaries between different properties, and I wasn't even sure if we were still on La Fleur land, which added a guilty thrill to my already complicated but highly excited feelings as Aaron led me in among the trees. We quickly found a quiet spot, shaded by a great twisting willow that created a cool space carpeted with little yellow leaves. Aaron kissed me again, more urgently this time, then casually tugged my dress up and off. Being in panties felt wrong, somehow smutty, so they followed my dress to leave me nude in the warm, dappled sunlight beneath the willow.

We began to kiss once more, Aaron's hands now moving over my body to a slow, sensual rhythm, teasing the nape of my neck and my back, the swell of my rear cheeks and the curve of my hips. I could feel myself giving in to him as my desire rose and knew he was reacting the same way, with his cock already making a firm bulge against my flesh. I imagined us lying naked together and reached a hand down to stroke him gently through his trousers.

'Let me undress you.'

He shook his head.

'Uh, uh. I prefer you naked. Look, I have to get back to London tomorrow, but I'd like to say goodbye properly, in a way I'm going to remember.'

As he spoke, he put his arms around me once more, pulling me in close and kissing me fiercely on the mouth. I responded in kind, melting easily into his embrace as I imagined myself laid down, the warm air full of the scent of flowers as my thighs came open to accept him, my entire being given over to a union we'd both remember for ever; but when I began to go down, he stayed as he was, his voice hoarse with arousal as he spoke again.

'That's a good girl. You know what to do.'

It was obvious what he wanted, and as I allowed myself to be eased gently down to my knees, I consoled myself that if our farewell wasn't going to be as romantic as I'd hoped, it would at least be intimate. That didn't stop me feeling resentful as I pulled down his zip and took his cock and balls out, but I was going to do it anyway, not laid down in a lover's embrace but put on my knees to suck cock.

He'd begun to stroke my hair, as if to soothe me and let me get over myself, as much as to turn me on. That did make it a little easier, but I still hesitated, wondering if I should say something as I tugged gently on his rapidly swelling shaft, only to decide that any protest would spoil the moment, such as it was. Maybe things would be different another time, but for the moment he wanted me to play the slut, so I kissed his cock very gently on the tip, then took him into my mouth and began to suck, teasing his balls at the same time. He sighed in response and then spoke.

'Good girl. That's the way, Elise. Now lick my balls.'

I let him slip from my mouth and glanced up with what was supposed to be an aggrieved expression, but his eyes were closed so I hid a sigh and got down to business. Taking him in my hand once more, I began to masturbate him as I flicked my tongue over the heavy, bulging sack of his balls. He gave a low sound, somewhere between a growl and a purr, followed by what was definitely a command.

'Right in your mouth. Suck my balls.'

This time I didn't even bother to look up, but did my best to comply, tugging harder on his erection as I struggled to cope with the mass of his balls. I now felt used, but there was no denying my excitement and in another instant I'd put one hand down between my legs. He didn't even notice, which made the raging sense of shame in my head all the stronger as I began to masturbate over what he was making me do, but I couldn't stop myself, rubbing harder and faster as his grip tightened in my hair and his sighs turned to moans, then an urgent spatter of dirty words.

'Yes, like that . . . suck on my balls, you dirty little darling . . . you dirty, filthy little darling!'

He finished with a grunt and I felt something warm and wet splash on my face, but I was coming too and I couldn't stop myself as I took his cock in my mouth once more, as deep as it would go, to swallow and swallow again as my body shook to wave after wave of uncontrollable ecstasy.

6

Aaron did apologise for his behaviour before leaving, but I still wasn't happy about the situation. His explanation was that I was so desirable he'd been unable to hold back his basic instincts, which I could have accepted if he'd been like an animal, taking me hard in whatever way gave him the most physical pleasure. Instead, he'd been deliberately dirty with me, and while there was no denying that I'd enjoyed every second of it, I couldn't help but feel that he was taking advantage of my sexuality. At the very least, I needed him to accept that just because it excited me to be dirty for him, that didn't mean I was any less worthy of his respect.

He was quick to reassure me, but even then I was beset by doubts, wondering if he'd simply been determined to add me to his list of conquests and was now playing along purely for the sake of potential business interests. On the face of it, that was ridiculous, as any money he could make by acting as my agent for the La Fleur wines in London would be small change in comparison to the levels of income he was used to, but the feeling wouldn't go away. If anything, it grew stronger over the next few days, as did my need to see him, and to talk to him, and to be held in his arms, and to be taken in whatever way he pleased. Before another week had passed, I had to admit it to myself. I was in love with him, with all the earnest yearning of the most powerful teenage emotion, with a deeper, more mature need, but also with a strange and frightening craving for the shameful ecstasy he'd taught me to enjoy.

Only he hadn't. It would have been nice to think my feelings related solely to Aaron as the man I'd fallen in love with, but there was no denying that it was Jean Belair who had triggered similar emotions by spanking Liselotte, while my wilder fantasies had often taken on a submissive edge. Aaron wasn't the only man who could make me feel that way, but he was very good at it, and I needed more.

I was going to get it, but not for a bit. My plans had to fit in with the seasons, and summer was drawing to a close, which meant vintage time and a lot of hard work. Even when I'd met Aaron in Bergerac, I'd noticed a fair number of rather rough-looking people, the casual labourers who migrate to the vineyards every year to help with picking. By the week after his visit, we had our fair share, first picking the Sauvignon grapes for our dry white wines, then the Merlot, which ripens first among the reds. I'd always been back at school in England by vintage time, so it was all new to me, showing me a very different side to La Fleur.

There were a million and one things to be done, many of them highly skilled and almost all of them exhausting. Luc was very much in charge, while all but the most junior of the pickers knew more than I did, save only when it came to organisation. Not wishing to feel useless, and conscious of Madame Belair's unending disapproval, I took over the management of our labour, not only making sure we had the right people in the right place at the right time, but resolving disputes over pay and conditions. All of it was immensely hard work, if less so than for those actually out in the fields, and at the end of each day I would be exhausted.

Evenings were very different – jolly, chaotic affairs with everybody gathered around long trestle tables set out in the new winery building and laden with dishes of ratatouille and baked pasta, with the cheapest of the previous year's wine available in never-ending supply. I joined in as best I could, refusing Madame Belair's pointed suggestion that I should eat separately and generally hold myself somewhat aloof, but I never quite felt fully part of it, especially later in the evenings when everybody would be laughing together and talking in rapid colloquial French I found hard to follow, or when couples would start to slip off among the bushes to become lovers, often those who'd only met that day, but Jean and Liselotte too. Then I would end up sitting rather uncomfortably at the head of the long tables, twiddling the stem of my glass as I listened to the talk of the older folk, wishing Aaron were there so that I too could give myself over to the same uncomplicated joys.

With the red wines safely in the vats, we moved on to what really mattered, and what lifted La Fleur above the level of being just one more producer among the thousands along the valleys of the Dordogne and Gironde: the sweet Monbazillac I'd always thought of as the nectar of the gods. By then, the mornings were cool, with mist rising from the valley to cover the vineyards in a soft white cloak that burnt off gradually in the heat of the sun. As Luc explained to me, the mist allowed the formation of noble rot, which robbed the grapes of their water to leave the juice far more concentrated and to add an exquisite flavour all its own. Conditions were perfect too, with an area of high pressure settled right over Aquitaine. But a single Atlantic storm could ruin everything. Each evening Luc would go into the village to pray, while he spent his days walking among the rows of vines with a hod on his back, selecting individual grapes for our top *cuvée* and keeping a critical eye on the workers. Jean would often be with him, learning the finer points of the craft and, like his father, constantly glancing at the sky as if searching for coming changes in the weather.

Work had slowed down by now, but we kept everybody on to make sure we could handle a final rush if the weather did break, and the evenings grew more lively than ever. Many of the pickers had formed attachments, or seemed to have long-standing seasonal agreements whereby they would return to old lovers on an annual basis, and it slowly dawned on me that the maze of hedges and little rustic seats I'd always found so magical was not merely a convenient place for lovers, but had been designed with lovers in mind. That was certainly the favoured place for late-night assignations, although some of the pickers were barely less restrained at table, and one giggling, drunken girl had even had her breasts bare and her lover's cock in her hand before a sharp word from Madame Belair sent them giggling into the night.

By then, my sense of missing out had grown to a physical ache, made worse by my detachment as the owner, alone and aloof with Luc and his wife to either side of me, while I knew from snatches of overheard conversation that I was considered very cool and very British. Nobody had approached me, not even any of the swaggering, testosterone-fuelled young men who made up a surprisingly high proportion of our workforce. I've never enjoyed unsolicited advances, and I knew it was mainly because I was the boss and very definitely not one of them, but I couldn't help but find it all a little galling. The girls they'd chase so eagerly in among the bushes were often no younger than me, and I hoped no more attractive or sexually appealing. Worst of all, Madame Belair had begun to share her little disapproving remarks with me rather than directing them at me, and I was very glad indeed when Jean drove into Bordeaux to collect some new barrels, and decided to stay over, leaving me with Liselotte's company for the evening. She'd been picking all day and was tired, but gradually brightened up as we ate and drank. I had to talk across Luc, and it wasn't until he retired and Liselotte and I were sitting back with glasses of *eau de vie* in our hands, that she mentioned Aaron.

'You're missing your man, the one who came here?'

'Yes, but he's not really my man, or not officially.'

'You fucked?'

I was taken aback by her directness and found myself blushing, but nodding too.

She shrugged. 'Then he is your man, even if he has another girl back in England.'

'I suppose so, but not in the sense that Jean is your man.'

'Jean? He will be in bed with some little Bordelaise tart right now, as likely as not.'

She laughed as she said it, and I found myself shocked.

'Surely not! He's devoted to you, isn't he?'

'Yes, when I am with him. Jean is a man, and he will do what men do. If I thought otherwise, I would be a fool.'

I made to reply, keen to reassure her of his good faith, but then thought of Jean and realised that he probably had no more concept of keeping faith than the bull he so resembled. He was also sure to attract attention and presumably knew quite a few people in Bordeaux, including girls who would enjoy a night in bed with him, quite likely married women too.

Liselotte carried on. 'Yes, I am jealous, but I would rather have Jean as he is than any other man all to myself. And you?'

'I'd want a man to be faithful, but I do understand what you're saying, or I think I do, anyway. Maybe I'm fooling myself, but I'd like to think I could give a man everything he needs.'

'When you're with him, yes, but when he's away and he's feeling lonely and turned on, and some pretty girl starts to make eyes at him? What's he going to do? The man who won't take her to bed is too weak to be any good.'

'No, surely not? A good man, a strong man, he wouldn't give in to temptation. He'd stay faithful.'

'Would Aaron, even if you were engaged to be married?'

I didn't have to think for more than a second to give my answer.

'No. I think he'd feel used . . . controlled . . . if he had to stay faithful to just one woman. When I worked for him, he was always with different women, usually gorgeous women. I don't think he could give that up, and if anybody tried to make him, it would only make things worse.'

'He's a man, then, like Jean, and better to have than somebody weak.'

'No. I want a man who's strong, loving, but faithful too.'

'Maybe in heaven.'

I didn't answer, stung by her cynical attitude but unable to deny that she understood Aaron and probably the great majority of men, or at least the attractive ones. Yet surely there had to be somebody, or was the idea of a Mr Right no more than a myth? Aaron Curran certainly didn't fit the bill, and yet just to think of him filled me with longing, and now with jealousy as I thought of what Liselotte had said and wondered if Aaron was even now with another woman – Vicky, perhaps. Liselotte was right. Life was much easier if you accepted that a man might stray, and yet all my life everybody I'd known had seemed to take it as read that a couple should be faithful to each other. I could understand why she hadn't minded me watching, too, and let him put his cock in my mouth.

The thought sent a powerful shiver through me, instantly followed by a touch of wry amusement at my own behaviour. Maybe Aaron was in bed with Vicky, but I couldn't pretend that I reacted to him and to him alone. Not that there was any reason I should, save that I'd always assumed that was how it would be when I fell in love, which in turn brought on the thought that maybe my feelings for him were simple lust after all.

I poured myself another glass of *eau de vie*, fuller this time, and then topped up Liselotte's glass. We were very nearly on our own by then, with nobody else at our end of the table and just a group of four playing cards and drinking at the far end. I was going to have to lock up before too long, and I knew I ought to try and get a decent night's sleep, but it was impossible to shake my feeling of dissatisfaction at ending one more evening so tamely, when just about everybody else was having such a good time. Liselotte spoke again.

'Anyway, there is love and there is pleasure. Jean takes his pleasure where he likes, and always will, but he loves only me.'

'I wish I could say the same for Aaron, but maybe, in time.'

She didn't reply immediately, and her eyes were still focused on the pale liquid in her glass when she spoke again.

'It was good, wasn't it, when you came to watch us down by the river? He had said he would spank me in front of you, and he did. I'll bet you enjoyed taking him in your mouth too. He is very fine, isn't he?'

'Like a bull, I always think. Yes, I enjoyed what we did.'

'And watching me?'

'That too, only . . . only it's hard to accept how you can allow a man to treat you like that, to spank you.'

'How do you mean? The man should take charge, no?'

'Not necessarily.'

'But it feels good when he does, yes?'

I thought of Aaron and the way he'd taken control

of my body, firm but gentle when he was loving, or simply using his greater physical strength to get me in the position he wanted me when he was being dirty.

'Yes, I suppose so, as long as it's what you want, of course, but doesn't it hurt? He wasn't exactly gentle, and your bottom was ever so red.'

She laughed.

'Of course it hurts, at first, but it soon starts to feel nice. Don't tell me you've never been spanked?!'

'Of course not, why should I?!'

'No, really? I thought you English liked that sort of thing?'

'We're not all perverts!'

She laughed, her eyes now full of mischief, then began to talk once more.

'I had an English lover once, a man who used to take a *gite* in the village every summer. Paul Kent was his name. He used to spank me, across his knee like Jean does it, or rolled up on my back with my knickers twisted around my ankles so I'd be showing everything. He even used to buy special knickers, white ones, a little too small so they'd be very tight.'

'What a pervert! How old was he?'

'Forty, forty-five, perhaps. Older men are better at spanking, more patient. Jean spanks me like he is really in a temper, ever so hard and fast. Paul would spend ages just holding me, stroking my bottom through my knickers and telling me how lovely I was.'

'The dirty old sod!'

'Yes, but it was nice. The man who bought you the roses at the fair, I bet he'd be the same.'

'Very likely, or worse, but not all Englishmen are like that. Aaron can be very gentle and loving, although he does get a bit carried away. He . . . he had me in the cellar, over one of the barrels. I . . . okay, I'll tell the truth, but this is secret, between me and you, but while he was doing it, from behind, that is, I was sort of wishing he'd spank me at the same time.'

I could feel my cheeks blazing with heat even as I spoke the words, and regret came in an instant, followed by self-recrimination for drinking so much that I'd admitted to such an awful secret, but Liselotte was laughing.

'You should have asked him! He'd have been hard on you, I'm sure, but it's good when a man's already inside you.'

'He'd probably just have thought I was perverted.'

'Maybe, but I bet he'd have done it. Who could resist you, with your long, long legs and your little round bottom? You're so lucky.'

'Thank you, I suppose, but you have a lovely figure too.'

She made a face and I found myself struggling to find the right words, hoping to reassure her without seeming to be condescending, but she spoke again before I could decide what to say.

'So really, you have never been spanked, but you'd like to be?'

'Yes, I suppose so.'

I'd spoken so quietly, I'd barely heard my own voice, while Liselotte had stood up and suddenly clapped her hands to get the attention of the men playing poker.

'Time for bed! There is work in the morning.'

They rose, grudgingly, and moved slowly away, talking all the while. I wasn't sure if Liselotte had even heard what I'd said, and the evening seemed to be at an end except that she was still holding her glass of *eau de vie*. She took my own glass as I locked up the big double doors, and we were alone in the warmth of the night, but for the trill of insects and a faint gasping to suggest that somebody was getting what she needed not so very far away. Liselotte put her finger to her lips and beckoned.

I followed her across the yard, with just the dull yellow light of the lamp by the gate to see by, but it was obvious where she was going. Whoever was making love was behind the great stack of new bottles we'd had delivered that day, six pallets in all, and which made a long, high wall across the far side of the yard. The far end was in shadow and I could tell we'd be able to see what was going on without being spotted ourselves.

Without the drink and Liselotte to lead me on, I'd never have done it, but as it was I'd quickly come up beside her to peer around the edge of a pallet. At first all I could see was vague movement in oddly patterned light created by the distant lamp shining through the bottles, but soon I realised that what I was looking at was a pair of muscular buttocks moving and squeezing to the rhythm of the man's thrusts, along with part of the woman's raised thigh. He was between her legs, one of the cocky young men by the look of it, mounted up on a girl whose gasps and squeals suggested that she was thoroughly enjoying herself.

So was he, thrusting away at a furious speed inside her, only to suddenly pull out, grab hold of his erect cock and finish himself off all over the girl's naked belly and breasts, his face now clearly lit – young, bearded and handsome, but twisted in ecstasy. The vision lasted only an instant and then I'd pulled back, sure he'd turn around or that she would sit up and see us. Liselotte was bolder, trusting to the darkness, but quickly caught up with me as I fled across the yard. She was giggling, and took my hand in playful, guilty companionship, to lead me around the side of the house to the front.

There wasn't a single light on, but the lawns and the façade of La Fleur were clear enough in the faint moonlight, and we'd soon made our way inside. Liselotte still had her glass, and quickly drained it, not letting go of my hand but instead leading me towards the staircase. I'd thought she'd go home, but I didn't want her to, and it was easy to push down my guilty feelings as we ran upstairs together, for everything I was pretty sure what she wanted.

It was so easy; I was hot with drink and arousal, frustrated and lonely too, so that when she kissed me,

I reacted with instinctive need. Our tongues met, we tumbled together onto the bed, and for the first time in my life I was making love to another woman for her own sake rather than to please a man. It felt good, though, but odd, with her body softer than my own and everything about her so abundantly feminine, but that didn't stop me and it certainly didn't seem to bother her. I'd had my dress pulled up and off in a moment. Her own followed as she climbed on top of me, riding me as if she were riding a man, so that her naked torso showed in the faint light, the curves of her softly rounded belly and heavy breasts making glorious shapes, her hair tumbling about her shoulders and her pretty face lit up with an expression of pure, joyful desire.

She leant forward and her breasts were in my face, full and round, so much bigger and heavier than my own. I took hold, marvelling at the feel of her flesh even as that same curious sense of weakness I'd felt before came back, and before I really knew it, my mouth had come wide and I was sucking eagerly at one stiff nipple. Liselotte laughed at my drunken, dirty enthusiasm and reached down to cup her breasts, lifting one and pushing it forward to help me suckle. I didn't need the encouragement, mouthing eagerly at her nipple as my thighs came up and open to let my hand down the front of my panties. She realised what I was doing and her voice was full of laughter as she spoke up.

'Oh, you dirty thing! I know what you need.'

I clung on as she tried to pull away, not wanting to stop, but she pushed me back down on the bed and climbed off my body as I found my voice.

'What are you going to do?'

'I'm going to spank you.'

'Spank me? But . . .'

'Ssh! Not another word, Elise. Just let it happen.'

My answer was a sob, and she was already rolling me over, pulling me roughly by one arm, and my panties, until I was face down on the bed. She paused long enough to wriggle out of her own knickers, then mounted me once more, settling her meaty bottom into the small of my back to leave me pinned down and shaking, with doubt, with need and with shame for that need, but completely unable to resist. Her thumbs pushed in down the back of my panties, and my mouth had come wide in a moan of mingled ecstasy and despair as I was laid bare behind, on show to her, to the woman who was about to smack my naked bottom.

I thought it was going to start, but she gave me a little rub instead, which was somehow worse, emphasising how helpless I was and making the act of spanking me more intimate still. She seemed to know how I was feeling, too, laughing as she stroked and squeezed my cheeks, even pulling them open for a moment to bring me a pang of extraordinarily intense shame. I was grimacing in consternation and had begun to wriggle underneath her, wondering if I could throw her off and turn the tables on her. She just laughed all the more, and then spoke.

'Spanking is always better when it's a punishment, so this is for peeping, Elise.'

'You were peeping too!'

'Not at the couple just now – at me and Jean.'

'You invited me!'

'And so? You didn't have to follow us. You certainly didn't have to suck Jean's cock. You deserve this, Elise; you deserve a smacked bottom, and that is what you are going to get!'

On the final word, she planted a single firm smack across my cheeks, both at once. It was hard, but my gasp was more out of shock than pain. I was being spanked, and not only on my bare bottom, but by another woman, a woman sat astride my back to hold me down, and as a punishment. She was right, that really got to me, the thought that I could be punished with a spanking, making me feel small and weak and utterly ashamed of myself. I'd begun to wriggle again even before the second smack landed, and as she set to work in earnest, I was squirming frantically beneath her, completely unable to cope with what was being done to me and desperate to escape but succeeding only in making a yet ruder display of my bottom.

She didn't even slow down, riding me with one hand gripped in my panties to help her balance and the other smacking down on my naked rear cheeks, again and again, laughing all the while and teasing me with remarks about the shape of my bottom and how much she could see when my cheeks came apart, and how wet I was. That was what made me give in, because she was right. I'd been turned on anyway, but the spanking had brought the heat to my sex in the most extraordinary way, leaving me wet and needy despite my aching shame.

It was too much, too good. I stopped fighting, lying beneath her, fighting my own sulky feelings and feeling determined not to let her see what she'd done to me. She knew anyway, tightening her grip on my panties and pulling on them to force me to lift my bottom, then telling me how I was showing everything behind as she continued to apply the smacks. Still I tried to hold back, but she was now bringing her hand down across the tuck of my cheeks, so that every slap sent a jolt of ecstasy to my sex. I began to stick my bottom up, unable to help myself, then to clutch at the bedspread, biting at it in my rising ecstasy. Finally, Liselotte spoke again, her voice now soothing.

'Let yourself go, Elise. Let it happen. Think how nice it is to be spanked by me. Think how you are, with your knickers pulled down and your pretty bottom all red. Think what you're showing to me between your little round cheeks and your thighs. Think how you need this; think how you need you bottom smacked, Elise!'

As she spoke, she began to spank harder still, and faster, creating feelings so good I could no longer hold back, but was moaning in ecstasy and squirming beneath her, with my bottom stuck up, high and open. I could feel myself coming in a way I'd never experienced before, and with feelings I seldom had; shame and ecstasy blended inextricably together as I pictured how I must look, face down on the bed in nothing but pulled-down white panties, my bottom stuck up in the air as another woman rode me and spanked me, punished me. A scream broke from my lips as my orgasm hit me, and Liselotte was laughing once more, in cruel, mocking delight at what she'd done to me; but that only added to my pleasure as I begged her to makes the smacks harder still.

She stopped the instant I was done, quickly climbing off and rolling me over to take me in her arms once more. We began to kiss again, now with raw, urgent passion, our fingers moving over each other's bodies as if each was determined to take in the whole of the other's being, but both of us focused on my hot, aching bottom cheeks. She even kissed me, twisting around to take me by the hips and pushing her face to my burning skin, once to the crest of each cheek, and once deep between them in an act so rude, so uninhibited, that it immediately shocked me.

'Liselotte!'

'Don't be prissy. Come on. It's my turn.'

We were head to toe, her bottom lifted into the pale light to make twin crescents of beautiful, feminine flesh, perfectly spankable. I needed my revenge too, to make me feel better about the way I'd surrendered my own dignity, and to make her come in the same utterly abandoned way I had myself.

'Okay, but I want you over my knee.'

'Oh no, not that. I want to ride you,' she insisted.

'Hey, you did me!'

I grappled with her, intent on getting on top long enough to warm her cheeks, then putting her across my knee once she was too turned on to resist. She had other ideas, fighting back and trying to get me down on the bed, and within moments I'd realised that she was far, far stronger than me. I'd been put on my back in seconds, straddled and pinned down with her ample bottom spread across my tummy. My legs were pulled up, my panties removed and my bottom given a few more smacks to punish me for trying to turn the tables on her. I still wasn't sure exactly what she wanted, until she moved further up my body, spreading my thighs open to her face and at the same time offering me her sex to lick as if in a sixty-nine, only to suddenly sit up. For one moment I was staring at the full, bare moon of her naked bottom, then she settled herself down, full on my face. All I could manage was a single muffled protest, and then I began to lick.

7

I've had my fair share of regretful mornings, generally involving alcohol and boys, but waking up next to Liselotte was a triple whammy: first the realisation that I'd slept with another woman, then that I'd let her spank me, and lastly that she'd sat on my face. There was at least some consolation in that I'd enjoyed every second of it, but that only made my embarrassment worse.

Liselotte didn't seem to care, but got up early to see to the pickers' breakfast with barely a word. I was left staring at the ceiling for a long while, trying to make sense of my feelings, before giving up and following her. We'd now got the bulk of our white grapes in, with only the Semillon left to pick from the cooler vineyards on the wrong side of the ridge, and even Luc was in an optimistic mood. It looked as if my first vintage as owner would see a profit, and that I'd have something really good to show off in London come the new year; but for the time being, I'd have to make do with the produce of the last three, relatively poor years, alongside a few older bottles to show what we

were capable of. Patience is not a virtue associated with
moneymen from the City, and I could predict exactly
how Aaron's friends and associates would behave, so
I spent the morning taking an inventory of our older
stocks from good years, and tripled the prices. I'd just
emailed the finished presentation off to Aaron when I
looked out of the window of the little room I'd made
my office to see a familiar figure coming in the gates
of the old yard – John Lambert.

The last he'd seen of me was my bare bottom as I
struggled to sort myself out in the rowing boat on the
Dordogne, and he was obviously here to visit me, so
my immediate reaction was to consider making a hasty
exit. Unfortunately, he looked up just as I stood up, no
doubt giving the impression of being eager to come
down and see him, so I was left with little choice but to
return his friendly wave and make my way down to the
yard. He'd been smartly dressed when I met him in
Bergerac, but now he looked like a wealthy landowner
on his way to a garden party. As I greeted him with a
friendly smile and prayed he had the discretion not to
mention the incident on the river, I was thinking that
I'd never seen such an obvious roué, an impression
confirmed by his opening line.

'Ah, Elise, I was hoping to catch you in, and may I
say that you are an absolute vision of beauty.'

'Thank you. Is there anything in particular? We're
not offering tastings today, as we're still finishing up
the picking.'

I'd judged my response to be a little cool, but he took no notice whatsoever.

'So I see, but I'm sure you'll excuse me when you hear what I have to say. This is strictly confidential, of course, so if you wouldn't mind walking a little way?'

He started towards the arch that led to the hedges, which I thought a little odd, but I followed, intrigued, half expecting him to take my arm and not quite sure how to react if he did. If he intended to proposition me, he was going a very odd way about it, asking about the size of the estate and our average production levels as we made our way round to the rose beds, then stopping to look out across the front of the house and the vineyards beyond.

'Impressive, although it's just a shame that so few people appreciate fine sweet wines these days, especially in Europe.'

'We do quite well.'

'Not well enough, sadly, with losses averaging just under ten thousand euros per year over the last decade – or rather, for the last ten years for which accounts are available – and last year must have been worse, a really rotten vintage, the worst since '65 some say. Fortunately, I have the solution.'

'You do?'

'Yes. As I think I may have mentioned, I am a land agent for property in the area, especially for foreign buyers. I have several clients who are interested in wine estates, although generally in the Gironde, but I think I might be able to raise some interest, up to a price of, say, two million euros.'

It took a moment for what he was saying to sink in, and another, rather longer moment for the full implications of the offer to register, but that was what sparked my indignation.

'Two million euros? Mr Lambert, I may be relatively young, and I may be a newcomer to the area, but I seem to remember that I already told you I'm not interested in selling, and I am not completely naive. For instance, I happen to know that Château La Rivière sold for about thirty million euros last year, and . . .'

'Ah, but with due respect to your property, La Fleur is hardly as grand as La Rivière, while the estate is half the size, and this is Bergerac, not Fronsac.'

'This is Monbazillac, which is every bit as good as Fronsac.'

'But it is not Bordeaux, while Fronsac is, and it is the name Bordeaux that draws in the big investors. Two million is actually a very generous offer, so much so that I doubt I can keep it open for very long, especially with the poor reports coming in on last year's vintage, while the eurozone crisis shows no real signs of letting up, and . . .'

'Mr Lambert, until recently I worked for a City broker, one of the best. Slick sales talk is not going to impress me.'

'I didn't mean to come across as patronising, but it

really is an excellent offer, and surely it's better to take it up now than wait until you're in debt?'

'I'm hoping to make the estate profitable.'

He gave a smug little chuckle before he replied.

'Ah, the optimism of youth, a wonderful thing! Who knows, maybe you will succeed, but if so, you will be very much the exception. Wine estates do not make a good investment nowadays. Indeed, most recent purchases have been made more for the sake of prestige than profit. Still, the offer remains open, for the time being; but more immediately, would you care for a spot of lunch?'

I was about to make an angry refusal, but he seemed oddly familiar with La Fleur, more so than he could have been merely from looking at the public accounts, and I wanted to know more.

'You're welcome to join us in the shed, although it's just ratatouille and bread and wine. How well did you know my aunt?'

'Everybody knew Adèle de Regnier, at least locally, but I wasn't thinking of joining your workforce at their bucolic feast, more of a little *tête-à-tête* down by the river, at La Poisson d'Or, perhaps, which is very good.'

'I really need to be here, thanks.'

'Another time, then, but do you mind if I take a look around?'

'Go ahead. I need to get back.'

It was a lie, as Madame Belair and Liselotte were perfectly capable of coping without me, and usually did, while they wouldn't be serving lunch for another half hour in any case. I knew I could easily resist his clumsy and avuncular blandishments, but I didn't see why I should have to try, especially when he was clearly just as keen to take advantage of me financially as he was sexually. He obviously wasn't going to tell me how he had known that what appeared to be a way into the stables also led to the gardens, which meant that not only had he visited La Fleur at least once before, and probably more often, but that he didn't want me to know.

As I walked back towards the winery, I was wondering what he was up to and trying to tell myself that it didn't matter as he had no power over me anyway. Unfortunately, I'm too sensitive to male arrogance, and too inquisitive, so quickly found myself wondering whether his attempt to flirt with me was a ploy to improve his chances of buying La Fleur, and if his offer to buy La Fleur was designed to help him get into my knickers. Neither possibility made any real sense, but he was definitely up to something, and I wanted to know what.

Jean was in the main yard, unloading the new barrels, and greeted me with a grin so broad and so knowing I immediately wondered if Liselotte had already told him about the night before. I found myself blushing, as usual, but gave him a non-committal nod and walked on to the shed, where Liselotte was setting out plates and cutlery. Her smile was no less familiar than Jean's, and there was no mistaking the warmth of her kiss as she greeted me, nor the implication of the gentle pat she applied to my bottom. I was sure Jean had seen, and my face was now burning hot, but he was as casual as ever, merely passing me a packet of paper serviettes to go next to the places she was laying.

I got to work, now wondering what I ought to say and what I wanted to say, but unsure of either, save that my feelings were far too complicated to be easily expressed. Then there was the possibility of what might happen now, which was bringing on my feelings of weakness and vulnerability as never before, which in turn made me feel guilty about Aaron, not because I couldn't resist, but because I didn't want to. If Jean and Liselotte suggested something, or tried to tease me into misbehaving, I could either refuse and end up feeling hurt and left out, or accept and end up feeling guilty. I couldn't be sure which way I'd jump, either, other than acknowledging that the decision would probably have a lot less to do with my morals than the amount of alcohol I'd taken on board at the time. '*In vino veritas*', as the saying goes, and in my case the truth was that I wanted them to take me somewhere quiet and spank my bottom then put me on my knees for oral sex.

My feelings had come on with the most extraordinary rush as well, changing from annoyance and puzzlement at John Lambert's behaviour to weak-kneed arousal in a matter of moments. I needed it, at a deep, visceral level, my body reacting without reference to my head and regardless of what I'd been taught to believe was acceptable or desirable. Only the appearance of Luc stopped me from propositioning Liselotte then and there, while also turning my mind back to John Lambert. Luc had been at La Fleur for maybe twice as long as I'd been alive and knew everybody.

'Luc, did you see the man who met me in the old yard earlier? Do you know who he is?'

'Don't you? He is an incomer, British, who lives in Colombier. John Lambert.'

'Anything else?'

'He used to come round, years ago, to visit Madame Adèle after her second divorce, but she wouldn't marry an Englishman and, anyway, she preferred Monsieur de Regnier.'

He'd made a rubbing motion with fingers and thumb as he spoke, hinting at money.

'Oh. So he's not that well off, then?'

He shrugged.

'Well enough, but not so rich as de Regnier. Don't let Lambert get his way with you. He would ruin us and sell out to the Americans or the Chinese.'

'Thank you, and I certainly do not intend to let Lambert get his way, as you put it. He's more than twice my age!'

Luc shrugged and smiled, perhaps pleased, perhaps cynical, then walked on to help Jean strip the plastic wrappers off the new barrels. I considered what he had

said as I finished laying out the serviettes. Lambert had
made his offer before he asked me out to lunch, and so
perhaps had hoped that I'd accept, but then, when I'd
proved obstinate, he'd changed his tactics. That made
sense, and if it relied on his extraordinary arrogance in
thinking I'd consider him as a lover, especially when
he knew I was with Aaron, then that was on a par
with his character. Liselotte had been listening to my
conversation with Luc and now laughed.

'I remember him now, the man who would come
round with roses, in an old black British car, a huge
thing.'

'I'm glad she had the taste to choose de Regnier.'

'Not until Lambert had taken her to bed a dozen
times, maybe two dozen.'

'Oh. How long ago was this?'

'More than twelve years now.'

'And he thinks he can move in on me – the cheek
of it!'

'You wouldn't be the first young girl to go for a rich
old man, and he is not even so very old.'

'He's twice our age, easily, maybe three times!'

She merely shrugged and moved away to collect a
box of glasses, leaving me seething with indignation
at John Lambert's arrogance and unscrupulous
behaviour. He was still in the grounds and I very nearly
went to find him to give him a piece of my mind, only
to decide that I was better off keeping what I knew to
myself and seeing how things developed. Just possibly

there might be some way I could turn the situation to my advantage, or at the very least punish him for daring to imagine I might give in to his wiles.

Madame Belair had come into the shed, carrying a great dish topped with silver foil, which she set down on the table before giving Liselotte a sharp command. Both women left the shed and I went to my place at the head of the long table and poured myself a glass of wine, which I sipped as I watched Luc and Jean rolling the barrels down into the cellar and brooded on John Lambert and why I seemed to grow aroused so often and so easily, far more so than when I'd lived in London. One possibility was the country air, which no doubt meant I was healthier all round now that I no longer spent my days breathing in fumes. Another was the constant presence of a man with far more than his fair share of testosterone – Jean – who managed to create more sexual innuendo merely by man-handling barrels than a dozen firemen going through a strip routine.

After a while, the first group of workers came in and I busied myself with the ratatouille, only to have Madame Belair reappear and insist on taking over, as if I were a five-year-old making a mess while trying to help out in her mother's kitchen. We began to eat, with Luc sat at my right-hand side as usual, and in expansive mood, laughingly telling me how my aunt had done her best to help John Lambert and Monsieur de Regnier avoid each other while both had been her

lovers. I couldn't help but laugh, despite Madame
Belair's occasional caustic remark, and was just about
to make a joke of how Lambert had propositioned me,
when his head appeared around the shed doors, which
we'd left open to let in the sunlight and air.

'Ah, Elise, my dear, might I take you up on your
kind offer of lunch after all? The aroma is too good
to resist.'

I bit back the angry retort that first came to mind,
deciding on a more subtle insult instead, something
more in keeping with the way he'd treated me. As
a guest, he should have sat near me, above even the
permanent staff, but the only free chairs were well
down the table. I waved casually towards them, leaving
him no choice but to accept my offer or go. Or so I
thought. Instead, he picked up one of the chairs and
carried it to the head of the table, giving me no choice
but to move over and let him take a place between Luc
and myself.

He immediately became the centre of conversation,
praising Madame Belair for her ratatouille and Luc
for the wine, remarking on how fresh and healthy
Liselotte and I looked, discussing the prospects for
the vintage and generally acting the suave gentleman.
I put up with it, all the while mulling over ways to take
him down a peg or two, although nothing immediately
suggested itself; and despite one or two near-the-
knuckle comments, he didn't say anything that would
have deserved the equivalent of the water cooler

treatment, in this case a large jug of red wine poured down his collar. It was tempting, but everybody would have thought I was nuts.

I contented myself with mentioning Aaron as often as possible and trying not to drink too much wine. He seemed indifferent, ever more expansive and relaxed, and if I was holding back on the drink, he wasn't. By the time lunch was over, he'd put back at least a litre of red Bergerac and had persuaded Luc to draw a cask sample of the previous year's Monbazillac, which he fussed over as if he were a critic and finally pronounced good for a poor year, an assessment Luc accepted with a solemn nod. It was time to get back to work, but he showed no signs of leaving so I asked if he'd help with the triage, a tough, skilled job that involved standing at a conveyor belt and sorting bunches of grapes according to how ripe they were. He accepted, presumably thinking I'd be working alongside him, which allowed me to escape, although when I offered to help with the washing up, Madame Belair told me it wasn't my job. Rather to my surprise, she then poured me a large glass of *eau de vie*, not the usual mirabelle, but a special recipe of Luc's made from the little wild peaches that grew against the walls of the old stable.

With John Lambert safely out of the way, I accepted the drink and spent a reflective few minutes sipping at it, before taking a hod and making my way down to the vineyards below the garden. A few bunches of grapes always get missed and are well worth picking later, and besides, I didn't want to feel useless or sit around indoors doing nothing. It was hot work and the grapes were ripe and sweet, tempting me to nibble a few as I went along, and I was beginning to feel pleasantly drowsy. I was still feeling horny, too, and all the more so for being so close to where Jean had given Liselotte her spanking and then taken us into the bushes.

It was rather nice to imagine it happening again, and I was just thinking that it was a shame they were both so busy, when Jean himself appeared from one of the entrances into the hedges. He saw me, waved and started down between the vines, which set my heart hammering despite the fact that he was alone and that whatever he wanted was almost certainly to do with work. Even so, I found myself thinking of how it would be for him to take me in among the trees for sex, my imaginings immediately followed by a flush of guilt about Liselotte and of shame at my own lack of faithfulness. Jean cocked a thumb back over his shoulder as he approached.

'Father says not to pick the last three rows of Semillon. He wants to try a winter harvest.'

'I know.'

'And Liselotte, she says you could use a little attention to your bottom.'

I swallowed hard, knowing exactly what he meant and instantly full of fear and arousal and burning embarrassment. Liselotte and I had talked the night before, as we lay cuddled together after sex. I'd been a little ashamed of myself for letting her dominate me so completely, so I'd joked about how silly and rude she'd looked while Jean was spanking her. She told me the experience was well worth a little undignified treatment, and I'd admitted I felt the same and would have enjoyed it too. Now she'd told him, and if I wanted it I could have it. All I needed to do was surrender and he'd take me in hand, but I found myself speechless, choking on my own pride. Jean favoured me with a knowing grin.

'She is right, isn't she?'

My mouth came open in a vain effort at denial, but I was nodding at the same time, unable to resist. Jean's grin grew broader still and he came close, to lift the hod from my back before taking me by the hand. We were just yards from the fallen willow he'd sat on to take Liselotte across his knee and he was leading me towards it, but that would mean anybody further up the slope would get a prime view as I was spanked, and that was well beyond what I could cope with. I gave a desperate shake of my head and pointed in among the trees, at which Jean shrugged and changed course to where a bush heavily overgrown with wild vines pushed out to make a sheltered enclave.

He was holding the hod, and carefully tipped out the contents onto a patch of dried grass, then turned it over. It made an excellent seat, just the right height to let him take me across his legs for my spanking, and as he patted his lap I found myself getting down into position, obedient and accepting, for all the tiny sensible voice in the back of my head screaming at me that what I was doing was a betrayal of every principle of female equality and self-respect.

I went down anyway, across his knee with my bottom stuck up in the air and my breathing deep and ragged, my entire body shaking and my heart beating at a crazy speed. He took hold, one heavy arm curled around my waist, so strong that I was able to tell myself I no longer had any choice, that I was about to spanked by a primal brute who'd do as he pleased, however much I begged for release and however much I struggled. It was a lie, as I knew full well he'd let me go if I asked him to, but it did make it ever so slightly easier to cope with my burning shame as he lifted one knee to bring my bottom into greater prominence and casually lifted my dress to show off the seat of my panties.

His hand settled across my bottom and, despite myself, I began to whimper, frightened of the coming pain, even though I badly needed what was coming to me. I shut my eyes and bit down on my lip, determined not to be a big baby about it but completely unable to still the trembling of my body or the weak jerking of the muscles in my legs.

He laughed.

'I haven't even begun yet!'

My answer was a feeble sob, and as his hand lifted from my bottom, I braced myself. Nothing happened, and after a moment I twisted around, wondering what he was doing, to find him reaching out towards the wild vine that cloaked the tree and on which hung clusters of golden-brown grapes, overripe and rich with decay. He picked a bunch, one of the largest, and held it up to nip off one of the few grapes that still looked edible. I couldn't help but protest.

'Just do it, you bastard!'

He ignored me, but bit off a second grape, shedding a drop of juice that splashed down on the bare skin of my back where my dress had been turned up.

'Jean! It's bad enough being over your knee, but at least pay me some attention!'

'Okay.'

He shifted his grip, to take me around the waist with the other arm, still holding the grapes. His free hand slid to my chest, taking hold of one dangling breast, squeezing and stroking to make my nipples pop out, but I choked off my instinctive protest at such rude treatment, reasoning that if I was his to spank, then it was hardly surprising he'd want to touch me up. It felt nice anyway, and I soon closed my eyes and let my mouth come wide in bliss, only to have it unexpectedly stuffed full of overripe grapes.

'Bfft'd!'

Jean laughed and pushed the now badly crushed bunch in down the front of my dress, smearing my breasts with sticky, reeking pulp. A quick jerk and my dress was down, leaving my boobs hanging free as he continued to rub the mess in, finally letting go to leave me thoroughly soiled, my entire face and chest slimy with pulp and bits of skin, juice dripping from my nipples and the tip of my nose. Finally, I found my voice.

'You pig! You utter bastard! I thought you were going to spank me!'

'I am.'

He'd adjusted his grip again, harder now, so that I had no possible chance of wriggling free. I was feeling pretty sorry for myself, with my bare boobs soiled and dripping and my face filthy with muck, but in a weird sort of way it was nice. It was like getting deliberately dirty, only not having to take responsibility for my behaviour, and I was going to be punished anyway. I stuck up my bottom, eager once more and less frightened than before. His grip changed slightly, a big calloused thumb went down the back of my panties and they were coming down, but only a little way before they were tugged away from my skin, at which I realised what he was going to do.

'Hey, no, Jean, not down my knickers! You can spank me, but . . .'

My words broke into a plaintive cry as a bunch of grapes was dropped in down the back of my panties, heavy and wet and slippery where some had burst as my waistband was released. Again he laughed, and as I turned my head I saw he'd picked another bunch, which was plainly destined to join the last.

'That's right, Elise, this one's for your cunt.'

I began to struggle, determined to spare myself
the final, awful indignity of allowing my sex lips and
the neat little triangle of fur under my belly to be
given their share of mess, but Jean merely tightened
his grip, pushed his hand well in down the back of my
panties and squashed the entire filthy, glutinous mess
full between my thighs. Some of it actually went in
up my vagina, while it was between my cheeks too,
soiling my bottom hole, then squeezing out around
the leg holes of my panties as he pulled them sharply
back up.

'Jean! You . . . you . . . Ow!'

He'd finally begun to spank me, landing one heavy
hand across my bulging panty seat to jam yet more
pulp up my hole and splash grape juice in every
direction. A second smack, a third, and the mess was
running down my thighs and spattering my back and
even my hair as I began to kick in my pain, only for
my panties to be whipped smartly down and the bulk
of the soggy, squishy mess to fall out onto the ground
with a wet plop. Not that I cared any more, kicking
and wriggling in Jean's grip as he spanked me, with my
hair tossing and my legs kicking frantically in my half-
lowered panties, my boobs jiggling and my bottom
cheeks bouncing crazily, a display I was very, very glad
nobody else was around to watch.

Jean spanked me hard, far harder than Liselotte had
done, and the effect was stronger still. With her, I'd
had at least some fight left in me once she was done,

enough to put up a little resistance when she'd decided to sit on my face. With Jean, there was no resistance at all. When he finally allowed me down from his lap, I went straight into his arms, to cling to him in a trembling, babbling mess until he'd freed his cock, which went straight into my mouth. I stripped as I sucked him erect, peeling off my filthy dress and my ruined panties to go nude at his feet, as both my shoes had come off during my spanking.

When he was ready, he simply took me, easing his cock in up me from behind as I knelt in the warm grass with my bottom pushed high, no more reserved than a she-cat on heat. He fucked me as well as he'd spanked me, hard and long, knocking the breath from my body to set me gasping and clutching at the soil, out of my mind with ecstasy. He made me come that way, something few men can achieve, and not just once but three times, before he gave me the same delightful treatment I'd seen Liselotte get, his cock pulled free and rubbed on my clitoris until I hit a fourth orgasm even more powerful than the rest.

Only then did he take his own pleasure, lying back on the grass to let me crawl between his legs and take him in my mouth once more, to kiss and lick and suck at his huge balls and the great straining tower of his cock. I was masturbating as I did it, with my knees set wide and my still-aching bottom pushed high, my body still slick with grape juice and also with sweat, lost in ecstasy at my own filthy behaviour as I reached my fifth climax just as he took his own down my throat.

Liselotte was right. I had needed attention to my bottom, and more.

8

The last of the grapes was in, our vats full and the hard work over, or at least that part of the work I could help with. I would be much more valuable in London and had booked myself a flight direct from Bergerac to London City Airport.

It felt strange stepping off the plane, evoking as great a sense of change as I'd ever experienced after a flight, even though I'd only come a few hundred miles. London felt different, not only in the smell of the air and the all-pervading buzz of the city, which I'd always taken for granted, but as if I'd travelled in time as well. In Bergerac, the autumn had been soft and warm, with the leaves turning slowly to gold in the still air, creating a languid, easy atmosphere. London was cold and damp and somehow sharp, with an air of urgency and bustle. It also made me feel small, with tower blocks rising all around as my cab took me in to the City itself, with more people on every short stretch of pavement than I'd have seen in a week at La Fleur. Most of all, it felt alien, no longer my home.

I'd assumed I'd be going into Aaron's office, which

would have felt stranger still, but he had apparently set up a tasting at Angel's, a hotel close to St Paul's. I was impressed from the start, both by the quiet refinement of what was obviously a small but exclusive establishment and by the woman who greeted me at reception, Rebecca Laindon. She knew exactly who I was and what was going on, while her tidy blonde hair, sharp suit and even sharper heels gave an impression of brisk efficiency entirely in keeping with her manner.

Aaron wasn't there, but was due within minutes, while they'd given us the Arbitrageurs Suite, which was apparently designed for tastings and similar functions. I'd sent the wines on by courier, along with instructions for how they should be served, and Rebecca and the rest of the staff seemed to know what they were doing and have an eye for elegance. Long tables had been set out at either side of the room, one against the windows so that the wines could be admired in the pearly north-light coming in through the net curtains, and the other against the opposite wall, for the buffet. The reds had been opened to allow them to breathe, as per my instructions, while each white had its own ice-bucket. Glasses, spittoons, linen napkins, cutlery and other accessories were all set out ready for use, so that all I needed to make the tasting complete was a few customers.

They were quick in coming, the first arriving a quarter of an hour before the tasting was due to start, with others close on their heels. I soon had more than twenty people to deal with, and while Aaron still wasn't there, he had certainly done me proud. Some of the guests were City friends, a few I'd even met before, while they in turn had obviously passed the word on to their own friends and colleagues. There were also several restaurateurs and catering managers from big companies and institutions.

Half an hour into the tasting and I had more than fifty people, forcing me to beg Rebecca to greet newcomers at the door, while I'd given up all hope of trying to control the order in which they drank the wines and how much they took. Half of them weren't even paying attention and had begun to discuss different topics, but I was in constant demand, with an ever-changing audience. The buffet was opened up and the pressure finally reduced a little, at which point Aaron arrived, as cool and dapper as ever, with a kiss for my cheek, a discreet squeeze of my bottom and a casual apology for being late.

There was no time to make an issue of his tardy arrival and he quickly began to prove his worth, extolling the virtues of La Fleur with an easy assurance that went far beyond the truth. Not even Luc would have made such ambitious claims, but aside from one or two doubtful glances from the more experienced restaurateurs, the guests seemed to lap up his assertions without question. I was soon taking orders, some large, some high value, while the extravagant prices I'd put on the older, rarer wines didn't seem to bother anybody in the least. Before long I was trying not to grin, and I was looking forward to Luc's astonishment at what I'd achieved, while even Madame Belair was going to have to admit I'd done well.

By the end of the tasting, I was well pleased with myself and with Aaron. I'd sold an impressive amount of wine, and perhaps more importantly had secured ongoing orders to supply four restaurants, plus two institutions with their own catering facilities. Most of that was red and dry white, but the private clients had taken plenty of Monbazillac, much of it at prices I'd never really expected to get. I was also exhausted, and despite my best efforts to spit out everything I'd tasted myself, fairly drunk.

When the final guest had said his goodbyes, I poured out the last of one of our most expensive bottles into a fresh glass and settled myself against the table. Aaron was at the far side of the room, talking to Rebecca Laindon, but when he saw that I was alone, he made his apologies and came over to me. She glanced towards us as he took me in his arms, and for a moment I thought I caught a curious look in her eye, perhaps amusement, even disdain. It was only for an instant, and I wasn't even sure if I'd read her correctly, but then Aaron was kissing me and I put her out of my mind. He wasn't quite as intimate as he might have been, but Rebecca was still standing in the doorway, so that wasn't really surprising, and there was no mistaking the passion in his voice as he broke away to whisper into my ear.

'I've booked us an executive suite, come on up.'

I'd been expecting to go back to his flat in Docklands, but if he wanted to splash out on my entertainment, that was fine, and it was a great deal easier just to go upstairs than to make our way across the City in the rush hour. His hand found mine and I was being led across the room, past Rebecca, who now wore a professional but somehow faintly smug smile and obviously knew exactly what was going on, and up two flights of richly carpeted stairs to a room that looked out at the cathedral. It was well appointed, neither too spartan nor too fussy, with a huge bed and a table beside it, on which rested an ice-bucket with a bottle of vintage Krug nestling among the frosty cubes. Aaron spoke as he closed the door behind us.

'I think I'd like you nude.'

'As you please.'

His words had brought a lump to my throat and set the butterflies in my stomach fluttering, but he seemed to want to play a game and I did my best to act up to his expectations, trying to remain cool and poised as I slipped out of my clothes. It wasn't a striptease, exactly, more the way I imagined a very expensive call girl would undress for a favoured client. He seemed to appreciate it anyway, watching from the bed as he dealt with the champagne, settling back to sip from his glass as I divested myself of my stockings, rolling each one slowly down and dropping them as I made my way into the bathroom with a taunting wiggle.

I'd hoped he would follow and take me in the shower, but he stayed where he was and I found myself hurrying as I washed, dried and helped myself to the luxurious complimentary toiletries to apply a little powder and scent where it would do the most good. He was still on the bed when I came out, laid out full length with his feet crossed and his back propped up on the pillows, champagne glass still in hand. I walked over, slow and easy, enjoying the way his eyes moved over my naked body, then climbed up onto the bed and crawled across to him.

His Adam's apple bobbed as my fingers went to the zip of his suit trousers, and I found myself smiling at having ruffled his composure even ever so slightly, before looking up to meet his eyes. He'd begun to tremble as I drew his zip down and burrowed my hand into his fly to squeeze his already swollen cock, and he gave a low moan as I pulled it all free. I don't know what it is, but I love the sight of a man in a really good suit, perfectly dressed but for his cock and balls sticking out of his fly. Aaron made the perfect example: the best possible suit and the best possible set of cock and balls, big and smooth and gloriously virile.

I began to kiss and nuzzle, to lick and finally to suck, bringing him quickly to full, magnificent erection and myself to a state of need so strong it took all my will power to keep my hands from between my thighs. He gave in only gradually himself, watching me and stroking my hair but letting out the occasional moan or sigh when I found a particularly sensitive spot or did something especially dirty. The state of his erection told its own story, the skin taut and the head glossy with pressure. Still I took my time, reaching out for the glass he'd poured for me and filling my mouth with the well-chilled champagne before going back down on him once more. He gave a deep moan, somewhere between pleasure and pain, as the cold fluid surrounded his cock, and I began to suck in earnest for a while before swallowing down my mouthful and repeating the trick before taking him in hand and applying my tongue to his balls as the cool champagne ran out over my lips.

With that he began to shake and push himself up into my hand, his famed reserve cracking under my careful ministrations. Feeling rather pleased with myself, I climbed on, straddling him and taking hold of his cock to guide him slowly in. I was wet and ready, not surprisingly, and took him all the way as I settled myself across him, keen to ride and hopefully make myself come before he did, or better still, to reach orgasm together in one perfect moment.

He let me have my way, his eyes still feasting on my naked body as I rode him, his hands moving gently up and down my wide-spread thighs, then to my breasts as I came forward a little, my pleasure already rising towards ecstasy. His grip tightened, he seemed to shift, and as I realised he was about to throw me off and change position, I started begging.

'No, please, Aaron . . . let me come . . . let me come . . .'

His cock jammed up into me as I broke off, and again, thrusting hard as his fingers found my nipples, pinching and pulling even as I began to wriggle on his cock, right at the edge of orgasm and then over. He laughed as he saw that I was coming, a sound as much of cruelty as of delight, and which made my ecstatic surrender all the deeper as I rode his cock through a long, lovely climax that ended only when I let my body slump slowly down on top of his. His arms came around me, hugging me tightly to his body for one wonderful moment before he spoke into my ear.

'Now my turn, you greedy little bitch.'

I didn't protest or even answer and he took my acquiescence for granted anyway, twisting himself over on top of me and pushing his cock deep once more even as my thighs came wide in welcome. A few firm thrusts and I was gasping and clutching him to me, only for him to take hold once more and flip me over onto my tummy. I'd barely had a chance to push my bottom up before he was in me again, driving deep with the hard muscles of his belly slapping on my bare bottom just as if I were being spanked.

Memories of Jean came back, and with them a flush of guilt, but I couldn't stop now, not with Aaron handling me like a rag doll as he pulled up my hips to get me into a kneeling position, face down on the bed with my bottom stuck in the air as he continued to thrust into me from behind. It was the same way Jean had had me, down among the trees by the river, and before I could stop myself I was begging Aaron to spank me, the words spilling from my lips in a barely coherent babble of rude, dirty pleas. He laughed to hear me, as cruel and amused as before, then brought his hand down across my bottom in a firm, punishing slap as he spoke.

'Why, you kinky little bitch! I might have known it, Elise . . . I might have known you liked a good spanking, and boy are you going to get it!'

He was still fucking me as he did it, driving his cock in over and over again as he smacked my upturned cheeks turn and turn about, hard, stinging slaps that quickly had me biting at the coverlet in a vain effort to stifle my yelps, although the sound of his hand cracking down across my bottom could probably have been heard down in the street. I was going to come, again, fucked and spanked in the nude with my bottom stuck in the air for my man, a man in an immaculate suit and still fully dressed but for his cock and balls, an unspeakably shameful situation to be in and so, so good.

Aaron got there first, by a whisker, crying out in ecstasy and jamming his cock in as deep as it would go as he filled me with hot come, holding himself deep for a long moment, then starting to pump once more, hard and fast, to a frantic crescendo of violent thrusts that pushed me over the edge one more time, setting me screaming into the coverlet and clutching at my sex in an utterly uninhibited exhibition of wanton desire that ended only when he finally pulled out. I collapsed, exhausted, my muscles aching and my bottom smarting badly, but perfectly happy.

'That was wonderful, thank you.'

'No, thank you. You really are the best.'

'By which you mean I'm a kinky little bitch?'

'I wouldn't have you any other way.'

He'd moved back into his original position on the bed and I snuggled into his chest, slowly relaxing. His arm came around me, to hold me to his body, another perfect moment, but again only brief before he busied himself with refilling our champagne glasses. As my excitement slowly faded to a feeling of warm satisfaction, it was marred only by a faint sense of embarrassment at my behaviour. I was hoping Aaron was enough of a gentleman not to say anything, but I was wrong.

'Do you know, I always thought you might be into kinky sex. It was one of the things that first attracted me to you.'

'Thank you very much!'

'That was a compliment, Elise, and besides, there's nothing wrong with being a little kinky. Girls like you often are.'

'How do you mean, "girls like me"?'

'Oh, you know, from a privileged background, well educated, the sort who never really have to worry because if everything goes wrong, Mum and Dad will bail them out. I suppose having that sense of security allows you to express your submissive side.'

I didn't answer immediately, because I was thinking of all my cares across the years as I'd struggled through my school exams and through college, after the death of my parents, to kick off my career in the City and to make my way up the career ladder. I'd never felt secure for a moment, and yet in a sense he was right, because even if I'd failed completely, I wouldn't have found myself on the streets, and I'd also had several opportunities to drop out of the rat race altogether by marrying a man with good prospects. Then again, what he called my 'submissive side' had been restricted entirely to my most private fantasies until I'd found myself the owner of La Fleur. It still seemed a bit unfair of him, especially as his background was far more privileged than mine, and I couldn't resist teasing.

'How about you, then? Do you enjoy a good spanking? No, let me guess, you like . . . you like dressing up in fancy lingerie? Or maybe you like to suck . . .'

I broke off with a squeak as he twisted me around to lie across his body, but I was laughing even as his leg came up to lift my bottom and his hand slapped down across my cheeks to deliver a dozen hard swats, for all that my laughter was broken by yelps and squeals. He then paused and began to talk, punctuating each word with a hard smack to my wriggling cheeks.

'I . . . am . . . the . . . one . . . in . . . charge. I . . . am
. . . the . . . boss. Who . . . am . . . I?'

'You're not my boss, not any more! Ow! Ow! Ow!'

He set to work, twisting one arm up into the small
of my back and spanking hard, regardless of my
desperate wriggling and squeals of pain, or my helpless
laughter and the occasional cheeky comment. Finally,
I gave him what he wanted.

'Okay, okay, you're the boss! You're the boss!'

'Good. I'm glad you see it that way. Now, another
half-dozen and you're done. Stick that cute little
bottom up.'

I obeyed, lifting my hips to deliberately offer him
my bare bottom for spanking, which was infinitely
more humiliating than being held down to have it
smacked. He knew it, too, grinning as he gave me my
six hard slaps, then holding his arm up to let me cuddle
into his side once more. I came up, now trembling
badly and clinging to him with a desperate need for
comfort, while he'd reduced my poor bottom to a hot,
aching ball; but for all my bruised feelings and sore
flesh, I needed more as badly as I needed to be held.

He seemed completely content – so typical of a
man after he's come, and perhaps typical of a man
when a girl he's just spanked is clinging to him as if
she never wants to be released. I was wishing I felt
the same, but the spanking had brought me back
on heat with a vengeance, and the week I planned
to spend in London now seemed impossibly short.

He'd put his arm back around my shoulder and was sipping champagne with his eyes half closed, making me wonder if he was going to drift off to sleep, but that would have been unbearable. I swallowed my own drink, then let my hand sneak down to the front of his suit trousers, burrowing in to give his cock a gentle squeeze. His response was a sigh that might have been contentment, or resignation, or even exasperation, but he didn't take my hand away and I was determined to make him respond, speaking softly as I teased his cock and balls.

'I have a confession to make. The night after I quit work, I . . . um . . . I thought about you tying me up . . . for sex.'

He raised his eyebrows in surprise as he replied.

'Oh yes? That was after you'd poured the contents of a ten-litre water cooler over my lap, was it?'

I managed a weak nod, then a shrug, sure he was going to spank me again, but he contented himself with letting one hand stray to my bottom, stroking my hot flesh as he carried on.

'So, would you like me to tie you up?'

'I . . . I suppose so, if you think I ought to be punished?'

It was an open invitation, and he did give me a gentle pat to each cheek, then continued.

'I see how it is. You like it, but you don't like to have to ask for it. Is that right?'

'Something like that.'

'Typical posh girl; demure on the outside, dirty underneath. So I can do as I please?'

'Within reason, yes.'

My throat was dry as I spoke, and despite his calm, amused attitude, he was reacting too. All the while I'd been stroking and squeezing his cock, and he'd begun to respond, swelling slowly beneath my hand. I looked up, wondering what I'd let myself in for, but he continued to pet me and to sip at his champagne. A quick adjustment to his trousers and I had his cock out once more, in my hand and then my mouth, sucking gently with my head resting on the hard muscles of his belly. I shifted around a little and his fingers stole down between my cheeks to tickle between. He laughed as my bottom hole tightened instinctively, gave me another light slap to each cheek, then spoke again.

'Keep sucking, and play with my balls, too.'

I obeyed, now feeling delightfully rude as I took him deep into my mouth and began to squeeze gently at his balls. He was growing hard, but only slowly, and I knew that this time it would be long, slow and probably kinky. What I hadn't expected was for him to turn on the TV, and the sudden, unexpected sound of an authoritative male voice commenting on the state of the stock market brought me up with a jerk. Aaron took a grip in my hair, pushing me back down onto his cock as he gave me a new order, sharper this time.

'Keeping sucking, I said. I need to see what price Geinsheimer and Cribbs is being floated at. Come on, Elise, right in, and what did I say to do with my balls?'

'Play with them.'

I sounded sulky even to myself, but I went back to work, now feeling distinctly resentful and determined to make him react to me beyond simply growing stiff in my mouth. He didn't even bother to keep his grip in my hair, sure of my continued obedience as he went back to stroking and patting my bottom, only to pause to turn the volume up slightly as the announcer began to discuss the item on Geinsheimer and Cribbs. I continued to suck, trying every trick I knew to get his attention, even nipping the head of his cock with my teeth, for which I was rewarded with a sharp slap to my bottom as he spoke again.

'Nine-forty-two, that's low. Right, I need to make a call, so keep on sucking, and if you stop, or bite me again, I swear I'll take your own hairbrush to your bottom. I take it you have one in your bag? Yes, I thought as much. No girl has hair like that without constant attention.'

I'd nodded on my mouthful of cock as he spoke and found myself shaking as I thought of the hairbrush in my bag, a small wooden one with a handle which was sure to sting like anything if used across my rear cheeks. Aaron had pulled his phone from his pocket and was soon talking to somebody at the office. I carried on sucking, his cock now fully erect in my mouth so that

I could get my hand around the shaft and tug as I used my lips on the head, listening all the while.

'. . . yes, at least twenty points, but don't start to sell until . . . Ow! Jesus fucking H Christ. Get off, you fucking maniac!'

I'd bitten his cock, quite hard this time, and right on the head, forcing him to snatch at my hair and pull me off before he could carry on.

'No, not you, Mark . . . sorry . . . sorry, start to sell if the price goes above ten. Call you back. Ow! Jesus, Elise, that hurt! Right, you asked for this!'

I had, but that did nothing to quell my very real fear as he dragged me across his body by my hair, where I was held in place as he rummaged in my bag for my hairbrush. He soon found it, and quickly changed his grip, letting go of my hair and snatching one wrist to twist my arm up, hard, into the small of my back before bringing the hairbrush down across my cheeks. The loud, meaty smack of wood on flesh was followed in short order by my yelp of pain, a sequence quickly repeated, and again and again as he beat me. It was impossibly painful, leaving me writhing and kicking across his lap and wondering how I could possibly have been stupid enough to deliberately seek out such an agonising punishment.

Yet even as I squirmed in his grip and squealed out my feelings, I knew. His cock was still erect, hard against my naked belly, and I knew exactly where it would be going once he'd taken his revenge on my bottom cheeks. What I didn't expect was the change in myself. One moment the only reason I wasn't begging him to stop was that I couldn't speak, and a few smacks later I was actively pushing by bottom up for more and my yelps had given way to gasps and moans. Aaron immediately threw the hairbrush aside, his voice no longer angry but full of surprise as he pushed me off his lap.

'You . . . you really are something else, Elise! Right . . .'

He'd got me by the hips, to lift me into the same rude position as before, kneeling with my face in the covers and my blazing hot bottom pushed upwards and open, completely available to him. I felt his cock between my cheeks, rock hard and urgent, then moving lower as he took it in hand. For one awful moment, I thought he was going to try and push it in up my bottom, but my protest turned to a gasp as he filled me, all the way, with one firm shove, and in the right place.

My head was swimming as he begun to fuck me, ruthlessly hard, with his fingers locked into the flesh of my hips. It had all been so sudden, so rough, and so good, my bottom spanked with my own hairbrush before I was put on my knees and taken, but one thing it wasn't going to be was quick. It was only minutes since he'd last come, and even the most virile of young men needs a little time to recharge, which meant plenty for me. Before long he'd slowed down, but he was in no mood to compromise, enjoying my body exactly as he pleased.

After a while, he began to spank me again, by hand this time but only briefly before spreading my cheeks with his thumbs to show me off behind, with his cock still pushing in and out. I could imagine the view he was getting, which added to the thrilling shame of being in such a rude position, along with the knowledge that my bottom cheeks were red from spanking. He seemed to guess my feelings, and to enjoy my shame, spreading my cheeks wider still and taking a moment to tease the tiny hole between until I'd begun to whimper into the covers and bite my lip.

He took his time with my bottom, then flipped me over onto my side to enter me once more in a very strange position, straddled across one leg with the other held high, so that not only could he see everything, but his balls were rubbing on the inside of my thigh as he fucked me. Another quick adjustment and I was on my back with my legs held up and wide, his hands gripping my ankles as he eased his cock slowly in and out. I took one boob in each hand, showing off for him as I played with my nipples.

That seemed to encourage him and his thrusts grew faster once more, until I was moaning with pleasure and wondering if he could really manage to come again so soon. If so, I wasn't going to miss out on my own satisfaction. My hands went down and I was rubbing myself, my pleasure all the stronger for making such a wanton show of my body and my mind full of images from the way he'd used me. I'd been made to strip and show myself off, leaving no detail of my body unexplored, however intimate. I'd been spanked, again and again, always hard and always while in the nude, with him fully clothed the whole time. I'd been fucked, in one position after another, my body used as if I were a pretty doll for him to play with, and to come in, which was what he'd done, deep inside me in a perfect, mutual orgasm so intense it drove me to the edge of losing consciousness before I finally collapsed, dishevelled, sweaty, sore, but strangely proud of myself.

9

I'd been surprised to discover that we'd be staying the night at Angel's, and I was even more surprised to find that Aaron had booked an executive suite for my entire stay. He'd even set up an account for me, allowing me to order whatever I pleased, regardless of expense. It was extraordinarily generous of him, but I didn't want to take unfair advantage and end up with him thinking of me as a gold-digger. So I made a point of eating and drinking in moderation and keeping my use of the paying facilities to a reasonable level.

He was there a lot of the time anyway, or at least as often as he could manage, and I knew how busy he was. I also had plenty of my own affairs to attend to, securing the orders I'd taken at the tasting and doing my best to give the business the personal touch. Despite all that, we saw plenty of each other, especially in the evenings, when Aaron would treat me to dinner followed by a night of uninhibited sex, sometimes loving, sometimes kinky, more often just plain rude. He loved to manipulate me physically, which in turn made me feel delightfully helpless and thoroughly appreciated. After four days, we'd worked our way through what must have been most of the positions in the Kama Sutra, while I'd got so used to being spanked, it felt odd if he didn't bother.

Aaron also seemed to have an almost miraculous effect on the hotel staff, who must have been used to wealthy guests but seemed extraordinarily eager to please him. Rebecca Laindon was especially devoted, so much so that at first I wondered if he'd taken her to bed. Her attitude to me was certainly a bit odd, as if I were a call girl Aaron had hired for the week rather than his lover and business partner, but after a while I decided that she was merely jealous and trying to impress him.

There were plenty of people trying to impress me, which was flattering but a nuisance too. Men who'd barely spared me a second glance when I worked for Aaron were now highly attentive, with attitudes varying from chivalrous regret, through flirtation, to open advances. I treated them all equally, doing my best to stay polite and businesslike but making it abundantly clear that I was with Aaron alone and not inclined to stray, while I now felt distinctly guilty for having given in to Jean in France. My only disappointment was that I'd hoped to see Vicky, as I'd barely been in touch with her and felt bad about it, but by sheer bad luck her holiday coincided almost exactly with my time in London.

The Saturday was busy, with lunch at one restaurant and dinner at another, followed by an evening of slow, sensuous sex as Aaron first massaged me with oil then took me from behind on the bathroom floor. The next morning, I awoke expecting him to be erect and eager for the use of my mouth, as he generally was, but when I tried to go down under the covers, he cuffed me gently away and told me to get dressed as we were going out. I did as I was told, intrigued and wondering what treat he had in store for me and why it meant saving himself for later, as it clearly did.

I'd always liked wandering around the City on a Sunday, especially in the morning when everything is strangely quiet, at least in comparison to the bustle of the working week. Aaron seemed to share my taste and intend nothing more, first stopping at a café for coffee and croissants, then taking me by the hand and leading me up through the alleys and little courtyards north of Cheapside until we came to the back of a tall grey tower. It wasn't the most attractive place, with windowless concrete rising on three sides and a rather forlorn-looking piece of modern art mounted on a plinth; and while the smooth, abstract granite curves looked to be the ideal place to make me bend over, there were no fewer than five security cameras in the immediate vicinity. The thought of being spanked and then fucked in the knowledge that any number of security guards would eventually see was thrilling but just too dangerous, especially as some joker was sure to put it all up on the Internet. Fortunately, Aaron had other ideas and had crossed to where a plain, functional concrete staircase reached the ground. He beckoned me to follow.

'Where are we going?'

'Up here. This goes right to the top.'

'What about Security?'

'That's taken care of.'

It was. A metal grille closed off the stairs at the first landing, but Aaron had the key, leaving me feeling a lot safer once he'd locked it behind us, but also pleasantly naughty. It was a long climb, with the panorama of the city slowly opening up as we ascended, floor by floor, until all but the tallest of the other buildings were below us. From the roof the view was better still, with just a squat parapet between us and empty air, and London spread out below and to the sides. Aaron came to put his arm around me.

'Impressive, isn't it? Nearly ten million people, and every single one of them the centre of their own private universe. How many windows do you think you can see?'

'Thousands, tens of thousands, if you go out far enough.'

'Hundreds of thousands, I'd say, but yes, most of them are too far away to be able to see much, which is a pity.'

I'd caught the faint tone of blended cruelty and amusement with which I'd become so familiar and looked around in alarm.

'What are you going to do?'

He'd drawn a hank of silk cord from his pocket, soft, thick and a beautiful golden colour that somehow made the thought of being tied with it all the more appealing, and frightening. Obviously that was what it was meant for, as he quickly confirmed.

'I'm going to tie your hands behind your back. Then I'm going to fuck you. You said you wanted to be tied up.'

'Yes, but . . .'

He'd unwound the cord as he spoke, to stretch a length between his hands, and I went quiet. We were safe, after a fashion, in that nobody could possibly recognise us, and nobody could get to us, as Aaron had presumably bribed the security guards. The parapet would hide most of my body as well, but that did very little to reduce my feelings of exposure and vulnerability, all of which Aaron clearly understood. He was grinning like a wolf as began to give me my orders.

'Turn around. Hands behind your back.'

I did as I was told, turning my back to him so that I was looking out across the City with the river beyond and the great grey-brown expanse of south London beyond that. My wrists went behind my back, crossed, and I felt the silk cord touch my flesh. A couple of loops and he had me secure, unable to defend myself, but he seemed determined to make a thorough job of it, lashing my wrists so tightly together that I knew there was no way I could escape. I thought that would be enough, as he could certainly have had me at leisure, but as I looked back I saw he'd taken a second cord from his pocket, equally thick but made of rough hemp rather than silk. At the end was a small but very solid metal hook.

'What are you going to do?'

'That's the second time you've asked that. Just trust me.'

I nodded, eager to show willing but more than a little nervous as I watched him walk over to the apparatus for supporting window cleaners' cradles, a sturdy gantry of green-painted beams. One of these stuck out backwards to support a counterweight, at least ten feet above the surface of the roof. Aaron threw the hank of rope over the beam and tied the loose end off to the bulk of the machine, leaving the hook dangling a few feet off the ground. He beckoned me over and once more indicated that I should turn around, allowing him to fix the hook to the silk cord between my wrists. A brief adjustment to the rope and my arms had been hauled up behind my back, forcing me to bend forward and go up on my toes at the same time, an awkward, painful position that left my bottom completely available to him. I'd never felt so helpless in my life, and I was already shaking with reaction, while my position left me with a clear view out over the London rooftops. My voice was breaking as I twisted around to look at Aaron.

'Okay, but not too long, please. This hurts!'

He responded with a complacent nod, but moved back to where the rope was tied off, adjusting it once more to allow me to stand a little more easily.

'How's that?'

'Better, thank you.'

I felt pathetically grateful, a bizarre reaction to a man who'd tied me into an awkward and humiliating position, but as I was learning very fast indeed, the feelings you get when you submit yourself to somebody sexually are more or less the reverse of what you'd get in normal life. That was certainly true now, with my helpless excitement soaring as Aaron came behind me to touch my bottom, the palm of his hand tracing out the shape of my rear cheeks as he explored me, slowly and casually. I hung my head, my feelings ever more muddled and ever more powerful as he completed his exploration of my bottom before pushing his hand in underneath me to find the button of my jeans. It came open and they were being tugged down, my panties too, baring my bottom to the cool autumn air, and to Aaron's cock. He did my top, too, easing it high and taking my bra with it to leave me bare-breasted before stepping away.

'Say cheese.'

'You bastard!'

He'd taken a photo with his phone, just as I turned my head, and from an angle that made sure he got a good view between my thighs from behind as well as of my breasts and face.

'Don't worry, darling, it's strictly for private use.
After all, you do live in France.'

I nodded my understanding as he put the phone
away, but I couldn't help but think of how I'd look in
that picture, bound and bare for his pleasure, an image
that gave no hint of my own feelings.

'Just promise you'll keep it to yourself.'

'Of course. Relax.'

He'd come up behind me as he spoke, to push
himself against my bottom, and from the feel of
the bulge in the front of his trousers, the game we
were playing appealed to him a great deal. I thought
he'd just unzip and take me then and there, because
he was certainly ready, but he contented himself
with rubbing against me for a moment, then pulled
back.

'Have you ever been caned, Elise?'

'Caned? No, of course not. You know that.'

'Well, then, it's probably about time you were, and
as you like to be spanked, I'm sure you'll love it.'

I wasn't at all sure and felt the first trace of panic as
he reached behind the doorframe of the lift-housing to
draw out a long brown cane with a crook handle. My
stomach started to churn and I found myself treading
up and down on my toes as he stepped close. The cane
touched my skin, cool and hard against the soft flesh of
my bottom, and I began to whimper, unable to control
myself, a reaction that seemed to give Aaron a great
deal of pleasure.

'Gently, please, Aaron. I'm not sure how much . . . Ow!'

He'd lifted the cane as I began to speak, then brought it suddenly down across my bare cheeks. It couldn't have travelled more than a couple of feet, but the sudden shock and sting had made me squeak and jump. He shook his head and gave a low sigh, as if disappointed by my performance.

'That was just a tap, Elise. You do want this, don't you?'

I found myself nodding automatically, although my feelings were more than a little mixed, especially as I hadn't known he was going to cane me when he'd tied me up. Yet I knew how I reacted to spankings and this was more of the same – less intimate, maybe, but more intense.

'Are you going to take it like a big girl, or shall I just fuck you?'

'I want it. Do it . . . fast . . . don't stop . . . don't give me a chance to think.'

My words had come out in broken gasps and I was shaking with fear, but I was determined to go through with my ordeal. Aaron nodded.

'Good girl. Six, then, and try to keep still.'

The cane came up, and down again, full across my bottom with a stinging pain far stronger than before, far worse than the hairbrush. I was yelling and kicking my feet in instant reaction, but before I could find my voice, he'd given me the second stroke, harder still, then the third, to send me into a crazy little dance of pain that grew more desperate with each succeeding stroke – four, five and six – until I was thrashing madly on the end of the rope and struggling to keep my balance.

Aaron dropped the cane and took me in his arms, holding my body to his and stroking my hair as I let out my feelings in a great rush of sobs and broken words, my body shaking violently and my eyes so wet with tears I could barely see. I could feel, though, and even as he whispered soothing words and told me how wonderful I was for allowing him to enjoy my body so thoroughly, there was no mistaking his reaction. He was hard, rock hard, his cock rearing up beneath the material of his trousers to make a rigid bar against my flesh where he was cuddling me.

He was good about it, though, waiting until my sobs and shudders had subsided before reaching down to undo his fly and free his erection into my mouth. I sucked willingly enough, as eager to please as I always was after attention to my bottom, for the hot glow of a good spanking had been replaced by the stinging fire of the cane. It felt right, too, to have the man who'd punished me in my mouth, and good to know that I excited him so much that he'd got hard without so much as a touch to his cock.

As soon as he'd had his fill of my mouth, he got behind me, to impress his erection between the cheeks of my bottom as he'd done several times before, only this time when he took hold of it, he pressed the head right between my cheeks. I immediately shook my head and started begging.

'No, Aaron, please, not up my bottom!'

He hesitated.

'Seriously?'

'Seriously.'

'What a shame. You have such a pretty bottom, and surely you understand how tempting it is for a man to put his cock up your tight little hole?'

I gave a desperate shake of my head, now close to panic as he continued to rub his cock between my cheeks, pushing against my anus. Finally, Aaron gave a soft chuckle and moved his cock lower down, to slide himself in to the hilt and fill me with mingled ecstasy and relief. I'd been promised a fucking, and I got it. My bound wrists ached terribly, my muscles were getting stiff and my bottom felt as if it were on fire, but all of that only made the experience stronger still as he took me firmly by the hips and began to thrust himself in and out. I'd wanted to be tied, and I'd got it, and more, strung up with my hands lashed behind my back, stripped bare, caned and finally fucked, an experience I knew would bring me to a climax beyond anything I'd experienced before.

Only it didn't. Aaron had been struggling to hold back even before he entered me, and he'd barely got his rhythm up before he cried out my name and whipped his cock free. I felt the hot droplets of his come spatter across my burning bottom and I was immediately begging him to bring me off, which might have been less perfectly ecstatic than being fucked to orgasm, but was still good, and exquisitely shameful. To my horror, he refused.

'Uh, uh, I don't want you coming just yet.'

'What? Why not?'

'You'll see.'

'Aaron!'

'Make me come, please? Please, Aaron, I'm begging you!'

'Not yet.'

He gave my bottom a playful slap and began to tidy himself up. I'd begun to whimper, but realised how silly I sounded and shut up, sure he was teasing me and would soon give me what I needed. If so, it was going to be pretty humiliating, probably a hand slipped between my thighs to masturbate me to orgasm in a casual, even clinical fashion, but that went perfectly with being tied up and used for his amusement. I could imagine the fantasy becoming a firm favourite, and being made to wait would be an important part of the thrill; but when he was finally content with his look, he simply came over and tugged at the knot on my wrists. It had been fixed with a bow and came straight open, letting me off the hook as well as freeing my hands.

The relief as I straightened up and stretched my aching arms was immense, but tempered by disappointment. I wondered if he wanted me so helplessly excited

that I'd do it myself, down on the hard concrete of the
roof in front of him, and as my hands went back once
more to squeeze and stroke my welted bottom cheeks,
I knew I couldn't resist. He was winding the rope up as
I squatted down, but came over as he saw what I was
doing.

'Hey, stop that! You amaze me, Elise, so demure,
but underneath it all you are the dirtiest little bitch
I've ever met!'

'Sorry.'

'Don't be, it's how I like you. Now look me in the
eye.'

I'd been staring at my feet, lost in a welter of
embarrassment and excitement, shame and submission,
but I forced myself to look up into his grey-blue eyes,
now alight with amusement and cruelty. He reached
up, his palm open, and cuffed me across the face,
very gently, but for my mind it was a thousand times
stronger than any smack he'd ever applied to my
bottom. At that moment I was his completely, as if he
owned me, and my voice sounded faint and weak as I
spoke to him.

'Shall I just cover up, then?'

'Yes, but this isn't over, not just yet. Don't bother
with make up.'

I didn't answer him, glad he wasn't finished with me
but afraid for what he intended, if being tied, beaten
and taken from behind wasn't the climax. A few quick
adjustments of my clothing and I was decent, if not

exactly presentable, with my mascara streaked and my lipstick smudged, but as he came to inspect me, he gave a pleased nod.

'Perfect, just the look. Now come with me.'

He took my hand, leading me not to the top of the stairs but around the lift-housing to the service door. Only then did I realise that there was a security camera there, hidden in the shadows beside a ventilator and trained directly on the space in which we'd been playing.

'Oh, hell! Aaron, look.'

He merely smiled as he turned a key in the door lock.

'I told you, Security has been taken care of. Come on.'

'If you're sure?'

'Oh, I'm sure.'

I followed him in, to the top of a concrete staircase beside the lift machinery, then down to the lift itself. He talked as we descended, amused and proud of himself.

'You see, there was a faint chance that somebody would spot us on top of the building and complain, or a dozen other things might have gone wrong. There might have been a maintenance crew up on one of the taller towers, or a TV crew. Maybe a helicopter would have flown over, and I doubt I could have got you untied and covered up in time to stop them getting a good eyeful. People tend to be a bit precious about female dignity, which is why it's so much fun to break it down, preferably in public. That does mean they tend to feel obliged to complain, though, or investigate, so I needed to be very sure we had our backs covered. Of course, it's impossible to eliminate all the risks, but that's half the fun; and while I like risks, I also like to keep the odds firmly on my side. You see, if anything had gone wrong, whoever came to express their distaste for our little game would have to get past Security first, and would naturally assume that Security are on their side.'

'And you've bribed Security?'

'Exactly. Jack used to work for me, before your time, and he's very loyal. He gave me the keys you saw me use, and one to an empty apartment on the eighth floor . . .'

'. . . and turned the CCTV system off.'

'No.'

'No?'

'No. That was part of the deal.'

'He watched us?!'

'Yes, why not? Be generous, Elise; security guard on a London tower block has to be one of the dullest jobs in existence. A man needs a little entertainment.'

'Yes, but . . .'

'Besides, it'll be a lot quicker now that he's enjoyed a little voyeuristic thrill.'

'What will be a lot quicker?'

'The blow job you're going to give him.'

We'd reached the ground floor and the doors were sliding open to reveal a wide, tiled lobby, on the far side of which was a glass-fronted security booth. In the booth sat a man, tall, solid, with close-cropped black hair and a face most politely described as rugged. He was grinning. Aaron took me by the hand as he carried on.

'Come on, Elise, this is what you need, isn't it, an excuse to do dirty things?'

'With you!'

'And for me. Please, Elise, this is what I want, and I've told Jack you'll do it, because I trust you. Please?'

I opened my mouth to answer him but could find no words to express my feelings and so ended up standing there gaping like a goldfish for a long moment before turning angrily to the security booth. Jack had been watching us with a happy grin, and as I opened the door, I realised that he already had his cock and balls out, sticking up from the navy blue trousers of his uniform, a sight at once obscene and horribly appealing. He'd also pushed his swivel chair back from his desk to make space, with the clear implication that I should get down on my knees to him, underneath, sucking his cock while he kept an eye on his monitors. There was plenty to watch, too, with the central screen of a bank of three showing me strung up from the iron gantry, my hands lashed behind my back, gasping and kicking in my pain as Aaron caned me. He'd put it on a loop, so that the humiliating scene was played over and over again, from the moment my jeans and panties came down to when Aaron released me.

I hesitated in the doorway, gaping at Jack's erect cock and at the screen, but Aaron gave me a proprietorial little pat to the seat of my jeans and I started forward again. Jack looked up, his eyes full of crude, masculine lust as he took in my figure, but it was Aaron he spoke to.

'She's lovely. Have her get her tits out, yeah?'

'Elise, if you would.'

Aaron's voice was cool, commanding and slightly amused. I gave him what was intended to be a resentful glare and pulled up my top and bra, exposing my breasts to his gaze and to Jack's. Then, scarcely able to believe what I was doing, operating on automatic but with a tiny voice in the back of my head screaming that I must be mad, I got down on my knees, crawled under the desk, took the security guard's cock in my hand, and after one final moment of self-reproach, in my mouth. Aaron gave a pleased nod and stepped out from the booth, presumably to keep watch. Jack finally condescended to speak to me.

'That's right, nice and deep, and you can lick my balls too, I bet you'd like that, wouldn't you? If anybody comes, go right in under the desk, okay?'

I didn't bother to answer, my mouth full of erect cock, while I'd begun to tease his balls with my finger-nails, eager to make him come as quickly as possible.

It certainly wasn't going to be long, to judge by the state he was in, and as I sucked I was thinking of how he'd have been watching and no doubt getting himself erect and ready for my mouth while I was being put through my paces on the roof. I'd given in to Aaron completely, showing absolute trust by allowing him to tie me up, as well as surrendering myself in body and mind, and all the while he'd known we were being watched by another man, a man I'd never even met, a man whose bloated erection was now jammed well down my throat as I did my best to make him come in my mouth.

My sob of despair as my spare hand went back between my legs can't have been audible, and Jack certainly didn't notice, but that made no difference to the depth of emotion it expressed. I should have felt used, and reacted in fury at what had been done to me, but instead I'd not only done as I was told but I was going to make myself come. Yet I just couldn't stop myself, tugging the button of my jeans wide and pushing my hand in down my panties to get at my sex, every bit the eager, wanton little slut Jack obviously imagined me. He saw, too, and gave a low, gurgling laugh, but that didn't stop me. I was rubbing hard, fiddling with myself in the dirtiest way imaginable as I began to play with his cock and balls in a deliberate effort to make my agonised feelings stronger still. He'd wanted his balls licked and I did it, sucking them into my mouth and rubbing my face against them as I jerked at his towering erection. I smacked his cock against my cheeks and mouth, used my tongue to trace a slow line from base to tip, kissed the straining, bulbous head and finally forced myself to take him so deep that I began to gag. With that he came, and so did I, in blended agony and ecstasy as I revelled in my own filthy behaviour while swallowing down every last drop of what Jack had to give me.

I came up and off his cock so quickly I banged my head on the underside of the desk, leaving me dizzy for an instant and unable to resist or complain as Jack reached down to take me by the hair and ease himself back into my mouth. He obviously hadn't completely finished and I let him, allowing my body to be used as I struggled with sudden guilt and self-recrimination; but there was no denying that Aaron had given me an extraordinarily strong experience, far beyond anything I'd have achieved if he'd told me in advance what was going to happen, and one that would make a very private but very happy memory for the rest of my life.

For the moment, though, I needed a reassuring cuddle from Aaron, and to be told that he loved me. He'd come back, and as I struggled up from under the desk, blushing and unable even to look at Jack, I went straight into Aaron's arms. He held on, stroking my back and hair, only to pull me gently away as he spoke.

'Now you can come, if you like? Do it while you hold me and Jack can watch.'

I shook my head.

'No, thank you. I already have.'

If Aaron had been generous and attentive to me before the incident on the tower block roof, afterwards it was as if he couldn't do enough. It was as though I'd passed a test, assuring him of my devotion, and I had certainly turned him on. As he explained in bed that evening, most of what we'd done up until then had been for my benefit, especially the spanking, but by allowing myself to be completely controlled by him, I'd fulfilled one of his deepest needs, and in particular by accepting his right to give me to another man.

It had taken a lot for me to go that far, and I still wasn't at all sure how I felt about it, but I was very happy with his response. Everything now seemed perfect, and I spent the last two days of my visit in a blissful haze. His attitude made it far easier to come to terms with my behaviour in bed, although there were still occasional introspective moments when I'd look back and feel shocked or embarrassed. That didn't stop me, and while there was nothing as wild or extreme as our rooftop adventure, we did have a lot of fun.

By the morning of my departure, I was ready to tell him that I was in love with him, a prospect that made me more nervous than any strange sexual escapade. I hoped he would say it first, especially as he'd told Vicky he was in love with me months before. Without that admission, I would never have accepted him the way

I had, but he was remarkably reticent about admitting to his true feelings and it looked as if I was going to have to go first.

I'd told myself I'd do it when we woke up together, but the moment just wasn't right. He had a raging erection and was in a thoroughly dirty mood, urging me to climb into a sixty-nine and suck him off while he spanked and licked me. I complied, and by the time we'd finished and tidied ourselves up, the breakfast we'd ordered had arrived, brought up not by a maid but by Rebecca Laindon, whose knowing, superior smirk as she put the tray down on the bed served to revive all my old concerns about her. Not that Aaron paid more than passing attention to her, simply thanking her for the breakfast and asking her to have an itemised bill ready by the time we came down.

Then came the bustle of leaving the hotel and making our way across the city, driven by a cabbie with an inexhaustible flow of trivial conversation. By the time we reached the airport, there was a huge lump in my throat and I was close to tears, but our time waiting in the departure lounge finally gave me a chance to talk to Aaron without distractions. He'd been brisk and efficient all morning, with no real display of emotion, but that was so like him anyway, and as I cuddled up to his chest I was sure I was going to get the reassurance I needed.

'That was a wonderful week, Aaron, thank you.'

'My pleasure.'

'I never imagined I could . . . that I could give myself to a man so completely, but you . . . I love you, Aaron.'

The pressure of his arms increased, holding me tight against his chest, but he didn't speak and it was left to me to carry on.

'You do feel the same, don't you?'

'Of course I do. How could it be otherwise? You're perfect.'

'Thank you, and we are together, aren't we, as a couple, I mean?'

'We could be.'

10

It was not what I'd been expecting to hear. At the time, I'd said nothing, but on the flight back I couldn't help but brood over it, and with ever-increasing resentment. I'd given my all to him, allowing him to indulge himself as he pleased, always on the assumption that we were in a secure relationship. It seemed an odd thing to say, as well, after he'd been so indulgent, which set me off on a series of increasingly negative trains of thought.

At first, the only explanation I could think of was that he wanted to keep me on my toes, perhaps worried that I'd start taking him for granted and not make so much effort to please him. That made a certain amount of sense, save for the way we worked in bed, which was for me to give in to him utterly. He decided what happened, and I'd always done as I was told, which seemed to suggest that he simply found me fun in bed and wanted to get as much use out of me as possible before he moved on to the next sucker. Yet if that had been the case, he could easily have lied to me, making a false declaration of love to keep me hanging on as long as was necessary. Or perhaps he was simply playing an elaborate game and enjoyed the thrill of toying with my feelings and not knowing what the outcome would be. After all, he'd said he liked risks, and in letting the security guard watch us, he'd taken a very big one indeed: the risk that I'd never speak to him again, even more so after making me suck Jack's cock. He'd also said he liked to keep his risks to a minimum, and the implication of that was clear: that he wasn't particularly bothered if he lost me.

Only as I was stepping off the plane in Bergerac Airport did another possibility occur to me: that underneath his cool exterior and easy confidence, he might be afraid of rejection. It was at least a possibility, and one that I did my best to convince myself was true as I made my way through checkout and up from the valley in a taxi with a driver no less loquacious than the one in London. It had felt strange returning to London, and it felt no less strange to be back at what was now my home. For one thing, the weather was hot and sultry, while there was still work going on in some of the vineyards. The day I'd left, Luc had been out in the yard checking the hoops and staves on old barrels, and he was doing the same when I was dropped off, as if he hadn't moved at all during my absence. He greeted me with a lazy salute, just as though I'd been gone for only a few minutes rather than a week, and I was left to haul my bag into the kitchen. Madame Belair was at the big table, rolling out pastry, and instead of her usual perfunctory nod, she gave me a hint of a smile, albeit a rather sinister one. I was keen to talk to somebody, but definitely not her.

'Good afternoon, Madame. Is Liselotte around?'

'No, nor likely to be.'

'Is she ill?'

'Not ill – at her mother's in Cahors. She and Jean argued, the little trollop.'

'Why? What happened?'

Her face set in an expression of obstinate disapproval, she went back to rolling her pastry. For a moment, I didn't think she'd answer me, but she finally spoke up.

'She was with that Englishman, John Lambert, down in the hedges.'

To judge from the tone of her voice, it was very obvious the two of them hadn't been doing a crossword puzzle together. I knew Liselotte was quite partial to older men, but it was still hard to take in.

'Liselotte, with John Lambert? Really?!'

'That is what I said. I caught them, her with her backside all rosy, on her knees, the little trollop.'

She didn't need to fill in the details. I remembered what Liselotte had said about being spanked by older men, and John Lambert was an obvious pervert, just the sort to want to smack her bottom for her, and to demand his cock be sucked in return. It also occurred to me that Madame Belair spent altogether too much time snooping around among the hedges, and that Jean was a hypocrite for objecting to Liselotte enjoying herself with other men.

'And he broke up with her?'

'They argued. She went off to Cahors in a fury. She'll not be back, not that one.'

'But her job? She works for me, here, and she's invaluable!'

Madame Belair merely shrugged and I made my way upstairs, feeling angry and upset but not really sure who deserved my indignation. Liselotte was playful, a free spirit and perhaps the most uninhibited woman I'd ever met, and yet I couldn't help but feel disappointed in her for having sex with John Lambert, especially kinky sex. It was as if she had let me down by not sharing my distaste for him, even though the sensible part of me knew my response was both irrational and unfair.

Jean's behaviour seemed unreasonable, considering he'd had me, but then that had been with Liselotte's approval and she had obviously gone with Lambert without asking. Presumably, that was what had annoyed him, perhaps along with her choice of partner, but it still seemed very harsh to break up, although it was Liselotte who'd actually left. Then there was John Lambert, whom I wanted to blame, but if Liselotte had been flirting with him, it was hard to see how he could have resisted. I knew what she was like, and for a dirty old man like him, the chance to play with a gorgeous and dirty-minded girl less than half his age must have been irresistible, especially if she'd asked to be spanked.

I was also cross with myself, even though that was irrational. Had I been there, I might have been able to patch up their argument, or at least stop Liselotte from leaving, and with that thought I realised what was really upsetting me. She was my only friend in France and I'd come to rely on her as somebody to talk to, and as an ally. Now I was left with Jean, who was simply too potently masculine to ever really be a friend, Luc, who was kindly enough but hardly the sort of person I could confide in, and Madame Belair.

As I sat down on the bed, I swore softly under my breath, then dug out my phone. The first thing to do was obviously to call Liselotte, offer my sympathy and assure her she still had a job if she wanted it. Unfortunately, her phone was off, which left me feeling frustrated as well as irritable. I considered going to talk to Jean, but I wasn't sure what to say, and I was also sure how he would react to me now that he was no longer with Liselotte. Sensitivity and tact were not his strong points, and he was sure to come on to me. I'd have to turn him down, for Liselotte's sake as well as my own, but those last three words Aaron had spoken to me at the airport kept coming back. Had they been three very different words then I'd have been absolutely faithful, in body and mind, but as it was I felt torn between a desire to prove my loyalty and a burning need to affirm my appeal as a woman. With Jean around and keen to pick up where we'd left off, it was going to be very difficult to stick to the right course.

In the end I went for a walk, out across the lawns and between the long rows of vines on the ridge, thinking all the while. La Fleur now felt like home, and yet I was missing London and Aaron, so that as I watched the sun move slowly down the western sky towards a line of cloud above the hills of Saussignac, I was at one and the same time lost in the beauty and peace of the moment and yet imagining what I'd have been doing at Angel's Hotel. It was about the time Aaron and I normally came back to our room, which meant kisses and cuddles at the very least, almost certainly leading to more: wet sex in the shower, maybe; or being taken roughly from behind on the bed, perhaps; even a deliciously embarrassing spanking, across his knee with my skirt suit turned up and my knickers round my thighs.

As I walked on, I was smiling at my own dirty thoughts and chiding myself for needing something so utterly inappropriate so badly. Yet there was no denying the truth. Up until my encounter with Liselotte, I'd never been spanked in my life, and now, just weeks later, I'd not only been dealt with by her and two men, but I'd got it that morning and less than twelve hours later, I wanted more. I wanted it from Aaron, too, and I tried to tell myself that he was what I really wanted, but that was only partially true. Yes, I wanted him, but I wanted spanking anyway, desperately.

I'd reached the very top of the hill, with high, trained vines all around me, leaving only my head and shoulders visible above the canopy of yellow-green leaves, even had there been anybody to see. My hand went back, patting the seat of my jeans, then again, harder, a purposeful smack that provoked a faint echo of the satisfaction I felt when Aaron did it, but also made me feel silly. It was ridiculous to be spanking myself, after all, and took away any last hope of pretending it was something I let people do to me rather than something I craved myself.

In an effort to distract myself, I tried Liselotte's phone again, but it was still off. I rang Aaron instead, keen to admit to my dirty thoughts as well as to tell him how much I was missing him, and perhaps even to resolve my feelings for what he'd said earlier. His phone was also off, which not only felt like a betrayal but had me imagining him in bed with another woman, perhaps even Rebecca Laindon.

I knew perfectly well that he was probably still in some important meeting, so I sent texts to both numbers and carried on walking, now feeling strangely isolated and more frustrated than ever. Looking back towards the house, I saw that Jean had come out and was doing something among the roses, so that if I turned back, I'd have no choice but to pass him, unless I went round in an enormous loop. I considered going to speak to him, perhaps trying to persuade him to make up with Liselotte, but I was simply too on edge.

Feeling rather foolish, I turned down towards the valley, telling myself the long walk would do me good.

I'd got about halfway to the river when my phone rang, causing my heart to leap and the butterflies in my stomach to go into wild flight as I saw that it was Aaron calling. He sounded exactly as ever, calm and cheerful, friendly and reassuring, if also rather hurried as he was apparently on his way from a meeting to the office, after which he had to catch a plane to Frankfurt. I found myself apologising for disturbing him, but he assured me there was nobody he'd rather speak to and that he wished he were back at Angel's with me that very moment.

As I ended the call, I was feeling blissfully happy, but with something nagging at the back of my mind. There had been a lot of background noise at his end, no surprise if he was walking along a busy street in the City, but there had been something odd about the quality of the sound, as if he'd been in a room full of people rather than outside. I tried to dismiss the thought as pure fancy, or as irrelevant in that he might still have been in the foyer of whatever building the meeting had been held in. Yet even at the end of a working day, few foyers would have been all that busy, and the noise had been different, more like a bar, or a restaurant, perhaps. That still didn't mean there was anything wrong, and as I continued on my way, I was telling myself I was being paranoid and pointlessly jealous, but my misgivings wouldn't go away.

I wanted to call back, but didn't want to seem

neurotic or clingy, while if he was up to no good, I was pretty sure whom it was with. After one last moment's hesitation, I called Angel's and asked for Rebecca Laindon, on the pretext of wanting to arrange another wine tasting in the new year. The young man who'd answered went off to try and find her, but quickly came back to say that she was unavailable. I asked if Aaron Curran had been in and was told he'd been there just moments before. With that I broke the connection, now imagining Aaron and Rebecca together at the hotel, in bed, laughing together as he told her how I behaved when I was turned on, or described how I'd willingly gone down on Jack the security guard.

Rebecca could have had a hundred and one reasons for not being at reception, and Aaron might well have been attending a meeting at Angel's, which had several conference rooms, but that didn't alter the fact that he'd said he was on his way to the office when he'd actually been at the hotel. It was suspicious at the very least, especially as they'd always been very friendly and Rebecca's behaviour towards me had been odd from the start, both of which were suggestive, if not of an affair, then at least of attraction.

I wondered how Aaron would have reacted if Rebecca had made a move on him the moment I left. He'd be alone and suddenly deprived of an assured supply of what I liked to think was exceptionally hot sex. She was attractive, too – petite and blonde and winsome – while something about her suggested that she'd be dirty in bed. He'd find her hard to resist, if not impossible, while it was difficult to imagine him considering being faithful as anything other than a weakness, or at best a restriction. There was no real doubt. He'd have taken her to bed.

By the time I'd got to that point in my train of thought, I'd reached the place where Liselotte, Jean and I had played together, which reminded me that I hadn't been entirely faithful myself. That had been before I went to London, admittedly, and Aaron and I hadn't really been together. Then again, to judge by what he'd said at the airport, we weren't really together now, for all that had happened between us. Possibly, he'd said it in order to salve his conscience, knowing full well he'd be taking Rebecca to bed within a few hours, or if not Rebecca, some other girl.

I sat down on the willow trunk where Jean had spanked Liselotte, brooding on the perversity of human nature. Looked at from an entirely rational perspective, it made no difference how many people Aaron took to bed while I was away, so long as he was there for me when I got back. In fact, it made perfect sense for him, and me, to take casual lovers when we were apart, especially in these days of contraception and protected sex. Yet it was a view hardly anybody I knew would have agreed with, while there was no denying my own, burning jealousy. To make matters worse, I couldn't be sure Aaron was cheating, which had my feelings swinging back and forth between hope and despair, devotion and a determination to make him feel as jealous as I did.

The situation between Jean and Liselotte was no better. They'd seemed so secure, with their easy acceptance of each other's needs and an open enjoyment of sex. I'd admired their self-assurance and had joined in without any feelings of jealousy, and apparently without provoking them, either. Liselotte certainly hadn't minded me going with Jean, as long as I accepted her place at his side. He'd been delighted at the thought of her going with me, but not with John Lambert, which struck me as typically male behaviour until I thought a bit deeper. The real issue was trust, which Liselotte had broken by not telling Jean what was going on.

Aaron was very keen on trust, but sexually rather than emotionally, asking me to put myself into situations where I was entirely reliant on his good will. He'd proven himself worthy of that trust, too, by not taking me up my bottom when he had me bound and helpless, and I knew that I could have backed out of my encounter with Jack if I'd really wanted to. The pay-off for my trust had been moments of intense pleasure I'd never have experienced without completely surrendering my control to him. After a lot more thought, I decided that I should give him the same trust emotionally, which did a lot for my peace of mind as I walked back up to the house.

With all the pickers now gone, and no formal occasion occurring, dinner was in the kitchen once

more, a simple affair of omelettes, salad and bread
washed down with wine drawn straight from the tank
and into a jug. Luc was his normal wry, talkative self,
his mood in tune with the fortunes of the vintage,
which were currently excellent. Jean was no less
voluble, and attentive to me in a friendly, admiring
way that made him hard to resent. I found it easy to
respond to their good humour, and even Madame
Belair was less censorious than usual, complimenting
me on my success in London. Liselotte's name was not
mentioned.

I excused myself early, not entirely sure of the
ability of my somewhat tender emotions to resist
the combination of Jean and the inevitable *eau de
vie*, while I was genuinely tired after what had been
a very long day. By the time I'd undressed, showered
and crawled naked into bed, I expected to be asleep in
moments, but it didn't happen. I was alone in bed for
the first time in a week, and sleep just wouldn't come,
partially because of the endless cycle of thoughts in
my head, but mainly because it just didn't feel right
without Aaron there to hold me.

After a while, I decided that being naked was the
problem, as Aaron liked me that way, so I put on my
usual combination of a baggy T-shirt and panties. That
only made it worse, as I was now too hot, even with the
covers pushed down, while having clothes on made me
feel I ought to take them off. I knew what I needed,
too: sex, preferably after a good, hard spanking, which

was something I'd had every single night we'd been together.

It wasn't long before I'd given in to my needs and decided to masturbate, a poor substitute for Aaron but all I had, short of sneaking out to Jean's cottage and climbing into bed with him. I was on my side with the covers twisted around me and rebuked myself for my dirty thoughts with a firm slap to my bottom, imagining that I'd confessed my sins to Aaron and asked to be spanked. It felt good, if slightly silly, and I gave myself another couple of smacks across the seat of my panties, then pushed them down to lay my bottom bare.

Even as I began to spank myself in earnest, there was a faint, regretful voice in the back of my head telling me I was well and truly addicted, but there was no denying the effect of the growing warmth of my rear cheeks and between my thighs, nor the delicious sense of vulnerability that came with having my knickers pushed down at the back. I imagined how Aaron would have treated me had he come into the room to find me misbehaving, walking quickly and silently to the bed to take me gently around the waist in a grip I had no hope of breaking, and telling me off for being dirty with myself as he spanked my bare bottom.

It was a good fantasy, but not quite his style. Aaron was always very sexual, enjoying me physically and enjoying my submission to his will, but never really getting into the mindset of the whole punishment thing. I'd been fine with that, but now I wanted to

feel that I was being punished, just to make the shame
and the pain more intense. My thoughts took a new
channel, of what might have happened had I refused
to suck Jack's cock. Aaron would have looked at me, his
eyes full of disappointment, then he'd have asked me
if I felt I needed a spanking. I'd have admitted I did,
expecting to get it back at the hotel room, across his
knee as he sat on the side of the bed in his usual style,
but he'd have told me it needed to be done in front of
the security guard.

That worked, and my bottom had begun to take on
the delightful warm glow I'd come to enjoy so much,
but it wasn't really hard enough. I bounced over on the
bed, first to turn on the light, then to burrow into my
bag for my hairbrush, the same one he'd used on me at
the hotel. With the light still on to make my feelings
of exposure stronger still, I got into the position Aaron
liked the best, face down and bottom up, not a single
intimate detail hidden from his eyes, nor his cock, and
my cheeks fully available to spank. A couple of smacks
with the hairbrush confirmed that it hurt every bit as
much as I remembered, and I let my mind drift back
to my fantasy.

I'd already been caned, and Jack had seen everything, but that would do little or nothing to soothe
my feelings as I'd be taken across Aaron's knee and
my jeans and panties eased slowly down to show off
my bare bottom. The security guard would have a
fine view, of the full moon of my bottom and the six

dark welts where Aaron had caned me, and between, every little fold of my sex and the tiny knot of my bottom hole bare for his inspection. He'd still have his cock out, and he'd start to play with it as Aaron retrieved my hairbrush, masturbating not just over my naked body but also for my embarrassment and my shame. I'd try to maintain a little dignity by keeping still and taking my punishment like a lady, but I'd fail miserably. The pain of the hairbrush would be more than I could stand and I'd soon be kicking in my panties and half-lowered jeans, wriggling in Aaron's powerful grip and squealing like a stuck pig.

I would have been, too, if I hadn't been biting down hard on the pillow beneath my face. The hairbrush stung crazily, but I was past the point at which I could have stopped, smacking as hard as I could and not too fussy about accuracy, with the smacks peppering my thighs as well as my bottom. It was noisy, too, and I was glad I was alone in the main house; but I sometimes scream when I come, and that might have drawn unwelcome attention, a thought that distracted me briefly from one fantasy to another. I knew what would happen if Jean caught me, and I knew I wouldn't try to stop him. A few more smacks and up his cock would go, deep inside me for a good, hard fucking in the same rude position I was already in, a taste he shared with Aaron. If it was Luc, he'd no doubt want a go too, and I was so far gone I wasn't sure that I wouldn't let him, as long as he used the hairbrush on me while we fucked. Madame Belair would just beat me, but that was a step too far and I forced my mind back to the original fantasy.

Aaron would spank me hard, a genuine punishment for disobedience, applying the hairbrush over and over again to my poor, beaten rear cheeks until he'd reduced me to a sweaty, dishevelled mess. I'd be in tears before he stopped, but I'd also be turned on, so turned on my resistance would be completely gone, my inhibitions spanked out of me. When he finally let go, I'd come into his arms, shaking as he cuddled me, my mouth wide for his cock, my burning bottom stuck out behind me on full show to Jack. I'd suck Aaron off, then and there, kneeling at his feet as I pleasured him, and when he was done and I'd swallowed every last drop of what he had to give me, I'd crawl across the floor and take Jack in my mouth in turn.

It was too much. I dropped the hairbrush and twisted around, spreading my thighs, tight in my knickers, and jerking my top high as I remembered how Jack had wanted my breasts bare while I sucked him. One hand went between my thighs and the other to one aching nipple, and I began to masturbate, rubbing urgently at my clitoris as I imagined the state I'd be in, crawling across the floor with my well-spanked bottom bare behind me as I came to him. He'd order me to pull up my top and bra and I'd obey, showing off my breasts for his pleasure before I got down on the floor at his feet to take his great, strong cock in my mouth and suck.

My back arched as I started to come. My teeth clamped to my bottom lip as I fought to stop myself screaming. My fingers dug into my flesh and my thighs came wider still, setting my entire body into near unbearable tension as I went into orgasm, but with my mind switching over and over between two things: the heat of my well-spanked bottom and the memory of how it had felt to have Jack's erection in my mouth.

Some orgasms are better than others. Sometimes, it's lots of little peaks, sometimes, one huge one. Occasionally, it's several huge peaks, and that's usually when I'm on my own and there's nothing to distract me from pleasuring myself. This one was among the best, long and hard and tight, but even before I'd finished and slumped back in exhaustion onto the bed, my guilt had caught up with me. I'd meant to come over my handsome young boyfriend, a man any woman would be proud to be with, but somehow, in the darkest, most frenzied moments of my fantasy, I'd switched my thoughts from Mr Wonderful to Mr Inappropriate, a heavyset, dirty-minded security guard whose cock I'd been made to suck as a bribe for his silence.

One thing was clear, regardless of issues of love or trust or any of the other things that are so important in relationships: I might be faithful to Aaron in body, but in my mind I was a dirty little cheat and either didn't deserve him or was no better than he was.

11

I felt a lot better for a good night's sleep. Aaron's behaviour was still worrying me, but I was able to focus on work. Luc was taken aback by the volume of orders I'd generated, and while he fussed about the extra work and plainly didn't enjoy letting rare and ancient bottles go from the cellar, he was also impressed. I volunteered to do the packing and despatching myself, which pleased him but drew a haughty sniff from his wife, followed by a half-pleading, half-cajoling remark.

'You are the owner of the château, Mademoiselle Sherborne. Leave these matters to us.'

I'd been doing my best to accommodate her strange attitudes, but this simply made no sense, especially as she already worked hard to keep the place in order and was in effect offering to take on Liselotte's share as well.

'I don't mind doing my share, Madame Belair, and besides, I brought the new London clients in and I know their details, and the way British addresses and so on work.'

'What of the paperwork – the customs documents, the TVA forms? They are in French.'

'Liselotte showed me how to do them. And speaking of Liselotte, shouldn't we do our best to persuade her to come back?'

'Let the little trollop go.'

She muttered the word '*salope*', and with an inflection that suggested she meant it in the worst possible way, implying that Liselotte was little better than a prostitute, but I bit back my instinctive annoyance and carried on.

'At the very least, I should go and talk to her. Do you have her mother's address?'

'How would I know that? She is gone and that is that.'

She was surprisingly vehement, although she always rose to Jean's defence as if he were a five-year-old having trouble in the school playground.

'I realise you feel offended, Madame Belair, but Liselotte was very much part of the team here and will be extremely difficult to replace. Besides, we shouldn't allow personal considerations to get in the way of business.'

'I am not having the little trollop back in this house.'

I was going to reply that it was my house, but thought better of it and simply walked away, leaving Madame Belair to believe that I'd backed down. Clearly, she didn't want me to contact Liselotte, which made me all the more determined to do so. I didn't believe the story about not knowing Liselotte's mother's address, either, especially as she'd mentioned that it was in Cahors.

Liselotte's phone was still off and she hadn't answered my text, but I was in no mood to wait, nor to be patient. As soon as Madame Belair was out of the way, I began to go through the records and quickly found an address in Pradines, just outside Cahors. Pradines was only a couple of hours' drive away, and I could see no reason to wait, so went to fetch the keys to the van, reaching it just as Jean came into the yard. It was the first time I'd been alone with him since I got back, and there was no mistaking the quality of his grin as he addressed me.

'Hello, Elise, are you busy? Why not walk a little way with me?'

My temper was up and I could see no reason not to tell the truth.

'Yes, I am busy. I'm going to see Liselotte.'

He was plainly surprised, even defensive.

'Liselotte? Why trouble with her? She is gone, out of our way.'

'How do you mean, "out of our way"?'

He stepped closer, his eyes looking deep into mine as his hands closed gently on my shoulders.

'Elise, let's not be foolish. I want you, just as you want me. Never mind Liselotte. She can have her old man, and we, Elise, we can have each other.'

There was real passion in his voice, and despite the

circumstances I found myself wanting to melt into his embrace but quickly pulled myself together.

'Jean! How can you say that? Liselotte's my friend, even if she did cheat on you, and besides, I'm with Aaron, you know that!'

'Forget Aaron. He is in London, and however much you try, you can never really love from afar.'

'Yes you can. Lots of people . . .'

'Not you. You have too much love, too much need, as I do. I love you, Elise.'

His face was just inches away, his eyes burning into mine as if seeking a pathway to my soul, his mouth slightly open, and before I knew what I was doing, I had accepted his kiss. It was a purely animal reaction, my mouth coming wide in response to his overwhelming masculinity and passion, while in my head I was wondering what the hell I was doing. He'd pulled me close, too, one powerful arm around my back and the other at my waist but quickly slipping down to allow a huge hand to cup one cheek of my bottom.

I really thought he was going to have me then and there, down on the dusty ground in the middle of the yard, without thought for who might come by, but he finally broke away, only to scoop me up in his arms. He was grinning as he started towards the house, and it was quite obvious what he was planning – a trip to my bedroom for sex – but for all my helpless physical reaction, I simply wasn't ready.

'No, Jean, please! Look, I'm with Aaron, and I need

to think . . . at very least I need to think. Put me down, you great oaf!'

He did, reluctantly.

'This is not the time to think, Elise. This is the time to give in to what your body is saying to you.'

'That's all very well, and I do like you, Jean, you know that, but it's not that simple. Aaron . . .'

'Aaron has many women in London. You told me that.'

'Yes, but that was before. Now we're together, sort of . . . Oh, I don't know! Look, it's really very sweet of you, and I am flattered, and I do like you, but . . . but I do need to think. Let's talk this evening, okay?'

He gave a smile and a shrug, stepping back, and I was able to straighten up and smooth my skirt down. Jean nodded.

'This evening, then, and will you go to Liselotte?'

'Yes. I have to, and I would even if it were just a matter of business.'

'Mind that what she says might not be true.'

He sounded genuinely concerned, and I nodded in response, fully aware that anything either half of a couple says shortly after a break-up should be taken with a pinch of salt. That applied to Jean, too, and to Madame Belair, but at the very least I wanted to hear Liselotte's side of the story.

I drove out from the yard faster than was strictly necessary, keen to get away, but my relief at avoiding Jean's advances was tempered by disappointment.

Leaving aside his declaration of love, which I wasn't at all sure I should believe, he was obviously strongly attracted to me, and there was no denying that I returned his feelings. Yet the sheer passion of his advances had come as a shock, and it would have been very easy to just give in. I'd have felt terribly guilty in respect to Aaron, and also Liselotte, but there was no denying that it would have been a wonderful experience.

As I drove down through the vineyards towards the main road along the Dordogne, I was imagining how it would have been, more or less at that very moment. Jean would have taken me indoors and, hopefully, upstairs. Knowing him, he wouldn't have bothered too much about preliminaries but simply given me a quick warm-up, either over his knee for a spanking or with my skirt pushed up and my knickers held aside so that he could lick me. Given the way he made me feel, it wouldn't really have been necessary, as I was ready anyway, even though nothing had happened, but it would have been nice.

Once he'd got me suitably eager, his cock would probably have gone in my mouth, if only because it's very rare for a man to pass up the chance to have a woman suck him. That wouldn't have been the end of it, though. He'd have had me, probably on my knees, a position a lot of men seem to like me in, but being Jean he'd almost certainly have played his little party trick, pulling out to rub me to orgasm with the head of his cock before finishing off inside me or over my bottom.

It was a painfully arousing thought, and by the time I'd turned on to the D660, I was wishing I'd brought a spare pair of panties. After an alarming moment with a truck trying to overtake me, I forced myself to concentrate on the road, which wound up into the hills between small fields and woodland full of overgrown limestone crags. It was the first time I'd been upriver of Bergerac since childhood, and I'd forgotten how wild and beautiful the countryside was, while it was a beautiful autumn day with the leaves already turning and the air extraordinarily fresh, all of which brought on a new mood of optimism.

Whatever my problems, I was in an enviable position: the owner of a magnificent property and a business that now looked as if it could make a worthwhile profit, with two extremely attractive and highly sexed men keen on me, and really no major worries beyond trying to balance everything so that I could feel I'd done the right thing and been treated well in turn.

My good mood lasted as I drove south and east, eventually reaching the river Lot and the village where Liselotte's mother lived. I'd already looked up the address on my laptop and knew it was up a lane at the back of the village, but Google Street View had stopped halfway up the hill and I wasn't expecting the track to be so rough, nor the cottage at the far end to be so small and tumbledown. It was in a typically old-fashioned French style, with crumbling yellow stone and deep windows closed off by once brightly painted shutters, and very pretty, with two huge oaks overhanging the roof and an ancient apple tree heavy with gold and red fruit to one side – all very idyllic, but with no signs of life at all. There was no car there, and no tracks to suggest that there might have been.

I was wondering if I hadn't somehow got the wrong address, when the front door opened and Liselotte herself stepped out. She saw me immediately, looking surprised and maybe a little wary, even cross, but she accepted a hug and a kiss to each cheek then stood back.

'Why did you come here?'

'To see you, of course. I heard what happened between you and Jean.'

'Oh, but . . . I thought that's what you wanted?'

'No, not at all. Why would I want that?'

'So that you could be with Jean, of course.'

'I don't want to be with Jean. I like him, yes, but I wouldn't do that to you, Liselotte.'

'He wants to be with you.'

'But I thought you broke up because Madame Belair caught you messing around with John Lambert?'

'That's the excuse, yes, but why should Jean care? We always understood each other, and anyway, it was only spanking. That wasn't even what the argument was about, not completely. Jean said he wanted to be

with you, and you would want to be with him, but that
you'd still play with me, but . . .'

Her voice had grown more hoarse as she spoke and
suddenly failed completely as she burst into tears. I put
my arms around her and carried on, doing my best to
soothe her.

'That's not true, Liselotte. Okay, Jean came on
to me this morning, very strong, but that was the
first time he's even hinted that there might be
anything between us beyond play. I turned him down
anyway, because I'm with Aaron now, and there is
absolutely no way I would have done that to you.
Anyway, I need you at La Fleur, to help me with
work and because you're the only friend I have over
here in France.'

'To help you? But Madame Belair said you think
I'm no good, that I'm not trained, which is true, and
that I'm no good at sales, either.'

'That's rubbish. I never said anything of the sort!
Madame Belair was lying, just to get rid of you, and
she told Jean you went further with John Lambert.'

'How do you mean?'

'You said it was just spanking, but she told him you
. . . you sucked his cock.'

Liselotte shrugged as I let her go, her face now
flushed with tears and also embarrassment.

'I did. It only seemed fair, because he'd got very
excited, and he did ask nicely, and . . . well, you know
how you feel when you've been spanked.'

I nodded my understanding, although I couldn't see myself getting into such a state that I'd go down on John Lambert. Nor could I imagine letting him spank me in the first place, for that matter, but it wasn't the time to start questioning Liselotte's taste in men. She'd been wiping her tears on the edge of her dress and managed a smile as she looked up once more.

'Come inside. I need to tidy myself up, and you probably need a drink. Are you going to stay overnight?'

'I might, if your mother doesn't mind?'

'My mother stays down in the village with her boyfriend.'

'Oh, right, I thought the house looked a bit deserted.'

We'd come inside, into a blue-painted hall with bare boards but full of sunlight from the open windows at the back of the cottage. It was tiny, just two up and two down, with a kitchen area at the rear. Liselotte had been putting her lunch together and there was a basket of freshly cut bread, a plate of cured meats, a dish of butter and a bottle of deep-purple wine on the table, set out as if it were a still life for an art class. She hadn't bothered with plates or cutlery, and reached up to open a cupboard as I sat down.

'Don't worry about me. I'll eat with my fingers.'

'I can't ask you to do that!'

I let her put the plates and knives out, wondering at the way both she and Madame Belair behaved towards me, as if I needed special treatment, although with both of them their respect was tempered by almost opposite attitudes, if very different to one another.

'I'm not made of china, you know, Liselotte.'

'You are Adèle de Regnier's niece.'

'Is that so important? I know she used to give herself airs, but my mum was her little sister and she was never like that.'

'Then your mother was a very modest woman. They were Montaubin, after all.'

'That was my mum's maiden name, yes, and I know they were an old family, but so what?'

'They are old barons, *noblesse d'épée*, which means they go right back to the Middle Ages.'

'Oh, I suppose that explains Aunt Adèle's attitude, but that sort of thing doesn't matter to me. If I have any worth, I want it to be on my own terms, not because of who my ancestors were.'

'I know, and Madame Belair hates that, but she thinks you are just being young and wayward.'

'And a slut?'

'Me too.'

She'd poured out glasses of the purple wine as we spoke, and we chinked them together and each took a swallow, toasting each other in defiance of Madame Belair's prissy attitudes. The wine was rich and heady, stronger than our own red and not the sort of thing I'd usually have drunk at lunchtime, but as Liselotte had invited me to stay, I refilled my own glass, then hers, as I carried on.

'Anyway, never mind that old harridan. I need you back at La Fleur.'

'That's nice of you, Elise, but I'm not sure I can cope with seeing Jean all the time, especially if you and he get together.'

'We're not going to get together. I'm with Aaron.'

'Everybody seems to think you are, and really, I don't mind, as long as it's not right in my face. There's Madame, too. She'll make my life unbearable. Sorry.'

'What if I were to sack the Belairs?'

'You'd do that, just to get me back?'

I considered for a moment and realised that it didn't really make sense from a business point of view.

'Maybe, if I could keep Luc on. Madame is more of a nuisance than anything, even though she knows the place like the back of her hand, and Jean is replaceable, but Luc's skills are what lifts our wine above the ordinary.'

'And he knows it, and that we could not afford the few others who have his skill and experience. He'd never agree to stay on alone, and besides, you'd get a terrible reputation in the district.'

'I know, and I can do without that, but still . . .'

'It's not worth it, Elise, not just for me, but you're always welcome to come and visit.'

'But what are you going to do?'

'I can easily find work with a local domaine, or one of the big wineries, maybe, especially if you give me a good reference.'

'Of course. You can write it yourself, if you want to?'

'Thank you.'

We began to eat and drink, talking of this and that as we gradually resumed our old familiarity. She was a little tearful, and clearly very upset over Jean, but not exactly heartbroken, happily describing the rival virtues of the young men in the village, and some of those who weren't so young, including her own mother's boyfriend.

'He's ten years younger than her, and quite a man by all accounts, and a terrible flirt, but that's one person I wouldn't touch.'

'I should think not!'

'Not at the moment, anyway. Maybe I can save him until later, if Mother gets bored with him.'

'Liselotte!'

'He'd be good, plenty of experience.'

'You like that, I know, so come on, tell me, why did you let John Lambert spank you? I know you like older men, and I'm sure he's highly experienced, but . . .'

I trailed off, not wanting to upset her by giving my candid opinion of John Lambert, but she evidently didn't care, her voice full of enthusiasm as she answered me.

'He's so good at it! I thought he might be because he reminds me of Paul, my old English boyfriend, and I know that look in a man's eye, and how they look at our bottoms, and you know just what they're thinking.'

'So what does he do that's so special? I mean, he can't be anything like as strong as Jean.'

'Oh, it's not that. He spanks hard, yes, but Jean's so rough and not at all imaginative.'

'He put grapes down my panties. I'd call that quite imaginative!'

'Oh, that. I suggested that.'

'You little . . . !'

'Was it fun?'

'Yes, I suppose so, but pretty humiliating, too.'

'Which you love?'

'I suppose so, but I find it a bit hard to get my head around it. Women aren't supposed to like that sort of thing.'

'If you really want to be free, do what pleases you, not what other people say you should do.'

'I know you're right, and I do like it, but I need the right man, and the right situation.'

'Don't we all? So Aaron, does he like to spank you?'

'He loves to be in control, so yes, and to tie me up. He took me to the top of one of the skyscrapers in the City and tied my hands behind my back.'

'To fuck you?'

'He used a cane on me first. It hurt so much, but it was what I wanted. He spanks me with my hairbrush, too, and after he'd had me on the roof, he . . .'

I trailed off, blushing hotly but eager to tell her. She wanted to know as well, her eyes bright with excitement and mischief.

'What did he do, Elise?'

'He . . . he'd bribed the security guard so that we'd be safe. The bribe was me. Aaron made me suck the man's cock . . . he made me crawl to him, this man I'd never met before, a big guy, maybe a bit like your mum's boyfriend, and I had to go under his desk and suck his cock.'

'Elise, you dirty girl! Was it good?'

I nodded urgently, now keen to confess and thinking of how I'd come under my own fingers the night before, but before I could reveal anything more, Liselotte had taken over.

'John said he'd like to cane me. He said he'd make me touch my toes and stand like that while he lifted up my skirt and pulled down my knickers. I'd have to stay like that while I got him hard in my mouth. Then he'd spank me, and cane me, and fuck me.'

My belly had gone tight at the thought and I had to know more, even if it was John Lambert she'd been with.

'But what did he actually do, just spank you?'

'Yes, but he took ages, and he was like Paul, only worse . . . better. He started by making me bend over the bench, as if I was going to be caned, but just for spanking. Then I had to lie on my back with my legs bent. He held me by my panties, around my ankles, and he kept touching, playing with me until he made me come, and again while I was over his knee, with my knickers in my mouth so I wouldn't scream, or that's what he said.'

'He put your knickers in your mouth? He is such a pervert!'

'Yes, but all that before he'd even taken his cock out. You'd love it.'

I gave an urgent shake of my head, but I was imagining how she'd have felt, held tight across his knee, nude from the waist down, with her panties stuffed in her mouth and her smacked bottom stuck well up as he fiddled with her until she came, no doubt putting his fingers in, and not just up her vagina, either. The thought made me shudder, but Liselotte was enjoying herself, and my reaction, so she carried on.

'Isn't it nice when a man really pays attention to you? Most of them just want to have their fun, and if we happen to like it too, that's good, but John really concentrated on me.'

'It sounds as if he was just getting his perverted kicks! A lot of men like to make women come, and not just to give pleasure, but to be in control.'

'You're so cynical. Come on, admit it, you'd love to be handled that way.'

'Not by John Lambert!'

'By me?'

I'd guessed she was going to make an advance on me and I was willing, just as long as she took the lead. She did, not even bothering to wait for my response but rising and walking around the table to kiss me, our mouths opening together and tongues touching as she put a hand to the nape of my neck. I shut my eyes in bliss as we kissed, and her fingers were doing wonderful things to the nape of my neck, soothing me and rapidly making me receptive to more. Her free hand went to my chest, touching the outlines of my breasts through the thin cotton of my blouse then moving to undo one button, and a second.

She was quite the expert, tweaking my buttons wide until she could tug the sides of my blouse apart, then pulling up my bra to bare my breasts. I let her do as she pleased, stroking my skin, gently teasing my nipples to erection, and kissing all the while until I began to shiver in her arms. She paused briefly, to pull her dress up and off, baring her heavy, naked breasts, one of which she took in hand to offer me her nipple. I accepted, letting her suckle me as she went back to stroking my hair and neck, a sensation at once so soothing and so erotic I quickly tugged up my skirt and slipped a hand between my thighs. Liselotte giggled to see me so excited, then spoke up.

'Oh, no you don't, not yet. First, a good spanking.'

Her grip had tightened in my hair as she spoke. I was allowed to suck for a moment more, then hauled up from my seat and over the table. My boobs had gone into what remained of my lunch, and my face was right over the butter, but she didn't seem to care, holding me firmly in place as she retrieved a spatula from the draining board. Two quick tugs and my bottom had been laid bare without the slightest ceremony, skirt up and panties down to leave me showing behind and ready for punishment.

I got it hard, a dozen firm swats with the spatula applied to each bouncing cheek, turn and turn about, until I was wriggling in her grip and kicking in my panties. It stung terribly, but I'd been spanked often enough to know what would happened, the pain quickly fading to be replaced by a glorious warm glow and a sense of need that comes no other way. Liselotte knew too, having been on the receiving end many times, and she ignored my struggles and cries until I'd begun to push my bottom up for more, when she finally spoke again.

'You're like a cat on heat, Elise. Right . . .'

She put the spatula down but kept her grip in my hair as she took hold of my panties, levering them down the rest of the way and then off. I guessed what was coming to me and twisted my head around, grimacing as I saw her packing the little scrap of pale blue cotton into a ball with her fist.

'Not that, please, Liselotte? That's so dirty.'

'Hush. Open your mouth. They're going in.'

'Liselotte . . .'

'What did I say, Elise? I said your panties are going in your mouth. Now open wide!'

I obeyed, too well spanked to put up more than token resistance, my mouth coming slowly wide. She gave a pleased nod at her victory, but instead of pushing my knickers straight in, she dipped them in the wine jug, soaking up the deep-purple fluid as I looked on in disgust, then cramming the now-soggy ball of cotton well into my mouth. My face must have been quite a picture as I began to suck on my now sodden panties, and Liselotte was certainly enjoying the view, laughing with happy cruelty as she retrieved the spatula and set to work on my bottom once more. It was even harder now, and she had me kicking and writhing in her grip for another dozen or so strokes before the heat began to get to me once more.

As before, she stopped just when it was getting nice, this time to reach across my prone body, tighten her grip in my hair, then slowly and deliberately rub my face into the butter, ignoring my muffled protests as she smeared it in. I shut my eyes and didn't dare open them again because of the butter coating the lids, while the smell of it was thick in my nostrils, mingled with wine and the scent of my own helpless excitement. She'd taken the dish away, and I'd been expecting her to go back to spanking me, but instead of the hard wood of the spatula, it was her hand that found my bottom, soft and caressing but also greasy with butter. I gave a little wriggle of protest and got a slap for my pains, and then her fingers were between my cheeks, rubbing the warm, slippery mess over my bottom hole and inside.

She'd been wise to gag me, or I'd have told her to stop and missed out on the impossibly rude but utterly delicious sensation of having her finger

eased deep in up my bottom. I couldn't have done it
with a man, not ever, and not just because it was so
embarrassing but because I knew exactly what he'd
want to put up there after his finger. With Liselotte it
was different, shameful but exciting, and a wonderful
addition to the humiliation I could no longer pretend
I didn't enjoy.

Her hand was still tight in my hair, pulling my
head back as she fingered my bottom, with wine and
rapidly melting butter dripping down my face. A few
touches in the right place and I was going to come,
but she wasn't finished with me. She finally let go of
my hair, but I made no effort to escape, now gripping
the sides of the table with my bottom stuck well up as
she set to work with the spatula once more, spanking
hard. More butter was slapped between my cheeks,
her fingers went up me again, now in both holes, to
open me up and set me gasping and squirming.
A finger found my clitoris, flicking at the sensitive
little bud as she continued to spank me, as hard as she
could, the spatula smacking down across my naked,
buttery flesh again and again. My mouth came wide,
releasing my wine-sodden panties onto the table
below me, my muscles went tight and I was there,
screaming out my ecstasy and begging Liselotte to
spank me harder and push her fingers deeper in,
which she did, stopping only when I finally went limp,
to slide slowly from the table and land on the floor in
a slippery, bedraggled heap.

When I finally dared to open my eyes, it was to find Liselotte standing over me, just pulling her knickers free of one ankle to go completely nude. I knew what she wanted and nodded my acquiescence, but if she noticed she didn't bother to acknowledge me, simply turning to present me with her bare bottom, then squatting down to seat herself neatly on my face, her cheeks spread wide to my eager tongue.

12

It was the second time I'd woken up in bed with Liselotte, but this time there was no guilt, nor regret, save for the bruises she'd inflicted on my bottom. Instead, there were happy, slightly fuzzy memories of the night before: hours of rough, rude sex punctuated by cuddles, which had inevitably led to yet more sex. I'd come more times than I could possibly have counted, and given her the same sweet ecstasy just as many times, if not more. She'd spanked me in a dozen or more different positions, and with as many different implements, as well as suckling me, putting clothes pegs on my nipples, slapping my face and tying me spreadeagled to her bed while she sat on my face one more time.

I'd enjoyed every moment, but my entire body ached, and when I finally left in the early afternoon, I had to stop in a lay-by and do some stretching exercises before I could drive on. By the time I got back to La Fleur, it was all I could do to eat a light supper before making for my bed. Jean wasn't about, which was a relief, but from what I'd learnt in Cahors, two things were very clear: that he had broken off with Liselotte because he wanted to be with me, and that she didn't mind if he and I got together.

At least she said she didn't mind, but it was a moot point anyway as I still felt it would be wrong of me to give in to his advances. Admittedly, if Aaron wasn't prepared to commit to me, then it was perfectly reasonable for me to see myself as a free agent until he changed his mind – somehow sex with Liselotte didn't seem to count – but I still felt it would be right to hold back. As I drifted towards sleep, my last thoughts were that I could wait for Aaron just as long as I could go on satisfying my need with Liselotte, and that all would come right in the end.

I woke to a very different feeling and to very different weather. The rain was hammering on the window and the sky was so dark I had to check my phone to make sure it really was eight o'clock. I felt strangely lost, too – sad for my lack of company and badly in need of comfort, although I wasn't sure if I wanted it more from Aaron or from Liselotte. Telling myself it was probably just a hormonal thing, I sent cheerful good morning texts to both, then washed and dressed. By the time I was ready to go downstairs, Liselotte had replied, with a cheeky suggestion that I ought to visit John Lambert for a spanking, which she knew would ruffle my feathers. There was no response from Aaron, but I told myself he probably wasn't even awake and carried on.

Madame Belair always rose early and already had the breakfast set out: coffee and croissants and bread with a choice of homemade jams. I tucked in, doing my best to be pleasant to her despite her appalling behaviour but mainly talking to Luc, who was in a fuss over the weather and desperate to pick the grapes he'd left on the vine for a late harvest before they took in too much water or the rain turned to hail. It was obviously a case of all hands to the pumps, so I put on what wet-weather gear I had and trudged down to the bottom of the vineyards. The next two hours were spent in relentless, driving rain, cutting bunches and piling them into the hod on Jean's back.

By the time we'd finished, I was soaked to the bone and aching in every muscle and joint, while Madame Belair's remarks about me not being suited to hard work didn't help. Again I refrained from comment and retired upstairs once more. I usually showered, but the state I was in called for the gigantic cast-iron bathtub with lion feet, in which I could float with my feet and head barely touching the ends. It took ages to fill, but it was well worth it, and as I lay floating in the hot, scented water I could feel all my aches and pains fading gradually away, save only for the faint smarting sensation in my rear cheeks to remind me of having had my bottom smacked, and of the odd sense of longing I'd had since I got up.

I had the door safely locked, even though the Belairs were all busy downstairs or in the winery anyway, so it was the easiest thing in the world to let my hands stray first to my breasts and then lower, soaping my skin and teasing myself at the same time. My thoughts began to dwell on everything I'd done over the last few months, how much my life had changed and how many new experiences I'd enjoyed. I was completely at ease, lazy, relaxed, slightly sleepy, and as I teased myself I found my memories flicking easily between Aaron, Jean and Liselotte. As I'd realised before, I was no Little Miss Faithful, devoted to one man and one man alone, and I was no longer even sure if a man was my ideal. Certainly, Liselotte had been wonderfully attentive, as well as extremely rude, but she'd also been more sympathetic to me as a person than either Aaron or Jean, and perhaps more importantly, she liked to cuddle for a long, long time after sex.

Was I, I wondered, a bad person? I'd certainly broken a few taboos, but I could now see the rules I'd always allowed to govern my life as both trivial and old-fashioned. I'd never really accepted the idea that a woman could only ever really love one man, or that if I waited long enough I would find Mr Right. There was no Mr Right, and there were no heroes or villains, either, only individual men, each with his virtues and his faults, so that the most I could expect was somebody whose tastes suited my own and who had sufficient respect for me as a person for us to get along. Aaron might possibly be that man, but if I wanted his trust, I was going to have to tell him about Liselotte and hope that he didn't mind me paying the occasional visit to Cahors.

My train of thought moved on to what he might expect in return, which brought a sharp and unexpected pang of jealousy. I was pretty sure Aaron was purely heterosexual, for all that he'd thoroughly enjoyed the sight of me sucking Jack's cock, so he wasn't going to ask for visits to a boyfriend. He'd be sure to want something, though, which meant another woman, maybe Rebecca Laindon. The thought hurt, so much that I began to wonder if I was in love with him or just jealous, even if love and jealousy weren't one and the same emotion by different names. It certainly wasn't the same with Jean, as the thought of watching him with another woman was rather appealing, even if I wasn't able to join in.

The thought led to memories of watching Jean and Liselotte, and a touch of sadness that it was very unlikely ever to happen again. Not wanting to get into a melancholy mood, I began to rub a little harder with the soap and tried to work out which of my recent experiences had been the best. It was hard to choose, but there was no doubt at all which kink I'd enjoyed the most, and that was spanking, preferably held firmly in place across the knee but very definitely on my bare bottom.

I rolled over, lifting my hips to leave the full, pale moon of my cheeks sticking out from among the soap suds and reaching back to touch my tender flesh.

Liselotte had given me quite a few bruises, and I could just feel the faintly raised lines from the set of welts Aaron had inflicted with his cane. I'd already seen how I looked in the mirror and fell to wondering what other people would think if they caught a glimpse of my cheeks and realised I'd been punished. Outrage? Pity? Arousal?

Whatever their response, it would be extremely embarrassing for me, and while that would have been awful if it had really happened, it made a nice fantasy. I continued to stroke, letting my fingers sneak down between my cheeks to tease myself as I imagined somebody peeping in at Liselotte's kitchen window while she buttered my bottom, but that wasn't quite right. I didn't want to think of some dirty-minded stranger getting himself off over the sight of me being rude, but of somebody who would be outraged by my behaviour and who would take it upon themselves to teach me what having my bottom smacked was really about.

I twisted over onto my back once more, now eager to come and knowing exactly how I wanted to do it. Lifting my feet clear of the water, I turned on the huge brass mixer tap to send a cascade of steaming hot water gushing into the bath. A quick check to make sure it wasn't dangerously hot and I slid forward, allowing my thighs to come wide until the jet of water caught me directly between them. It felt wonderful and also left my hands free, allowing me to tease my breasts and between

my bottom cheeks as I let my spanking fantasy evolve
in my head. Aaron was no good. He liked it too much,
and besides, he hadn't even bothered to respond to my
text. It was hard to see Jean as a disciplinarian, either,
while Liselotte would be more suited to being dealt
with herself. That gave me the answer: a man I'd never
met and so could easily be made into the perfect fantasy
spanker, stern and strong, with rugged good looks and
hands like spades. Liselotte's mother's boyfriend.

Liselotte had assured me we were perfectly safe at
the cottage, but it was easy to imagine getting caught,
and from then on it would be pure routine. He'd
tell us off for being a pair of dirty little bitches then
inform us, quiet casually, that we were going to be
spanked. Our protests would be ignored as he played
on our guilt and secret arousal to make us accept our
punishments, then it would be over his knee with
my panties pulled down in front of Liselotte for the
spanking of a lifetime.

I'd got my position just right, my legs well spread
and my feet curled around the mixer tap to hold
myself into position, with the water gushing full onto
my open sex. A little more and I was going to come,
with one nipple pinched tight between my fingers
and the other hand squeezing at my bruised bottom
and tickling the little hole between my cheeks as I
imagined the appalling embarrassment of having a
complete stranger pull down my knickers in front of
my friend and spank me.

He'd be very thorough about it, dishing out a genuine punishment, both to myself and to Liselotte, but that didn't mean he wouldn't get turned on by having us squirming and bare across his knee. There would be plenty of touching while we were being spanked, our breasts felt and our vaginas penetrated, maybe our bottom holes too, both to shame us and because he was enjoying himself. Then, once he was done and we were both red-bottomed and contrite, he'd pull out his cock so that it stood proud from the fly of his rough work clothes over a pair of enormous balls, just the way Jean's had when he first made me suck him.

I couldn't help myself, with my muscles already tight in orgasm as the subject of my fantasy changed, and as I came I was thinking of how good it would feel to be kneeling at Jean's feet with his magnificent cock to suck on and my well-smacked bottom stuck out behind. My mouth came wide and I screamed out his name, followed by a babble of random, dirty words as I begged for what I wanted, all of which came to an abrupt halt at the sound of a sharp knock on the bathroom door. A voice followed, asking if I was all right – not Madame Belair's as I'd been expecting, but more embarrassing still, Jean's.

'Elise? Are okay? Do you want me in there?'

'No! I, er . . . go away!'

'Do you really mean that, Elise? I don't think you do.'

'Go away!'

'Okay, if you're sure, but I am here for you.'

He moved away from the door, his heavy footsteps fading down the passage, and I was left with my embarrassment and the ruins of what had been a truly beautiful orgasm. I needed more, and there was a moment of regret for having turned him away, followed by self-recrimination for being such a slut, and finally irritation, at him, at myself and at the world in general for expecting women to be the representation of sexual desire and then labelling us with nasty names if we acted in kind.

It was always the same, and as I hurriedly dried myself off, I was thinking back to college and the aftermath of the occasion when Lucy and I had stripped as a birthday treat for a male friend and finished off by giving him a helping hand with his cock. He'd loved every second of it, and promised to keep it to himself, but in the end he hadn't been able to resist the chance to boast. Suddenly, he was the big stud, while Lucy and I were a pair of sluts, but whatever was said about us, we'd suddenly become extremely popular with the other male students.

I was still brooding over the basic unfairness of life as I wrapped a fresh towel around myself and peered out into the passage. There was no sign of Jean, to my mingled relief and disappointment, and I padded quickly down the corridor to my room, where he was sitting on my bed, grinning. I stopped in the doorway, then caught the sound of Madame Belair's voice from downstairs and hurried inside as I addressed Jean.

'What are you doing?!'

'You called out for me. Here I am.'

'Yes, but . . .'

'You want me, Elise, just as I want you. Give in to your feelings, or if you want it another way, perhaps I should spank you for playing with yourself in the bath?'

'You . . . you bastard!'

He didn't answer, but moved forward a little on the bed to make a lap, a lap I was expected to lie across while he spanked me. Obviously, he'd heard more than just his name when I'd cried out in the bath, so there was no point denying what I'd been doing, or what I'd been thinking about. He put out one massive hand and gave his leg a meaningful pat.

'Come on, over you go.'

I shook my head, but it was only my stubborn pride holding me back, with thoughts of Aaron, and Liselotte, and outrage at Jean's sheer arrogance all racing through my head. He spoke again, sterner this time.

'Come on, Elise, over my lap. You need to be spanked, and you know it.'

My knees seemed to have turned to jelly, and I was going to do it, but the perfect excuse came to me.

'I . . . I wouldn't mind, but your mother's downstairs. She'd hear!'

'True enough. Come with me, then.'

He got up, took hold of my hand, and I let him lead me from the room, wanting it, knowing it was pointless to pretend I didn't, and yet still desperately searching for an excuse to get out of what I had coming.

'But Aaron . . .'

'Aaron is in London, and don't you think he'll have lovers there?'

He'd hit the weak point in my argument, and I remembered that I'd agreed to talk properly to Jean the other evening once I'd visited Liselotte. Of course, I'd become distracted by the delicious buttery escapade with my friend, and had forgotten all about my promise to Jean, but now I had other worries, as he was leading me down the corridor towards the servants' staircase. That seemed to imply he was planning to deal with me in the kitchen, which was unthinkable.

'Jean, no! What about your mother?'

'She is making lunch.'

'Yes, in the kitchen. You can't spank me in front of her!'

He just laughed.

'Don't be silly, Elise. I am taking you upstairs.'

We'd reached the end of the corridor, and sure enough, he turned up the narrow staircase to the second floor, which was largely closed up or used for storage. I could remember it from childhood – a secret and forbidden world, full of ancient treasures and strictly out of bounds by edict from Aunt Adèle – but I'd only explored it briefly since taking over at La Fleur. Jean seemed to know where he was going, though, closing the door that shut off the servants' area and leading me into a square, dusty room, dimly lit due to the rainswept vineyards outside. It was full of furniture, most of it under dust covers, while everything visible was old and sturdy and very fine, including a beautiful dappled rocking horse at least twice the size of the one I'd had as a child. He grinned and nodded.

'That's a thought. Climb up on the rocking horse. I'm going to beat you while you ride it.'

He'd let go of my hand, and as he spoke he pulled the belt from his trousers with a soft, leathery noise that made my stomach go tight and brought a lump to my throat. I'd been expecting a spanking, bare over his knee and delivered by hand, the way I liked it best, but this was something entirely different.

'I um . . . I'm actually a bit tender, Jean . . . you know, tender behind.'

'Show me.'

I turned around, looking back at him over my shoulder as I tugged my towel up to bare my bottom. He registered surprise.

'Who's been at you?'

The blood was rushing to my cheeks as I answered him, but somehow it was important for him to know that he wasn't the only one to give me discipline.

'Aaron likes to spank me. He caned me, too, and Liselotte . . . Liselotte spanked me, and beat me with a kitchen spatula, and my hairbrush, and an old ruler, and this sort of dog whip thing we found, and . . .'

'You have been a busy girl, and I guessed you went to Liselotte yesterday after all, but we'll talk about that later.' He clearly hadn't forgotten the talk we were supposed to have. 'Okay, then, let's have you over my knee before you go on the horse.'

He sat down on what looked like a low table beneath its dust covers, once more making a lap for me. This time, I got down, dropping my towel to let him see me nude, then getting down into what was now becoming a familiar and favourite position, but no less shameful for that, across a man's legs with my bottom presented for spanking. I knew it would be hard, too, because this was Jean, and I was shivering with apprehension as much as embarrassment as his hand cupped my rear cheeks, so big he could just about hold me. His other arm came around my waist to hold me firmly in position, no escape, his hand lifted and a single firm swat landed full across my cheeks, and it had begun.

Liselotte was right. He was rough and ready, and he was rude, too, spanking me so hard I lost control from the start, kicking and wriggling in his grip, but constantly pausing to stroke my cheeks or tease me between them, to pinch my already sore flesh or to cup my sex and rub me as if he was going to make me come. I'd have let him, for all the shame and guilt still raging in my head, and I was very glad indeed that he was holding me so firmly, and had found out my dirty little secret, because that made it so much easier to submit to him, both mentally and physically.

He quickly got me hot, and as so often seemed to happen, the moment I began to stick my bottom up for more, he stopped, laughing at my eager, dirty response before pulling me to my feet. I stood back, now sweaty and dishevelled, to reach behind me and take hold of my blazing bottom, squeezing and stroking my cheeks to dull the pain and add to my already powerful arousal. He watched for a moment then made a little turning gesture with one finger, indicating that I should show him my rear view. I obeyed, imagining his eyes feasting on my smacked cheeks and the gentle valley between, on my bottom hole and the lips of my sex, every rude detail fully on show, and he without a stitch out of place, save for the belt that he'd put to one side, ready for use. It felt good, though, and I was ready for his cock, but he was far from finished with me.

'Now get up on the rocking horse.'

I obeyed, too warm and needy to refuse, straddling the rocking horse as if I were riding it at a full gallop, with my back to him and my bottom pushed well out so that I was completely available to him, his belt and his cock. He gave a pleased grin.

'You're learning, Elise. Hmm . . . now that's a thought.'

He stepped close, but his belt was still where he'd left it, so at first I had no idea what he was doing as he ducked down at my side. Only as he lifted one side of the thick leather girth strap that held the rocking horse's saddle in place did I realise, and an instant later he closed the two sides across my back. As he tugged the strap through the buckle, I was pulled forwards onto the back of the rocking horse, forcing me to lift my bottom into a yet ruder and more revealing position. With the buckle fastened, I was completely helpless, shaking badly, but ready, and now clinging to the neck of the horse as he retrieved his belt.

Jean doubled the belt over, flexed it in his hands and made a quick adjustment to the very obvious bulge in the front of his trousers. I braced myself, expecting the crack of the belt across my naked bottom at any instant, and the pain that would follow, but he seemed content to admire the view.

'You are very beautiful, Elise; such a lovely little bottom.'

I made to answer just as the belt whipped down and my words broke in a scream as it lashed across my cheeks, causing Jean to throw a nervous glance towards the door.

'Not so loud, Elise!'

'I can't help it; it hurts! You'd better gag me.'

He looked around, and was about to pick up my towel when he seemed to have second thoughts. Easing down his zip, he pulled out his cock and balls then came to my head, offering himself to my mouth.

'This will shut you up.'

'You bastard!'

'Come on, Elise, in your mouth.'

I let him do it, opening wide to allow him to feed me his already half-stiff cock. He took up the belt once more, and as I began to suck I was thinking how right it felt to be sucking cock for the man who'd spanked me, just as I had for Jean before, and for Aaron, and as Liselotte had for John Lambert, only now I was doing it while my bottom was attended to instead of afterwards. It wasn't easy, either, trying not to bite every time the belt cracked down across my cheeks, and getting hotter and hotter behind all the while, with the huge erection in my mouth adding to my arousal, but unable to touch myself.

He didn't seem to want to stop, either, smacking the belt down across my bottom again and again as I did my best to suck him, and as he grew more excited he began to fuck in my mouth. I thought he was going to take it all the way, and braced myself for the inevitable climax of his excitement, with his cock pumping in my throat as he thrashed me, something I wasn't at all sure I could cope with, although it seemed I had little choice.

It never came, the smacks growing harder and faster and his thrusts deeper and ever harder to cope with, only to suddenly stop. He pulled back, mumbling something about not wanting to hurt me, and a great wave of gratitude swept over me. Not that he was finished; his cock was still hard in his hand as he withdrew from my mouth and got behind me, then he was in me once more as he spread my aching bottom cheeks apart with his thumbs and slid himself up me until I could feel his balls pressed to my sex.

The instant he began to fuck me, I knew I was going to come. I was spread so wide across the rocking horse's rump that every single thrust pressed his balls to exactly the right spot. He began to beat me again, too, holding the belt one-handed and smacking it down across my cheeks in time to his thrusts. I was just praying I'd get there first, and it seemed likely, with my ecstasy already rising in my head as his cock began to move ever faster and the slaps of his balls on my clit grew firmer.

I cried out once, right on the edge, begging him to fuck me harder and to beat me harder, utterly surrendered to him and to what was being done to me, then again, a wordless, ecstatic scream as I hit my orgasm, as hard and tight as any I'd had before, and wonderfully long. He didn't stop, riding me as I hit peak after glorious peak, and beyond, still thrusting into me as I lay limp and gasping across the back of the rocking horse, held in place only by the thick leather strap around my middle and the cock inside me.

He'd stopped spanking me, though, and had slowed down, no longer pumping into me, but holding on to my hips and pulling back and forth so that he was barely moving at all but the rocking horse was. I giggled as I realised what he was up to, amused by the thought of how I'd look, strapped down on the rocking horse as it moved back and forth on its casters, his cock easing in and out of me from behind. He didn't take long, though, enjoying me slowly until he could hold off no longer, then suddenly jamming himself in as far as he could go to make me cry out one last time as he came deep inside me.

And that was that. I'd given in to him, once more surrendering myself to the needs of my body in spite of all the reasons I had to hold back, which left me happy but more than a little guilty as I scampered back downstairs with my towel clutched tight around me and Jean going ahead to make sure nobody was about. He kissed me at the door to the bathroom, and made a fresh declaration of his love before sending me in with a pat to my bottom. I wasn't sure I believed him, but whatever his feelings towards me, they certainly included a great deal of lust, and mine for him weren't so very different.

After a quick shower, I returned to my bedroom, dressing quickly in order to be in time for lunch, as the combination of hard work and harder sex had left me with a ravenous appetite. Only when I was fully dressed and ready to go downstairs did I bother to check my phone, to discover a single text message, just five words, from Aaron:

Missing you. I love you.

13

Having had sex with three partners in less than a week, I had well and truly surrendered any claim to be Little Miss Faithful, but that did nothing to reduce my guilt. I'd actually been having sex while Aaron sent the message, which somehow made it even worse. No doubt he'd been busy, as he always was, and had answered as soon as he'd had a spare moment, and all the while I'd been indulging myself in dirty, kinky sex with another man, to say nothing of spending more than twelve hours of unbroken depravity with another woman the day before.

I was completely at a loss to know what to do. Logically, I knew I should keep quiet and pray he never found out just how badly behaved I'd been, but inside I was crying out to confess everything, apologise and beg him to punish me. It would have to be hard, and done in a way that both satisfied him and made me feel I'd paid for my sins, something way beyond what I'd normally accept.

With any other man it would have been unthinkable, an offer sure to draw down contempt as well as rejection, but with Aaron there had to be at least a chance. After all, he loved to punish me, and to push my limits. He'd also made me suck Jack off, so he obviously wasn't completely averse to the idea of me having sex with other men. There was a big difference, though, in that Jean was very definitely a rival, while Jack had been firmly under Aaron's control. Then there was Liselotte, but men being men and Aaron being Aaron, he was sure to be more turned on than angry at the thought of me going with another woman. There was still a chance that he'd simply tell me to get lost, but it was a risk I had to take. I also knew what to suggest in the way of punishment, a penance I was sure would greatly increase my chances of forgiveness from Aaron. It had to be done face to face, though, as he was far more likely to reject my apology if it was made by phone or email, which meant that for the time being I was stuck.

I'd also made it very clear to Jean that my feelings for him were more than just casual, and I'd promised Liselotte that I'd visit her again before too long, which put me in a very difficult position. When Jean suggested spending the night together that same evening, I used what's probably the oldest excuse in the book and told him I was on my period, to which he gave what's probably the oldest response in the book and asked if I'd suck him off instead. That left me with three choices: an angry refusal, and after what had happened earlier that day, I'd have been left looking like a flaky, bad-tempered bitch; to tell the truth and try to explain the situation, which would be sure to make him angry and leave me feeling even worse; or to get sucking.

Ever since I walked out of the gates of St Agnes' Convent School on the last day of the last term of my school career, I'd felt I'd left Catholicism and the nuns' teachings firmly behind me, but I now realised there was something in their philosophy after all. If I was going to beg Aaron to forgive me my sins and award me a penance, then the slate would be wiped clean, and as every good Catholic knows, you can go on sinning until the moment you enter the confessional. At least, that was what I was telling myself as I got down on my knees to unzip Jean's trousers and flop his huge, heavy cock into my mouth.

By the time he'd finished and I'd swallowed dutifully, I was telling myself I'd done the right thing, if only to buy myself a little time to think. I slept alone, with my thoughts moving between guilt and arousal, happiness at the thought of being with Aaron and worry about the practicalities of our relationship. I didn't want to leave France, and I certainly didn't want to be a trophy wife. The alternative, and by far the more sensible solution, was for Aaron to sell up and come and live at La Fleur. His business had to be worth many millions, which would leave us in a comfortable position financially, with his skill at investment allowing us to bring in far more than the château could possibly lose, however many bad vintages or natural disasters we suffered. I'd then be able to concentrate purely on quality, raising the level of our wines far above those of our neighbours. That in turn would ensure our reputation with buyers in the UK and all over the world. It was a happy thought, and one I clung on to as I drifted gradually towards sleep.

It was also my first thought in the morning, which found me in a brisk, practical mood. I could even see sense in Madame Belair's attitude, in that my true responsibility lay in considering the overall strategy for the château rather than worrying about minutiae. In Aunt Adèle's case, that had meant marrying a series of rich men, and I intended to do the same, only better, marrying one very rich man. All that remained was to get Aaron Curran to sign on the dotted line.

That clearly meant being with him, which in turn meant going back to London without delay. With any luck he'd see my almost immediate return as a beautiful, romantic gesture rather than merely daft, while I'd also be able to escape temptation in the forms of Jean and Liselotte. I could then make Aaron as happy as I knew how on the first night, and if the situation seemed right, I would make my confession on the second, followed by penance and, hopefully, a mutual declaration of everlasting commitment.

I obviously couldn't tell Jean what was going on, and I did feel bad as I fabricated a story about being given a chance to pull in a major client who insisted on seeing me in person. Jean accepted it without comment and volunteered to drive me down to the airport, leaving me feeling more guilty still as he talked cheerfully about the quality of the vintage and what a bright future we all had at La Fleur now that I was in charge. I did my best to answer in kind, even when the conversation began to get more personal, growing ever more ashamed of myself but still convinced I was doing the right thing. He completely failed to notice my agitation, and his conversation grew more intimate still. I wasn't entirely surprised when he pulled off the lane we were driving down to park in the shade of an ancient willow. I knew what was coming and did my best to make excuses.

'Shouldn't we be getting to the airport? I have to check in . . .'

'In just over an hour. I can be there in twenty minutes. Come on, I am going to miss you, Elise, and I need this.'

'Yes, but, isn't this a bit public?'

'Not many people pass this way, and if they see the van they'll only see me, because your head will be down in my lap, on this.'

Even as he spoke, he'd pulled his cock and balls free of his trousers, and if there's one sight I find hard to resist it's a well-endowed man with everything showing but otherwise fully dressed. He was half-stiff, too, and obviously turned on merely by being with me, which was flattering, while I knew that sucking him would help assuage my guilt for choosing Aaron over him, and I had yet to make my confession.

'Okay, but be quick.'

'That's not what you girls usually say.'

I ignored the quip, still hesitant, only to give in, telling myself that one last time wouldn't make any real difference. He settled back, making himself comfortable, and down I went, bent across to take him first in my hand and then in my mouth. As I began to suck, his hand went to the back of my head, taking me gently by my hair to keep me in place, which I've always liked. It felt strange, though, and I couldn't help but think of my situation: on my way to see the man I loved, and who loved me, but with another man's cock in my mouth.

They always say that when you really love somebody then nobody else matters. You shouldn't even think of another man, not in a sexual way; you certainly shouldn't suck other men's cocks, and if you do, then you definitely, absolutely, should not enjoy it as much as I was, as Jean grew fully hard in my mouth. Yet I couldn't help it, lost to the feel and taste of his magnificent erection, and to the situation I was in, parked at the side of a sunny lane deep in rural France while I pleasured my man.

He was at least as good as his word, quickly taking hold of the base of his cock and tugging urgently up and down to get himself off as quickly as possible. I tried to tell myself that was for the best, even that he'd coerced me into it, demanding a blow job because I'd be late for my plane if I didn't give in. It was a blatant lie, but I couldn't help enjoying the fantasy, imagining my resentment and shame as he held me by the hair and masturbated into my mouth.

It was simply too much. My skirt came up and my hand went down the front of my panties to find my sex, warm and wet and needy. If Jean remembered the excuse I'd made for not going to bed with him the night before, he didn't say anything, but merely chuckled as he saw what I was doing. No longer able to pretend I was in a hurry, I came up off his cock, to rub his erection in my face and kiss and lick at his balls as I masturbated, now revelling in his abundant masculinity and determined to come before he did.

I got there, just, sobbing with mingled ecstasy and shame as I brought myself off under busy fingers, with his cock back in my mouth as deep as it would go, deliberately choking myself on maleness. He'd kept his grip in my hair all the while, now painfully tight but so right for the moment, and at the very peak of my orgasm he pulled my head up, just far enough to let him get a good grip on his shaft, and finished himself off in my mouth. I was still coming as I swallowed – a last perfect moment I knew I would treasure even if everything between us turned sour, which seemed all too likely. It was a thought that brought me to the edge of tears, but my eyes were watering anyway and Jean failed to notice.

We were quickly underway, but kissing Jean goodbye at the airport left me feeling worse than ever, and urgently wishing polyandry was acceptable in our society. Not that it would have worked anyway, as neither he nor Aaron would have been content with any role but that of alpha male. Even as it was, if my plans came to fruition, Aaron would be to all intents and purposes his boss, which was sure to cause friction, maybe even lead to him moving on.

I was still following this rather melancholy train of thought when I noticed a familiar figure striding across the concourse towards the executive departure lounge: John Lambert, and he was not alone. One man walked beside him, three more behind, all very much in the same stamp – smart in dark, well-made suits, relatively short and compact in build, and very obviously Chinese. That was no great surprise, given his job and the Chinese interest in French wine estates, but I couldn't help but wonder if their presence related to his offer for La Fleur. I'd started towards them without another thought, successfully heading them off before they could disappear from sight.

'John, good afternoon! Good afternoon, gentlemen.'

He looked less than pleased to see me as he turned, but rallied quickly.

'Ah, Elise, what a pleasant surprise. Gentlemen,

this is Elise Sherborne, the proprietor of Château La Fleur. Elise . . .'

The effect of my name was extraordinary, the men smiling and bowing with such obvious interest and respect that I might have been a major celebrity. I responded equally politely while John Lambert made the introductions then began to discuss the La Fleur estate. It was the obvious choice of subject, and I was keen to know what they were doing in Bergerac. That had John Lambert glancing at his watch with poorly concealed agitation, before trying to change the subject.

'Where are you off to, Elise?'

'London. I'm working to expand our export market, with considerable success.'

The senior Chinese businessman showed immediate surprise.

'But you are selling, yes?'

'The estate? No, absolutely not. La Fleur has been in my family for many generations. It would be unthinkable to sell.'

He and his colleagues nodded, now puzzled, while John Lambert looked far from comfortable. I would have carried on, perhaps managing to drop Liselotte's name into the conversation, but at that moment my flight was called and I was forced to withdraw. It came as no surprise that John Lambert had been negotiating with the Chinese, but from his reaction it looked as if he'd given them a less than fully accurate impression of the availability of La Fleur. My statement must have been inconvenient for him, to say the least, maybe disastrous, a thought which had me grinning as I hurried for my exit.

I had no sympathy for him at all. The offer he'd made me was clearly far below what the Chinese were prepared to pay, if the level of their interest was anything to go by. In fact, I was somewhat taken aback by their enthusiasm, especially as one of them had referred to La Fleur as a First Growth, a term that to the best of my knowledge only applied to a handful of superlative estates in Bordeaux itself. Possibly it was something John Lambert had invented, as I had no doubt whatsoever that he'd say or do anything to maximise his profit.

The incident helped to soothe my feelings over Aaron and Jean during the flight, but as we banked over London and the familiar towers of the City and of Docklands came into view, it all came back with a vengeance. Yet there was no way out, no clever manoeuvre or tactful explanation I could use to make sure everybody was happy. I was going to have to go through with my plan as it stood and hope the consequences weren't too dreadful.

As before, London was much colder than Bergerac, but this time clear and crisp, with the tall buildings seemingly etched against a sky of perfect eggshell blue. I was growing ever more nervous as my taxi drove in among them, now worried about how Aaron would receive me, or if he would be there at all. There was a fair chance he'd be away on business, in which case I was going to look a complete fool when I sent him a text saying I was in London.

By the time I'd been decanted onto the pavement outside the warehouse conversion where he lived, I was imagining yet worse outcomes, so that as I pressed the buzzer, I half expected Rebecca Laindon to answer. She didn't, but nor did anybody else, and I was feeling very silly indeed as I pressed for a second time, only to start as a familiar voice spoke from directly behind me.

'Elise? What are you doing here?'

Aaron sounded surprised, but also very, very pleased. The next instant, I was in his arms, taking a long, delicious kiss before I began to babble my explanation.

'I had to see you. When I got your text. I got the first flight I could, today. I hope you don't mind?'

'Of course I don't mind, but what about La Fleur? I thought you had a lot to do.'

'Yes and no. This is more important, anyway.'

'I'm flattered.'

He let himself in and I followed, what few suspicions I had left fading as we rode the lift up to his suite on the top floor. Had he been with anybody else, she'd have left telltale signs around the flat, something feminine I'd be sure to notice, but if anything he was more eager to get inside than I was. I still found myself glancing around for anything suspicious the instant I was through the door, but it was hard to imagine a more masculine space, nor one that better reflected his personality.

The flat was almost entirely given over to one huge room, on two levels, with the whole of one wall taken up by a gigantic picture window overlooking Blackwall Basin. What little furniture there was had a functional but clearly expensive look, while there was a broad area of bare, polished boards around a central steel pillar. The kitchen and bathroom were at the back, along with doors to what appeared to be a gigantic walk-in wardrobe, while the bed was on the upper level. One curious detail stood out: a sort of bracket about halfway up the pillar, from which hung a golden silk rope that was painfully familiar to me. Aaron caught me looking, so I asked the obvious question.

'That's a whipping post, isn't it? Who gets tied to that?'

'You do, later, maybe, but for now . . .'

He simply picked me up, curling his arm around the back of my legs and hoisting me up over his shoulder with no more difficulty, or dignity, than had I been a roll of carpet. I protested, thumping my fists on the hard muscles of his buttocks, just for the sake of it and then for real as he started up the stairs so that I had an upside-down view of Blackwell Basin over a hundred feet below. He just laughed and put his hand on my bottom, first to apply a playful smack, then to flip up my skirt to leave my panties on show as we reached the top of the stairs.

'Hey! Ouch!'

A second, harder spank had landed across the seat of my panties, followed by a third before I was dumped unceremoniously on the bed, skirt up and legs wide. He was standing over me, grinning like a wolf, but only for an instant before he reached down to take hold of my panties and haul them down and off. They got tossed aside, and he climbed on top of me and pulled my blouse open, shedding buttons and drawing another weak protest from me before I simply gave in to his lust.

My bra came up, his mouth fastened to one nipple, then the other, sucking and nipping at each erect teat until I was gasping and clutching at his hair. His hand went down, fumbling for his fly, and I felt his cock touch my bare sex, hot and urgent. A few quick tugs and he was hard enough to put it in, while I was already wet and receptive, making it easy for him to enter me. Our mouths opened together as he began to fuck me, his cock growing fully hard in just seconds, while a minute before I'd been standing in the doorway with my cases in my hands.

I got it hard and fast, as I'd expected, just taken then and there because he knew he could and he knew I wanted it. There was no lack of passion, though, his arms tight around me and our kisses hard enough to bruise as he drove into me, fast and faster still, barely pausing until he'd reached orgasm inside me with a last few furious shoves. He rolled off, spent, to lie back on the bed with his cock and balls sticking up from his suit trousers, a sight I didn't even try to resist.

Rolling over, I laid my head on the hard muscles of his belly, to take him in my mouth and suck up my own juices. My legs were still wide, my hand busy between them, rubbing eagerly in an effort to get myself off while he was still nicely erect, and trying to think about how he'd taken me so rudely rather than the fact that I was doing almost exactly what I had been with Jean a scant few hours earlier.

We made love again before we went out for dinner, in a more leisurely and far more loving style, naked in bed together and with Aaron on top. It was the first time he'd gone all the way with me without taking control, and almost the first time he hadn't finished with me on my knees with my bum stuck up in the air. I took that as a positive sign of his affection but made a point of telling him that I liked the way he handled me and that there was no reason to go easy all the time, an offer he happily accepted for later.

Once I'd washed and changed, we went out, first to a floating restaurant where we could watch the lights reflected from the Thames as we ate and drank, then to an exclusive club where waiters in full white tie and tails served us ancient brandy as we talked together by candlelight. It was gone midnight by the time we left, and I was a little conscious that he had work in the morning, but he didn't seem to care. We took a long route back to his flat, walking hand in hand alongside one of the docks and across a little arched bridge, where he took me in his arms, kissed me and told me he loved me. I answered in kind and we began to kiss again, a long, perfect moment that left me blissfully happy and eager for more of the same, or anything else he cared to do.

I'd guessed what it would be, and sure enough, he'd barely shut the door behind us before he was slipping my dress from my shoulders and guiding me towards the whipping post. My dress reached the floor and I stepped clear, but as I made to kick off my shoes, he shook his head.

'You'll be needing those.'

'Why?'

'Because I like you that way, now get your panties off and let's get your wrists tied, shall we?'

I obeyed, stepping out of my knickers to go fully nude and holding out my wrists. He took the silk cord, binding my arms with a few expert and clearly well-practised twists, then threading the rope through the bracket and pulling on it to force my arms up above my head. When he'd tied the rope off, I was on tiptoe and very glad of the extra inch my heels afforded me, because without them I'd barely have been able to touch the ground.

As it was, he had me completely helpless, with my belly pressed to the cool steel of the pillar and my back and bottom and legs vulnerable, also visible. I hadn't found it in myself to say anything, and I'd been half hoping I could pretend the bruises Liselotte and Jean had inflicted on me had lasted since my previous trip to London. From the expression on Aaron's face, I knew it was hopeless, but while his voice was both surprised and accusing as he spoke up, there was no real venom in it.

'Who's been spanking you?'

It was time for me to confess, as least partially.

'I . . . I spank myself. I need it, ever since you started doing it to me. I need it so badly.'

It was the truth, but by no means the whole truth. He looked doubtful.

'Just that? You look like you've been done with a strap, hard, and accurately, too. Who was it, Elise?'

'Liselotte . . . my friend Liselotte. I asked her to, and . . .'

'Liselotte? The dark-haired girl with the big boobs?'

'Yes.'

'And she spanked you?'

'Yes.'

He drew in his breath, while the already noticeable bulge in the front of his trousers had now grown, clearly outlining the shape of his erect cock. A weak giggle rose up in my throat, half fear, half excitement.

'Do you want to punish me for playing with her?'

'You'd like that, wouldn't you?'

I nodded, relieved that he didn't seem cross but not at all sure how he'd take the news that I'd let another

man spank me, too, never mind the sex. That part of
the confession could wait, and as he drew something
from a nearby chest, I was glad I'd made that decision.
It was a whip, a long, black coil of plaited leather, the
sight of which set my tummy fluttering and put a lump
of fear in my mouth. Yet I trusted him, knowing he
would stop if I really needed him to, while a whipping
was certainly going to make me feel better about my
behaviour, even if it wasn't the penance I had decided I
deserved. He came behind me, shaking the whip out so
that for a moment it seemed to be a long black snake
wriggling across the floor as he spoke again.

'So, Liselotte spanks you . . . what with? Not just
her hand, I'll bet?'

'No . . . yes, usually her hand, over her knee, but she
bent me over her kitchen table too and used a kitchen
spatula. Then there was my hairbrush, in the bedroom,
and an old ruler, and a dog whip . . .'

'So this won't be the first time you've been whipped?'

'She was quite gentle . . . oh, God!'

I twisted around, unable to resist a chance to watch,
and as he hefted the wicked-looking thing in his hand,
I began to shake and lever myself up and down on
my toes, a sight that made him smile and set his eyes
glittering with cruelty and lust. A sharp snap as he
cracked the whip just inches from my skin and I cried
out, not sure I could handle the pain when he hit me,
but desperately willing myself to be brave.

Again he hefted the whip. Again he flicked it out,

this time to crack the sting smartly against the skin of my bottom to make me yelp and kick out. The blow had hurt, a sharp, hot pain that left me trembling harder than ever, full of fear and full of desire, eager to be punished and yet dreading exactly what I needed so badly. Again the whip snaked out, and again it cracked against my defenceless flesh, on the other side, so that I knew that each cheek would now be topped with a rosy mark. He stepped back.

'Now tell me. Tell me how Liselotte spanks you; tell me while you're whipped.'

I nodded and he adjusted his cock, then pulled down his zip to take it out, his balls too, standing proud from his suit trousers, a sight that had me whimpering.

'Yes, like that, Aaron, stay like that while you whip me, please!'

'I intend to. Come on, you said she likes you over her knee?'

He'd drawn the whip back as he spoke, flourishing it as he took his cock in his other hand. I began to talk, fairly sure I knew what he'd like to hear.

'Yes, over her knee with my knickers pulled down . . . Ow!'

The whip had caught me full across both cheeks, hard enough to set me kicking and squirming against the hardness of the pillar. He drew it back again, his other hand moving slowly up and down on his cock, and again the whip lashed down across my cheeks to add a second burning welt to the first and set me

jerking in my bonds for an instant before I could get
my balance and find my voice.

'Bare bottom over her knee, but that's only the
start. She likes to sit on me . . . Ow! She likes to sit
on my back and spank me . . . Ow! That's how she did
me with my hairbrush . . . Ow! And the ruler, on her
bathroom floor, in the nude . . . Ow! And she . . . she
turned me over and sat on my face, Aaron . . . She sat
her bare bottom right on my face.'

He dropped the whip, leaving me with six burning
welts across my naked bottom cheeks, and from the
wild look in his eyes and the way he was hammering at
his cock, it looked like I'd driven him to the edge. Sure
enough, he came forward to grab me by the hips and
ease himself up me from behind, as deep as he could
go. I tried to push my bottom out to make it easier for
him, but he didn't seem to care, thrusting into me with
crazy abandon.

Every push jammed me hard against the steel pillar,
and with my hands tied, all I could do was brace my
legs apart and let him get on with it, while his thrusts
were so hard they were making me gasp and moan,
both from pleasure and sheer breathlessness. I was
constantly reminded that I'd been whipped, too, with
his hard belly smacking against my aching bottom
with every push, so that it was like being spanked by
a giant hand. The same treatment in just about any
other position, even if just a tiny bit less awkward, and
I'd have come. As it was, he simply got me dizzy with

ecstasy and begging for the touch of his fingers to my sex, before he abruptly pulled out to finish himself off all over my well-whipped bottom with a few swift jerks of his hand. I was still begging, my voice a barely coherent gabble of dirty, pleading words aimed at getting him to make me come.

'. . . please, touch me off, Aaron . . . touch me, rub me . . . please, I'm begging you, make me come. Use your cock . . . use your lovely big cock between my legs . . . rub me with it, like Jean does, please?'

'Who the hell is Jean?'

14

People always joke about crying out the wrong lover's name at the moment of supreme ecstasy, but I had never, ever imagined that I would do it, let alone when I wasn't actually coming. Admittedly, I had drunk quite a lot, and I had been whipped, and fucked, but I still felt extremely foolish as I stood in front of Aaron, looking at the floor and fidgeting my toes as he untied my wrists. I was telling myself that I had meant to confess, so it was just that the moment had come rather sooner than I'd anticipated, but that didn't make it any easier as he repeated his demand.

'Who is Jean, Elise?'

'You . . . you met him. Jean Belair, at La Fleur.'

'The one who looks like a gorilla?!'

I shrugged, not really wanting to accept the description, but unable to deny it, either.

'And what's he been doing?'

'He . . . we had sex a couple of times, before I knew you were in love with me, or I wouldn't have done it, I promise. Please don't be cross, Aaron? I love you, but he was there, and he is very attractive, in his way, and . . .'

I trailed off, rubbing my wrists as I looked up to find his steely gaze locked with mine. He blew his breath out, plainly angry but still under control, then spoke.

'Okay, okay, I suppose I'd no right to expect you to be faithful, not up until now, anyway, but you might have told me!'

'I was going to, I promise. I wanted to confess, and then, maybe . . . if you wanted to, you could punish me?'

He smiled, to my immense relief, then went on.

'How am I supposed to punish you, Elise? You like your bottom smacked, and frankly, you can take as much as I feel comfortable dishing out.'

I leant forward to whisper a suggestion into his ear, my face hot with blushes. As I moved back, I saw that his smile had spread into a broad grin.

'That will do nicely, thank you.'

I found myself swallowing and looking at my feet again, immensely grateful, a little scared, but with the excitement that had broken when I spoke the fateful words now rushing back. He began to undress, and to talk again.

'Okay, I'll accept that, and we need to talk anyway, if we're going to be in a relationship, but tomorrow. It's gone one o'clock and I've got a breakfast meeting with the people from UYT.'

'So you're not cross?'

'No, not cross, exactly, and as you ran straight here

when you got my text, I'm guessing you prefer me anyway?'

'Yes, of course.'

'And did you tell him that whatever there was between you is over?'

'Um . . . no, not yet, but I will.'

'Fair enough. But hang on, weren't Jean and Liselotte together?'

'Yes, but not any more. It's complicated.'

'But she's spanked you? And him?'

I was looking at my toes again.

'Um . . . yes. Sorry. That's how it started, you see. He likes to spank her, and . . . and they let me watch, and it really turned me on, so I let her do me, then he wanted to do the same, and . . .'

'Elise.'

'Yes, Aaron?'

'You really are an absolute disgrace. What are you?'

'An absolute disgrace.'

He was naked now, his lean, muscular body beautiful in the pale glow from the single lamp he'd turned on when we came in. I managed a weak smile, hoping he would take advantage of the situation and put me through my paces one more time, or at least help me to come.

'Into the bathroom with you.'

As I turned, he gave my bottom a firm smack, making me jump and raising my hopes of further misbehaviour. He followed me into the bathroom, a square space as spartan as the rest of the flat, with a big, walk-in shower but no tub. I climbed into the shower, helped by another pat to my bottom, and again he followed, tempting me to make an offer.

'Would you like me to soap you?'

'Behave yourself, Elise.'

'I need to come, Aaron.'

I'd gone pink as I said it, but his response was a casual chuckle before reaching for the soap.

'And you like to be punished?'

'Yes, but . . . I mean, having my mouth washed out with soap?'

'Open wide, Elise.'

His voice was firm, uncompromising, and I found myself unable to resist, wanting it despite myself. I made a face but obeyed, opening my mouth to allow him to cram the bar of soap inside, and all the while wondering what it was about my nature that made that sort of treatment so exciting. There was no denying the effect, though, with the combination of my whipped bottom and having my mouth washed out with soap combining to send my arousal soaring once more. Aaron was thoroughly enjoying himself, too, which made the thrill of humiliation I'd come to love stronger still as I let myself slide down the wall to sit splay-legged in the bottom of the shower, with the end of the bar of soap sticking out from between my lips but most of it in my mouth.

He stood over me, watching, his face set in mild

amusement, his cock and balls right in front of my eyes as I let my fingers steal to my sex. The soap tasted foul, but I held it in, even sucking on it in my rising excitement until there were bubbles coming out from around my lips, the suds washing down over my chin in the water from the shower and falling in clots to my chest. I wanted Aaron to see, and tilted my head up, deliberately showing off as I masturbated, nothing hidden as I ran over what he'd done to me, and what he was going to do: first tied me up and whipped me, then fucked me rudely from behind, and finally made me wash my mouth out with soap in front of him. But there was more, and worse, to come, which was the thought I held uppermost in my mind as I reached orgasm.

When I woke the next morning, Aaron was gone, which was no surprise as his meeting had been for 8.30 and it was nearly 10.00. The day was my own, but my thoughts were focused on his return and there was nothing I particularly wanted to do. For a while, I lay in bed, just drinking in the scent of him from the sheets and the very personal and very masculine atmosphere of the flat. Eventually, I got up and padded down to the bathroom, naked, to wash and inspect myself in the mirror, admiring the fresh set of welts he'd put across my bottom. They stung a little, which was an exciting reminder of the night before, while to see myself with the evidence of a whipping so plainly written across my skin made me feel wonderfully wanted, almost as if I were owned.

There was the post too, with the golden silk cord still in place – a small thing, but a reminder of what Aaron did to me, what Aaron did for me. Again and again I found my eyes drawn to it as I sat and sipped coffee, thinking of how it felt to have my wrists bound, leaving me helpless and vulnerable to him, trusting him with my body in a way that went far, far beyond ordinary sexual intimacy. I would have masturbated again, but I wanted to keep myself on edge all day and so held back, merely making another inspection of my whipped bottom and spending a moment teasing my nipples with the tip of the golden silk cord before getting dressed.

As I was putting my lipstick on, it occurred to me that, if I was showing him a great deal of trust, then the same was true the other way. I was alone in his flat and could stay there all day. That surely meant he had nothing to hide, and that all my suspicions about Rebecca Laindon and other women had been groundless, based on nothing more than jealousy. If that were true, and he had been faithful to me since he came down to Bergerac, then it made my behaviour doubly sinful and my need for penance stronger still.

I wanted it then and there, and tried to fight my impatience by going shopping. Even that only went so far to calm me down, but I still made the best of it, picking up some stylish clothes for the winter and breathing on the shop windows in Bond Street as I wondered if Aaron would actually ask me to marry him, and if so, which of the myriad beautiful rings he would offer me when he proposed.

By the time I got back to the flat, it was dark, but there was still an hour or so before he was likely to return. I wanted it that way, keen to make the experience really special, while there were also certain practical considerations to be taken care of, very intimate ones, so much so that by the time I was done, I was shaking and ready for sex. I was naked and decided to stay that way, completely accessible to him, but I didn't want him to rush into it, either, so I put an apron on and busied myself cooking a dinner of duck breasts smothered with honey and accompanied by green peas. The aroma was beginning to make my mouth water, when I heard the door open, then Aaron's voice.

'That smells delicious. What is it?'

'*Caneton au miel*, the way my mum used to do it.'

'I'm honoured. Have you chosen something to go with it?'

'A bottle of our Vieilles Vignes '01.'

'Sweet wine with duck?'

'Trust me.'

He'd come up behind me as we spoke, saw that I was naked but for the apron, and gave me the familiar pat on my bare bottom, something that now felt deliciously proprietorial. I stuck it out for him and was rewarded with another couple of swats, but with a magazine, which he then threw down on the work surface.

'Here's something that might interest you, other than as an implement for smacking your delectable *derrière*. There's an article that mentions La Fleur.'

It was a copy of a publication called *Cellar Master*, apparently a wine magazine to judge by the picture and information on the cover. I wanted to look, but he'd begun to kiss my neck and run his hands up and down over the swell of my hips, which made it hard enough to concentrate on my cooking, never mind anything else.

'Not yet, darling. Let's eat first. I'm going to serve your dinner for you like this, naked.'

He made a pleased noise in his throat but didn't stop kissing me, while his hands merely moved higher, slipping in under the apron to cup my breasts. My nipples were already stiff and it was impossible to hold back a moan. Encouraged, he began to nibble at my neck and rub at my nipples, while he was now pressed so closely against me that I could feel the bulge of his cock through his trousers.

'Turn the gas down.'

'Aaron, no . . .'

'Shush, do as you're told. You wanted to be punished, and you're going to be.'

He adjusted the gas himself, twisting the control to its lowest setting, and then he took my hand to make me put the spatula I'd been holding down on the chopping board. I'd more or less given in, and allowed him to guide my hand behind me towards his crotch.

'Take it out.'

His grip was tight on my wrist, and my fingers were shaking as I struggled to pull down his zip and burrow my hand inside. He was already quite hard, as he always seemed to be around me, and it took a moment to get both his cock and balls free. I began to pull at his shaft and rub the head against my bottom, drawing a happy sigh as he continued to nuzzle at my neck. He was getting harder very quickly, and he steered my hand to make me rub him between my cheeks, his voice a purr as he spoke again.

'That's right, darling, you know where that's going, don't you?'

I managed a weak nod and forced myself to push my bottom out so that I could rub his cock right between my cheeks, feeling the now swollen head bump against my anus. Now sure I was compliant, he let go of my wrist to take himself in hand, rubbing his cock firmly against my bottom hole as if he was going to push it up.

'No, Aaron, not yet. I can't manage that! I want to be punished, but . . .'

'I know, that's okay. Just relax.'

That was easier said than done when I'd agreed to take his erection up my bottom. It would be my first time, and while I knew it was something he wanted to do and felt would be a fitting punishment for my behaviour, that didn't make me any less nervous.

Aaron let go of his cock and I took hold again, pulling on the shaft and rubbing him against myself. He could have penetrated me easily, and for a moment I did slip the head of his cock in, only to receive a warning smack.

'Oh no you don't. If I want to fuck you, I'll do it.'

'Yes, Aaron. Sorry, Aaron.'

'Good girl. Is that duck-fat?'

He was indicating the little Pyrex cup full of golden-brown grease I'd put to one side of the stove.

'Yes. You have to pour some off, or the honey won't brown properly. Careful, it's hot!'

'Not that hot.'

He'd stuck his finger in, scooping out part of the crust from the congealing fat. I immediately realised what he was going to do.

'Aaron, no, please, that's so dirty!'

'Shush.'

I went quiet, pouting in consternation as he slipped his greasy finger down between the cheeks of my bottom and in up the tight little hole I'd always guarded so carefully against male intrusion. It felt nice and I was quickly sticking my bottom out in wanton acceptance of my penetration, for all that my head was already full of shame and an odd, weak sense of self-pity. He simply pushed deeper, making me sigh, but while I'd agreed to let him use my bottom, it really was not sensible to do it over a hot cooker. I knew he wouldn't do that, either, but to move away was the final acceptance of my fate, and I just couldn't do it, even though I was still tugging at his now fully rigid cock.

As usual, Aaron took control. With his finger still deep up my bottom hole, he took me firmly by the scruff of my neck and pulled me back from the cooker to frogmarch me the few shorts steps across the kitchen to the table. I was pushed down, one breast now free above the edge of my apron and squashed out on the hard wood of the table top, my bottom pushed high, with his erection rearing above my cheeks. He took hold, tugging gently on his shaft as his eyes feasted on my rear view, then reached out to pick up the spatula I'd been using to cook the duck breasts.

It was all I could do to manage a sob of protest before the spatula smacked down across my bottom, drawing a yelp from me at the sudden pain on my still tender flesh. Another smack and another yelp, then he set to work in earnest, spanking me hard and fast as he held me down by my neck, until I'd begun to kick and wriggle. Still he spanked, indifferent to my cries and my ever more urgent writhing, and all the while with his eyes fixed to the rude, slippery crease between my cheeks. He knew what he was doing, too, now practised enough at beating me to recognise the signs as my pain gave way to warmth and need, but instead of dropping the spatula and simply taking me up my bottom, he placed it carefully on the very top of my cheeks, resting between them.

'Stay still.'

He left the room, still nursing his erection but also whistling to himself in a casual, cheerful fashion that somehow made the situation I was in stronger by far, as if my humiliating punishment were no more than a piece of light-hearted entertainment. I knew what he was doing, too, and already had my wrists crossed meekly behind my back when he returned with the golden cord. Still whistling, and with his cock a rigid bar between the cheeks of my bottom as he worked, he wound the cord into a tight cinch and tied it off.

I'd given in anyway, completely accepting what was about to be done to me, but being put in bondage added the final awful, beautiful detail and I was shaking with reaction and gasping in my breaths as he went back to spanking me. The first few stung, but I soon began to warm up again, yet he seemed to be in no hurry, and even when I was sticking my bottom up in my best imitation of a cat on heat, he continued to spank. Finally, I broke.

'Go on, Aaron, do it, please? Please, Aaron?'

'Do what?'

He was going to make me say it.

'Oh, you bastard! Ow!'

'Manners, Elise, or do you want your mouth washed out with soap again?'

'No . . . but please, please punish me the way I said . . . the way I asked . . .'

'Which is?'

'To . . . to put your cock up my bottom, you bastard! Ow! Ow! Ow!'

He'd been spanking my thighs, a cruel trick as every blow stung far more than when administered to my bottom, but with far less erotic effect. It was really unfair, too, as I'd said the dirty, crude words he wanted to hear, setting my face ablaze with blushes, but he wasn't satisfied.

'That's right, Elise, you asked me to put my cock up your bottom, to punish you, but what for?'

'For . . . for going with Jean, for letting him spank me!'

'And?'

'And for sucking his cock . . . and for letting him fuck me! Oh, you bastard, Aaron! I'm being punished by having to take your cock up my bottom for letting Jean spank me, and for sucking his cock, and for letting him fuck me. Now please take me, Aaron . . . fuck my bottom . . . sodomise me! There, is that dirty enough for you, you bastard?'

He laughed, dropped the spatula, which he'd been using across my bottom and thighs all the while, and pushed his cock down into the slippery valley between my cheeks. Even as the head of his cock touched my anus, my mouth had come wide in a sigh as much of relief as of ecstasy, and then I could feel myself

spreading slowly open behind, accepting him, and it
was done. For the first time in my life, I had a man's
cock up my bottom, a thing so shameful, so dirty, I'd
barely ever been able to get my head around it, never
mind surrender myself to it. Now I had, and it felt
so good, not just really nice but filthy rude, and yet
acceptable because I was being punished.

I started to cry as he pushed himself in deep, a little
out of regret for my surrender, but more for the sheer
force of my emotions, good and bad, but mainly good,
while the delicious, weak feeling I'd been growing to
enjoy more and more was stronger than ever. He was
going to get me there, too, because my head was awash
with filthy thoughts and his balls were pressing against
my empty sex in just the right way, rubbing with every
push. Even before he'd really got his pace up inside
me, I was gasping and moaning, while my smarting
bottom cheeks and the feel of the rope around my
wrists helped to push me higher still.

Aaron's hands had locked on to my hips, and his
powerful fingers sank deep into my flesh, holding me
exactly where he wanted me as his thrusts grew harder
and deeper still. My entire body, my entire being,
seemed to centre on his cock, even more so than when
he was inside me normally, while the thought that what
was being done to me was being done as a punishment
was raging in my head, a mix of physical and mental
ecstasy that finally came together in an orgasm so
intense, I screamed with all the power of my lungs.

I heard Aaron's laughter as he realised I'd come with his cock up my bottom, but he wasn't stopping and even as my orgasm began to fade, I felt a second welling up, more powerful still. He was pushing faster, too, taking me to the point of pain, only to suddenly stop as he cried out in bliss, and I knew he'd given me the perfect climax to my punishment by coming inside me. With that, my second orgasm burst, setting me screaming and kicking out, my body jerking on his cock and my hair tossing wildly, my every muscle in contraction, so hard and so long I nearly lost my senses.

It took quite a while to come down from my first experience of anal sex, and rather longer to sort myself out in the bathroom. Aaron was much quicker and took over the cooking, as cool, calm and collected as ever, while I struggled to come to terms with what I'd done and just how much I'd enjoyed myself. Of one thing there was no doubt, though. I'd done my penance and earned Aaron's forgiveness.

We ate slightly burnt *caneton au miel* together by candlelight, Aaron still in his work suit and me now stark naked, which felt right. I was quite sore, despite having applied copious amounts of cream to my bottom, and sitting down didn't help, but that went with my nudity to keep me in a state of permanent, mild arousal and deep satisfaction. Aaron was happy too, chatting cheerfully about his recent successes at work and making suggestions for how I might be able

to improve sales in London, which finally allowed me
to ask the all-important question.

'How are we going to manage, then, when I'm
living in France?'

He gave a thoughtful nod.

'Yes, that's a tricky one. Obviously I can't take much
time off, so . . .'

'No? How about this, then? The company must be
worth many millions by now. If you were to sell up, we
could live together at La Fleur.'

'Sell up? I couldn't do that. This is my life. I'd go
stir crazy in a week.'

'You could help me run the business, or you could
run the company from France.'

'No. I'm sorry, Elise, but it's impossible. I have to be
in London. There are too many things I have to do face
to face, and it's a world hub, too. If it were Paris, then
maybe, but Monbazillac is the back of beyond. Sorry.'

'Oh. But surely, if you want to be with me?'

'I do, Elise. I've been in love with you since the first
time you came in for your interview. You were wearing
a blue two-piece, I remember, and you'd made so
much effort to look the part, but your hair was in a
high pony-tail and you looked as if you ought to be in
the sixth form. I couldn't resist you.'

'You took your time to show it.'

'It was difficult. I was in a complicated relationship
– well, a set of relationships – with one girlfriend in
Frankfurt and another in New York, and . . .'

'Did they know about each other?'

'Gisela knew about Bailey, but Bailey didn't know about Gisela. Americans tend to buy into the monogamy myth.'

'The monogamy myth?'

'You know, one everlasting love and all that nonsense. I thought you'd be the same, because you seemed so prim and proper, and you seemed to be very much wrapped up in mainstream culture, but in the end I just couldn't do without you. When I broke off with Bailey, I invited you to New York . . .'

'. . . and I poured out a ten-litre water bottle over your lap.'

'Yes, and I dare say I deserved that. I shouldn't have been so arrogant with you, but as it goes, that technique usually works.'

'Not with me.'

'No, which made me even keener. Then you left and I followed you to Bergerac, and you know the rest, so here we are.'

'Okay, but what made you change your mind about me after I left London? You seemed doubtful.'

'I wasn't sure how we stood, and I did want to be with you, but I wasn't sure you could cope with my lifestyle. Then Rebecca . . .'

'Rebecca Laindon?'

'Yes. She rang La Fleur to answer some query you'd made about tastings and spoke to an older woman – Madame Belair, I imagine – who told her you were out at a restaurant with John Lambert, so . . .'

'John Lambert?! I was not!'

'No? So you didn't go out with him?'

'No! He's a dirty old man, and the next best thing to a con artist. He offered me two million euros for La Fleur when he'd already struck a deal with some Chinese businessmen, undoubtedly for far more. I wouldn't be seen dead with him!'

'Fair enough, but that's not what Madame Belair said. In fact, she implied there was something between the two of you.'

'Madame Belair has some explaining to do. I'm guessing she wanted to put you off, but I can't think . . .'

I trailed off, because I knew exactly why she'd done it: to improve her own son's chances. Aaron carried on.

'So I sent you that message, hoping to keep my hat in the ring. I was going to come over and see you as soon as I had time, but you came to me first. I was a bit surprised when you confessed to me about Liselotte and then Jean, but left out Lambert. I just imagined you were too embarrassed.'

'I would have been, and I really am sorry about letting myself go with Jean, however much I enjoyed what we did.'

'You're forgiven, and besides, I'm no better.'

I was gripped by a sudden sinking feeling.

'No. I did see Gisela when I was in Frankfurt, and I

did end up in bed with Vicky Bell the night after you'd gone, and a couple of times since.'

'But I thought you were in love with me? You told Vicky . . .'

'I am in love with you, but a man can love more than one woman.'

I shrugged, wondering what love even meant.

'And Rebecca?'

'No . . . well, not recently, but she and I have an arrangement. I bring her plenty of business and she makes sure I don't run into difficulties. Bailey used to stay at Angel's when she was in London, and Gisela too.'

'Oh.'

I felt cold inside and bitterly jealous. Really, he'd done no more than I had, with two partners over the same period, but I'd been in an agony of guilt over it, while he didn't seem contrite at all. My reaction must have showed in my face, because he reached out to take my hand as he carried on.

'Don't be upset, Elise, we can work this out. One thing I really like about you is that you don't believe in all this monogamy rubbish, so I'm going to make you an offer I never thought I would. Come and live with me in London. You'll have a wonderful life.'

'What about La Fleur?'

'Either sell to this Chinese group, in which case you'll be reasonably well off in your own right, or appoint Luc Belair as manager, which he is anyway in all but name, as far as I can see. You can then run the London end of operations, so you won't even get bored. Come on, you know it's good.'

'And what about Gisela?'

'I'd see her when I was in Frankfurt, yes, but you'd know. We'd be honest with each other – isn't that the important thing?'

I nodded, struggling to get my head around what he was suggesting, which did make sense in a way, except that I couldn't shake my feelings of jealousy. Yet his idea did at least free me from the obligation of having to refuse Liselotte, which was going to hurt, and although it didn't feel completely right, I would presumably be able to enjoy myself with Jean while I was in France.

'So we'd have an open relationship?'

'Yes, more or less. You'd have to give up Jean, of course.'

'So you'd expect me to be faithful to you, but you're not going to be faithful to me?!'

'Come on, don't be like that. You know it makes sense, Elise. Men can't cope with that sort of thing; women can. It's just nature, the dominant male with a group of females, but you can't have two dominant males in the same group, certainly not me and Jean. Come on, Elise, say you'll be with me. You could even bring your girlfriend over. Now that would be fun, or I could probably persuade Gisela to join in . . .'

I stood up, lifted the half-full bottle of Monbazillac Château La Fleur Vieilles Vignes 2001, and very slowly begun to pour it over his head.

15

I felt numb as I made my way to the airport. The taxi driver was chattering about some minor celebrity he'd had in his cab a few days before, but his words were no more than background noise. All I could think about was Aaron, how much I'd done for him, how much I'd given him, and still it was not enough. I'd been prepared to compromise, to make sacrifices I'd never considered before, and the very thought of which would have horrified me just a few months earlier, and yet he hadn't been prepared to budge an inch – his only offer being to allow me to be part of his private harem.

I'd spent a tearful night in a hotel near the airport, finally falling asleep with dawn already making a grey square of the curtains. The cleaners had woken me mid-morning and I'd been operating on automatic ever since. Even the tedious process of getting a last-minute ticket out to Bergerac seemed to pass in a haze, but once I was in my seat, two rows away from the window and next to a middle-aged woman who seemed to have been stuffed and mounted, it became impossible to avoid brooding.

Perhaps the worst thing of all had been Aaron's attitude after I'd poured the wine over him. I'd expected anger, certainly some sort of indication of hurt feelings, but he'd been amused, still trying to persuade me to accept his offer even as I slammed the flat door behind me. His last words were still ringing in my ears: 'You'll be back.'

I wouldn't. Of that I was absolutely determined. I had other choices, after all, principally Jean. He had his faults, and a typically overweening male ego, but at least he wasn't planning on collecting me like some pretty butterfly in a case, stuck through with a pin and spread out for all the world to see, which was more or less how I'd have been with Aaron. Jean also shared my interests, and in many ways would make a sensible choice as a husband, given that when Luc retired, he would be able to run the winery and cope with local issues, something I still knew next to nothing about.

The trouble was that I didn't really love Jean, for all that he turned me on like few other men, and I knew that if I accepted him, it would be at least partially for the sake of revenge on Aaron. That was no basis for a relationship, let alone a marriage, and I would always feel I had settled for my second choice, a thought that left me feeling hurt once again. I was determined not to start crying in front of all the other passengers, so I dug into my bag for the wine magazine Aaron had bought. Opening it at random, I spent a minute trying to read about a comparative tasting of the wines of

Volnay, but the words on the page seemed barely real and without sensible meaning, while my eyes were blurry with tears.

Aaron had said La Fleur was mentioned, and the index listed a news article on the resurgence of old systems to grade estates according to their worth. Monbazillac was mentioned, and I quickly found the reference.

> The INAO has accepted an application to allow the use of a nineteenth-century system of classification for Monbazillac. The system, introduced in 1863 to mirror the famous Bordeaux classification of 1855, covers twenty-three estates, of which eight are classed as First Growths and fifteen as Second Growths. These are . . .

A list followed, with the third of the First Growths struck through with a green highlighter pen: La Fleur. I read on, intrigued.

> There has, perhaps inevitably, been some controversy over the classification, but unlike the Bordeaux classification, the rankings rest as much on *terroir* as on market prices. Individual châteaux also stand to gain, even if they are not included in the classification, due to the publicity generated for the region. While difficult to

predict in the current market, the First Growth
châteaux are likely to see an increment of at least
fifty per cent on their release prices, possibly a
great deal more.

I folded the magazine, my eyes still hot with unshed
tears, but now at least I had something else to think
about. If what the article said was true, I would be
financially secure, while my efforts to promote La
Fleur in the City would put me ahead of the game. I
could make the estate work, without Aaron's money,
or anybody else's, for that matter. We'd print new
labels with the words 'First Growth' prominently
displayed, and maybe the 1863 date in order to add
a little gravitas, if we could get away with it. La Fleur
had the quality to match its status, too, especially with
the best vintage for years now maturing in our cellars.
My London clients could hardly fail to be impressed,
and according to the article, I'd gain an even stronger
advantage in the US than the UK, and stronger still in
the Chinese market.

With that, a new thought occurred to me. The article
was the first I'd heard of the classification system, but
negotiations had obviously been going on for some
time, possibly years. It seemed highly likely that John
Lambert had known about it, and that it had been a
factor in his efforts to secure La Fleur for his Chinese
clients. I wondered just how much he would have
made, which was certainly likely to have been in the

millions, and exactly what his overall plans had been. Judging by his behaviour, he'd intended to take me under his wing, and to bed, where he would no doubt have taken full advantage of my delight in having my bottom smacked. Then, once he'd reeled me in and pretended to sympathise with the financial situation at La Fleur, he'd have made his offer, below market price but not so far below as to raise eyebrows with the French authorities. He'd then have sold La Fleur on to the Chinese, leaving himself several million euros the richer, while I would have been dumped for the next pliable and naive young girl he could coax into bed. Fortunately, I hadn't been as pliable or naive as he'd hoped, but that in no way excused his behaviour.

Another thought then occurred to me. If it was likely John Lambert had known about the classification issue, then it seemed even more likely that the Belairs had too. After all, if La Fleur was one of the prospective First Growths, then surely the governing body of the local AOC would have been in contact? The letters would have gone to the winery, which meant they'd have been opened by Luc, or possibly Madame Belair. Neither of them had said a word, which almost certainly meant they'd deliberately kept me in ignorance of the situation. Yet I'd have been sure to find out eventually.

It was hard to see what they had to gain by not telling me, but as I ran over the facts in my head for a second time, I still couldn't find a fault in my chain of logic. They had to know, and they had to have a reason for keeping me in the dark as long as possible. Then it struck me. According to the article, it had been by no means certain that the classification would be accepted, which meant they might well have learnt the news while I'd been promoting our wines in London. During that time, Jean had broken off his relationship with Liselotte, and for reasons that didn't really add up. He'd then turned his attention to me, while Madame Belair had done her best to damage my relationship with Aaron by as good as telling Rebecca Laindon I was having an affair with John Lambert.

According to their plan, Jean and I would have ended up together, married, after which – unless I had taken legal steps to retain sole ownership, as my aunt had – the estate would have been as much his as mine. Having no reason to mistrust him, I would have happily shared everything with him, giving him a strong claim on La Fleur, while within nine months we'd have started breeding little Belairs to carry on the family name. Without such a plan, and with the estate worth far more and now profitable, they might have thought I'd sell out. The new owners would almost certainly have brought in new staff, and the Belairs would have been out. With the estate struggling to make a profit, it would have been a sensible choice for me to marry Jean, one I might even have made. But not any more.

'The bastards! The slimy little bastards!'

The stuffed-looking woman leapt in her seat as if

she'd been electrocuted, then pulled as far away from me as she could get, even as I stammered out an apology. I picked up the magazine again and read through the article, looking for any minor details or subtle nuances that might give me further information. There were plenty. One of the other First Growths and two of the Seconds were on the same ridge of land as La Fleur, nearby neighbours who knew the Belairs well. Samples of wine had been submitted to the INAO in Paris, obviously including wines from La Fleur, and just possibly by my Aunt Adèle, but far more likely by Luc Belair. Finally, there was the information that the new details would be permitted to appear on labels for the new vintage, something I could scarcely have failed to notice when the wine was bottled in about a year's time. By then I'd have been married to Jean and safely tucked up out of the way, owner in name and useful as the last of the Montaubin family to ensure impeccable lineage, but otherwise irrelevant save as a pretty fuck-toy for my husband.

I'd never been so angry. Aaron was bad enough, but at least he'd been reasonably honest in his intentions, however unacceptable they were. The Belairs had clearly had it all worked out in advance, plotting between the three of them, perhaps even before my arrival, but certainly once they'd been sure of the situation. Poor Liselotte had been quickly got out of the way, casually dumped because she came from a poor background, and Jean had set to work on me, using his masculine allure and knowledge of my personal foibles to draw me in. He'd very nearly succeeded, and as I sat there trying not to grind my teeth, I was even thankful to Aaron Curran, for his assistance, even though it had been blind chance.

It seemed to take for ever to reach Bergerac, and then the normally swift passage through customs was a nightmare. That at least gave me a chance to cool down a little, and to realise that it was not a good idea to go straight to La Fleur and confront the Belairs. First, I needed to be sure of my facts, and that meant a visit to Colombier and John Lambert. Not that I expected him to be pleased to see me, but one way or another it had to be possible to get him to confess. I also wanted to give him a piece of my mind.

As my taxi drove up into the hills, I was conscious of a change in my feelings towards my surroundings. Beforehand, regardless of what was going on, everything had been tinged with the rosy glow of my childhood memories. That was still there, but now the countryside evoked bittersweet feelings; it was still a place of peace and beauty on the surface, but undercut by the dark taint of malice and intrigue. No longer were my sympathies with the ordinary local people, but with my Aunt Adèle, who had held herself with such poise as she coped with everything life could throw at her.

Colombier is tiny, just a couple of dozen houses loosely clustered around a huge and ancient church with a bell tower visible for miles. I had no idea where John Lambert lived, but had soon tracked him down to a spacious, yellow-stone house at the edge of the village, set in a garden of unmistakably English character. The downstairs shutters were closed, but those of the first floor had been thrown open, with a curtain flapping in the light breeze.

A knock on the front door didn't get any response, but his car was in the driveway and I wasn't giving up so easily. Making my way to the back of the house, I saw a small round swimming pool and a newly laid patio of the same yellow stone as the house. A pair of French windows opened onto the patio, wide to the warm autumn air but with heavy curtains blocking the view within. From beyond the curtains, I could hear noises: sharp, fleshy smacks punctuated by giggles and little squeals of mingled pain and delight. A girl was being spanked, and I had a pretty good idea who she was, while there was no doubt at all who was doing the spanking.

I considered bursting in on them but thought better of it and instead moved quietly up to the curtains to peer inside. John Lambert was sitting on a plain wooden chair, bolt upright, his face split into a lustful, dirty grin, and it was obvious why. Liselotte lay across his legs, her pretty blue dress turned up onto her back and her panties pulled well down, the classic spanking position and one of which he was taking full advantage. Her bottom was flushed rosy red all over, while, with every rude detail between her cheeks and thighs on show, it was quite obvious that she was turned on, very turned on. So was he, with the head of a stiff, white penis poking up from where it was rubbing on the soft flesh of her hip as he spanked her.

It was hard to know what to do, as despite the temptation, I couldn't bring myself to burst in. I told myself I didn't want to watch, either, since I hadn't been invited and it was John Lambert who was spanking her, but I'd only pulled back from the crack in the curtains for a matter of seconds before my curiosity got the better of me. Even though the thought of John Lambert spanking a girl about one-third his age revolted me, there was no escaping the beauty of Liselotte's bare rear view, nor the pleasure of watching her get what she had dished out to me so vigorously. It was also a powerfully sexual situation, and at another time and place I might have risked slipping a hand down the front of my panties to play with myself while I watched, but my still boiling emotions, and the thought of John Lambert's reaction if he caught me, made that an impossibility. So I watched, holding myself dead still, with my eye to the crack in the curtain.

They'd been at it for quite a while, that much was clear from the state of Liselotte's bottom and her obvious excitement, his also. He'd begun to get dirty with her, too, alternating the smacks with some very intimate touching, his long, bony fingers repeatedly cupping her sex, pushing in up her vagina and even loitering between her cheeks to tease her anus, all of which struck me as unspeakably rude. She evidently didn't think so, or if she did, she was enjoying it, pushing up her bottom and purring with satisfaction as he molested her, and I couldn't think of it any other way.

Had I ever ended up in the same position, I'd have been bursting with resentment and consternation, not to mention fighting tooth and nail to escape, but not Liselotte. Even as his wandering fingers became more intrusive still, she had twisted around and reached back to take hold of his cock, jerking on the shaft and rubbing it against the softness of her flesh. Not surprisingly, he got even more excited, now smacking and groping at her bottom with a fevered abandon as he told her how lovely she was in words that set me blushing.

That just made her worse, her hand yanking up and down on his cock ever faster, until at last his words broke to a near animal grunt and he came, spattering her back and bottom with drops and streaks of white – a sight at once utterly disgusting and compelling in a way I wouldn't have thought possible, as the thought rose unbidden to my mind of how it would feel to be made to lick up his mess up from Liselotte's well-spanked bottom.

She had no such doubts, crying out in pleasure at what he'd done to her, and keeping her grip on his cock even when he was done. He was considerate too, whatever his faults, his hand now between her thighs, masturbating her as he went back to spanking her bottom, indifferent to the mess and concentrating fully on the task in hand until at last she came with a long, happy sigh and a series of piping squeals that reminded me irresistibly of a litter of hungry piglets fighting over their mother's teats.

They were done, and I was suffering from hot flushes and had serious difficulty in coping with my feelings, but I'd come there for a purpose. With my back against the wall, I counted to one hundred, reckoning that would give them enough time to cover up but still leave John Lambert off guard. I then knocked smartly on the glass of the French window and stepped through the curtains, only to discover that I'd been a little optimistic in my assessment. John Lambert was just putting his cock away, and instead of covering up, Liselotte had peeled off her dress and was in the act of stepping out of her panties. She saw me first, gave a squeak of surprise, tripped over her knickers and sat down heavily on the chair he'd been using to spank her on.

'Elise?! I thought you were in London!'

'Yes, it's Elise, and no, I'm not in London. I want to talk to you, John Lambert.'

I couldn't help but be impressed by his composure as he made a final adjustment to his fly then turned to me.

'Is it too much to hope that you have reconsidered my offer?'

'Yes, it is. I want the truth, please. You were planning to buy La Fleur and sell it on to your Chinese friends, weren't you?'

He shrugged, and answered without the slightest hint of embarrassment or discomfort.

'Certainly, I'm a businessman.'

'And how much were you hoping to make on the deal?'

'Half a million, maybe.'

'Oh yes? And what about this, then?'

I tossed the magazine down on the table, but I'd opened it at the wrong place and he merely gave a puzzled look at the picture of a group of wine tasters sniffing seriously at glasses of Volnay.

'I mean this.'

As I turned the page, he at least had the decency to look slightly ruffled, but there was a chuckle in his voice as he spoke.

'Ah, yes, that. Okay, maybe six or seven million, but I don't see what you're so angry about. You could have negotiated, and in any event, we'd both have ended up with a tidy sum in our pockets.'

'I am the proprietor of Château La Fleur!'

I stamped my foot as I spoke, not intentionally but by instinct. He finally reacted, taking a quick step backwards.

'Good heavens, I see you've inherited Adèle's temper as well her, um . . . predilections.'

'What do you mean?'

He was grinning.

'Didn't you know your auntie liked to be spanked? No, I don't suppose there's any reason you should, but it's true. Goodness knows how many times I've had her squirming across my knee. It's often the case, you know, with you hot-tempered, imperious women, all fire and attitude on a day-to-day basis and then begging to be put over the knee for a good bare-bottom walloping as soon as you've decided to let your knickers down.'

I'd started to blush and he was thoroughly enjoying my discomfort, but I wasn't going to let him distract me so easily.

'Never mind that. I just want you to know that I think you are a . . . no, never mind that, either. What I really need to know is whether the Belairs would have known about the classification business?'

'Yes, of course. In fact, Madame Belair made a point of asking me not to tell you, which was of course in our mutual interest. I was rather hoping that you might prefer my offer to theirs, though.'

'Your "offer" being to seduce me and buy La Fleur for a pittance, then move on to your next victim!'

'Come, come, you do me an injustice. Had you succumbed to my charms, I would happily have set up house with you, perhaps with Liselotte here as our housekeeper. Think what fun we'd have had!'

We'd been talking in English, and Liselotte merely looked puzzled, while it took me a moment of gaping at him in sheer outrage before I could find my voice.

'I was going to call you a slimy confidence trickster and a dirty old man, but the description doesn't do you justice! You really thought that I would be willing to live with you, and let you have Liselotte too?'

He gave a shrug, no more ruffled than before.

'It was worth a try.'

I didn't answer immediately, rendered temporarily speechless by his extraordinary insouciance and arrogance, but then I returned with difficulty to the issue I really wanted to sort out, switching to French so that Liselotte could understand.

'So the Belairs knew La Fleur was about to become far more valuable and tried to pair me off with Jean so they'd gain control? That's why Jean dumped you, Liselotte – not because you were playing with John, not because he had fallen in love with me, but so that he could end up as master of La Fleur.'

John Lambert nodded.

'That does seem to make sense. Welcome to the world, Elise.'

'Are you implying that I'm naive? No, don't answer that. Right, I'm going to fire the Belairs, all three of them.'

'French employment law can be tricky. You need strong grounds for dismissal, but then again, you probably have them. You're going to need a new winemaker too, and Luc Belair is good. Still, now that La Fleur is classified as a First Growth, you'll be able to pick and choose, not from among the very best, perhaps, but you could certainly hope to get somebody with experience in Sauternes, perhaps the current assistant from one of the top châteaux.'

I nodded, surprised he was being so helpful when I'd not only insulted him, but also scuppered a deal that would have left him rich. There was an easy explanation, of course, which was that he still hoped to get me over his knee, no doubt in tandem with Liselotte. But he wasn't the only one who could play games. I let my voice soften as I posed a question.

'I'm going to need a local lawyer. Can you recommend somebody?'

'Duluc Par. I've been with them for years, and they acted for your aunt.'

'Yes, I remember the name on the papers. So now what? The Belairs think I'm still in London, so maybe I should go to the lawyers first.'

I was thinking aloud, not really addressing him, but he answered anyway.

'That's a sensible move. Take them by surprise. You're very welcome to stay here while you sort yourself out, if you can bear to be in the same house as a slimy confidence trickster and a dirty old man, that is?'

'I'm sorry I called you that, but you must admit your behaviour was pretty underhand.'

'For the first part, I behaved as any competent businessman would, aiming to maximise my profit. I see no shame in that. For the second, I may be getting on in years, but I'm not actually dead, and a man would

need to be in order to resist your charms, even if we
didn't share the same tastes.'

'I'm sorry. I'm just not into older men. In fact, I'm
not really into men at all, just at the moment. Do you
know what Aaron was planning, Liselotte? He wanted
me to be with him, either in London or France, but
only one of several girls, while I had to stay faithful.
And he expected me to give up La Fleur!'

Liselotte made a face then answered with a single
word.

'Pig.'

'Yes, and Jean's worse. What is it with men, especially
the good-looking ones? They're so fucking arrogant!'

John Lambert had taken a cautious step towards
what seemed to be the kitchen door.

'Would you like a cup of tea, or perhaps something
a little stronger?'

'Tea, please. So, Liselotte, are you in this with me?'

'Yes, of course, but for now, I know exactly what
you need.'

'Not from him!'

'No, from me.'

She extended her hand and I took it, allowing
her to lead me upstairs to a spare bedroom, sparsely
furnished but with everything we'd need. I locked
the door behind me as she took her seat on the bed,
knees extended. She patted her lap and I unfastened
the button of my jeans to make it easier for her to
pull them down, then draped myself across her legs

in the now familiar position that would allow her to lay my bottom bare and spank me. The sense of relief as she took down my knickers was exquisite, all my tension and ill feeling draining away to be replaced by a sensation of blissful surrender. She began to spank me, gently at first, each and every smack sending a delicious little shock through my body, both erotic and wonderfully soothing. As the smacks grew firmer and my bottom began to warm up, I was reflecting on how right she was to say I needed spanking, and not only because it turned me on. I'd found the perfect therapy, and the perfect person to administer it: my Liselotte.

Epilogue

The first new buds were beginning to break on the vines, worryingly early with the chance of a frost still quite high, but one way or another their emergence signalled the start of my first full year as the owner of Château La Fleur. How it would go was largely down to nature, but the team I'd installed at the winery was capable of getting the best out of whatever nature provided, and in the traditional style, with nearly forty years of experience between them. I'd installed a new press as well, and replaced a lot of the older machinery. The house was looking smarter, too, with the shutters newly painted in a delicate eggshell blue, while the arch over the main gates was also freshly painted, with my new handyman just touching up the metalwork I'd added in gold. Just to see it was immensely satisfying, the newly wrought letters below the old: 'Château La Fleur', then 'Propriétaire Mlle Elise Sherborne de Regnier'.

When I'd first ordered the new work, the *forgeron* had given me a quizzical look, and then asked if it were wise to have the abbreviation Mlle for Mademoiselle in the middle, suggesting that the chances were high it would soon be changed to Mme for Madame. I'd assured him that I knew what I wanted, and he'd responded with a typically Gallic shrug and asked me how I'd be paying for my order. His work was now almost complete, and with the gold paint already beginning to dry in the warm spring sunshine, I finally felt that I had replaced my Aunt Adèle as owner, and in doing so I had come to realise that I was far more like her than I would ever have expected, and that she must have realised that when she named me as her successor. I'd also realised the nature of the mysterious scandal, her love for spanking, and with that my feelings for her had changed to sympathy, while her presence no longer seemed to haunt the house. The Belairs were gone too, and I was now firmly in charge, save only in the bedroom.

There I spent a great deal of my time having my bare bottom spanked, often with my hands tied behind my back, or my own knickers in my mouth to gag me, generally followed by the insertion of a large cock where it would do the most good. The cock would belong to Esteban, the bronzed young Adonis currently applying the final touches of paint to the letters of my name, just as he would shortly be applying his hand to both my bottom and Liselotte's. Half-French, half-Spanish, with a combination of lean, dark good looks and an uninhibited attitude to sex, he had the great advantage of being naturally dominant in bed and a useful, skilled employee, providing me with the best of both worlds, and Liselotte too.

Once he'd finished and climbed down from the ladder, he gave me a brief, appraising look, challenging me to criticise his work and hinting at what would happen if I did. It was a situation I was coming to love, and I made a deliberately dismissive remark, knowing full well it would put me over his knee with my knickers down as soon as we were in the bedroom. His dark eyes immediately hardened, and his mouth curved up into a smile, before he turned to Liselotte with a casual remark that sent the blood to my cheeks. I was still in charge, though, and paused a moment as he gathered up his things, allowing me to admire the view through the freshly painted ironwork and down the drive. I then reached out to take Liselotte by the hand and walked in through the gates of Château La Fleur.

Also by Monica Belle:

TO SEEK A MASTER

Work hard, play harder. . .

Eclipsed by the high-powered businesspeople that surround her, shy Laura Irving spends her time absorbed in her own workplace-fantasies.

So when the masterful and arrogant man known as 'The Devil' begins to show interest she is both terrified and thrilled. And there is nothing she wants more than to call him 'Master'.

A classic Black Lace tale of a love-hate affair and an explosive relationship.

BLACK
LACE

Also available form Black Lace:

DIAMOND

By Justine Elyot

**Her name is Jenna Diamond.
She is about to meet her match...**

Since the painful breakup with her famous musician
husband Jenna has returned to England and bought a
crumbling old house back in her hometown.

But Jenna discovers a mysterious stranger hiding out
at Holderness Hall. Logic suggests she should alert the
authorities, but when she looks at her sexy, young house
guest Jenna finds it all too easy to let her heart rule her
head...

**Book 1 in the Diamond trilogy, a glamorous erotic
romance, from the bestselling author of
*On Demand***

BLACK
LACE

Also available form Black Lace:

WRAPPED AROUND YOUR FINGER

By Alison Tyler

A story of submission

Samantha is loving her 24/7 BDSM-lifestyle: costumes, erotic toys and role-playing fulfill her dirtiest dreams. And Jack, the ultimate dominant's Dom, pushes Sam's boundaries to the limit, making her do things she'd never thought she could do.

Yet can she manage to stretch her love for Jack to incorporate his carnal need for his male assistant, Alex, as well?

Take the ride with this deviant trio. This diary of a submissive ups the ante with intense sensuality that will have you hanging on by your handcuffs!

BLACK LACE

Also available form Black Lace:

UNDONE

By Kristina Lloyd

*I can't recall my first thought that morning:
that I was in a strange bedroom; that an unfamiliar man
was naked beside me; or that a woman was screaming
somewhere in the distance.*

When Lana Greenwood attends a glamorous house party she finds herself tempted into a ménage a trois.

But the morning after brings more than just regrets over fulfilling a fantasy one night stand. One of the men she's spent the night with is discovered dead in the swimming pool. Accident, suicide or murder, no one is sure and Lana doesn't know where to turn.

Can she trust Sol, the other man, who is an ex-New Yorker with a dirty smile and a deep desire to continue their kinky game?

**A dark erotic thriller from the author of
*Thrill Seeker***

BLACK
LACE